"Mr. Chaney…?"

It was almost a whisper and seemed to come from outside the door to the dressing room.

Lon Chaney's eyes snapped open. Only then did he realize he had dozed off in the chair. His fingers burned and he looked down to see the long ash of his cigarette ready to fall on the carpet. He quickly extinguished the cigarette in a potted plant then glanced toward the door.

"It's open!" He shouted. But no one came in and for a second he began to wonder if he'd imagined the voice in his half-asleep-half-awake state.

But then he heard it again.

"Mr. Chaney…?"

It was louder and this time came from the short dark hallway that led to the kitchen and bath.

"Is someone there?" The perplexed actor called out.

"Lon Chaney…?"

It was more of a hiss this time, coming from very close by, practically in his left ear.

Startled, Chaney swung around to the source of the sound and found himself staring into the scarred, bone-white countenance of…a living skull.

"They call me Erik," the skull said. Then its hand shot up to Chaney's face. It was holding a rag moistened with chloroform.

As Chaney struggled, the figure closed the rag over the man's nose, until Chaney's body went limp.

MASQUERADE

JOHN MCCARTY

For the Grandkids
Isobel, Shane, Brennan and Harrison
Nurture a Love of Reading and Never Be Bored.
—Pop-Pop

PART ONE

PARIS
1909-1920

ONE

Subterranean Lake
Beneath the Paris Opera House

The popular press called him the "Opera Ghost" — a man of mystery about whom little was known except he was disfigured and went by the name Erik, which was very likely false.

He was hyperbolized as a master of legerdemain on account of his eerie ability to seemingly walk through walls to elude capture; his adroitness at throwing his voice into different rooms at once to evade detection; and his uncanny knack for disappearing like a perfectly timed wisp of smoke into the bowels of the Grand Opera House Garnier whenever the arms of the law drew too near.

In the public's imagination he was perceived as some kind of tormented genius, an embittered impresario, an obsessed lover, or all three. But to the members of the police who hunted him, he was nothing more than a common thief, kidnapper, and murderer — with some not-so-common tricks up his sleeve.

He was branded a thief because he had stolen the mystique of the Grand Garnier, a jewel of Parisian cultural life, as a palace

3

of joy and inspiration, and sullied it into a nest of terror and death.

He was a common kidnapper because his fixation upon one of the opera's ingénues—Christine Delfont—led him to abduct and conceal her in his lair—where he attempted to bully her to become his personal diva and possibly his lover, as well.

He was a murderer because he had cold-bloodedly strangled an all-too-curious stagehand as a warning to others to stay away. Then, in a fit of pique, he had brought down the Opera House's architectural centerpiece, the huge glass chandelier looming above the audience, sending it, in the middle of a performance, crashing upon a crowd of screaming, fleeing patrons—injuring many and killing an elderly, infirm woman in a pile of twisted bronze and shattered crystal.

So far the fiend had gotten away with these crimes. But *not tonight*!

These were the determined thoughts of *procureur* Pierre Donnay as he maneuvered along the precipitous landing that ran from the Opera House proper past a honeycomb of open storage cellars to a narrow landing of brick, mortar and stone alongside the building's foundation. It had been put there to keep the surrounding water at bay.

Donnay saw an old wooden boat a few yards away. It was tied to the landing, an oar dangling in the water, rats crawling upon it then tumbling into the boat as it bobbed uselessly in the darkness.

The boat was likely the fiend's favored mode of transportation when he had the luxury of time to move around, Donnay surmised. But the fiend had no such time now and was breathlessly trying to flee on foot.

Donnay held up his hand, signaling those behind him to stop. With his other hand he extended the lantern he'd carried onto the landing and listened. Over the gentle lapping of the water and squeaking of the rats, he could hear the criminal's boots slapping against the wet landing as he fled.

Physically, *procureur* Donnay was not as imposing as his foe. Standing a little over five feet eight, and slender, with a thin, dark mustache, he reminded people of the comedian Max Linder. But there was nothing comic in his determination to run the "Opera Ghost" to ground. In his quest to do so, he was very much like a lion's grip on its prey, which was why he'd probably gotten the high-profile assignment in the first place.

In the French system of justice, it is not the National Police, or Sûreté, that leads the investigation, but the prosecutors in the Office of the Public Prosecutor at the Ministry of Justice. Assisted by the Sûreté and its organization of detectives (*les inspecteurs*) and policemen (*les flics*), it is the job of the prosecutor (*le procureur*), once a suspect has been identified, to lead the inquiry into that suspect's guilt or innocence until the person is either charged with a crime or released.

If the suspect is charged, the same *procureur* conducts the prosecution of the case in court until a verdict is reached. It was reasoned that by this method of overseeing every aspect of the investigation and subsequent trial, the *procureur* would ensure that no clue was missed, no lead unfollowed, no task undone.

At age thirty, Pierre Donnay was not the youngest public prosecutor at the Ministry of Justice, but he was among the youngest, and definitely the most youthful to be handed such a huge assignment as capturing the notorious "Opera Ghost." But tender age or not, he was already a veteran of solving several almost-as-challenging assignments, each of which he had brought to a successful conclusion.

Donnay had launched his search for the slippery "Opera Ghost" by dismissing all the rumors of the fiend's alleged magical powers. He knew his quarry could neither walk through walls nor disappear like smoke, but was a creature of flesh and blood, and thus subject to the laws of physics like any other human being. There had to be some other explanation for the "Opera Ghost's" miraculous escapes.

And he soon found it—in an expedition to the Bibliothèque Nationale where he had arranged to view the original designs of the Opera House by architect Charles Garnier that were preserved there.

In addition to elaborate sketches of the opera's spectacular auditorium and magnificently ornate grand entrance and lobby, he found in these intricate drawings a labyrinth of trap doors and sliding panels designed for stage effects, as well as hidden rooms for storage purposes that stretched deeply underground. So deeply, in fact, that the original construction workers had struck ground water that quickly poured into the site, and could not be stopped.

Believing the water might serve as a precaution against fire, it was therefore decided to let it continue to seep in. Eventually, it swelled into a large subterranean lake that fed into the sewers of Paris and ultimately the Seine.

Donnay made several trips into this labyrinth both during the daytime hours and at night until he was convinced he had solved the mystery of the fiend's extraordinary disappearances. He had also discovered the fiend's lair—an expansive, watertight series of subterranean rooms, complete with living quarters, a soundproof music room with an old organ probably fashioned out of stolen parts, and a mirrored torture chamber to have been used to kill the ingénue's fiancé, Alain, an attempt Donnay had thwarted in the nick of time.

In retaliation, the fiend had hidden behind a secret panel within the office of the opera's management and projected his disembodied voice into the room, threatening the managers' lives if they did not call a stop to this meddling in his affairs by the authorities. Instead the managers had contacted these same authorities right away and the chase was now on.

"I heard him—he's not that far ahead of us," Donnay whispered to his men. He waved them onto the landing. "This way."

Carrying a second lantern was the red-haired detective-sergeant Etienne Verneuil of the Sûreté, who emerged first, followed by three *flics* with carbine rifles.

Six years older than Donnay, Verneuil chafed at a system that made him take orders from a much younger man without his criminalist expertise. Nevertheless to be in on the capture of the most infamous criminal in Paris was almost sufficient compensation and Verneuil was determined to make the most of it.

Donnay led his men to the edge of the nearest corner of the foundation then signaled them again to stop as he peered around it. The landing stretched out before him at almost the length of several city blocks, but the way was clear—except for the fleeing "Opera Ghost" himself.

He was several hundred yards ahead, running swiftly for the farthest corner, his black cloak with red silk lining flapping behind him, the torch in his hand throwing long, flickering yellow reflections upon the walls. The white plume of his foppishly broad-brimmed, musketeer-style hat bobbed and swayed as he ran.

From his earlier explorations into the opera house's dark nether regions, Donnay knew rounding that far corner, which was the fiend's obvious goal, would do him no good. There was no way of gaining entrance to the opera house from there, no way to get inside and disappear. Only the sewers that emptied into the river would remain at hand. Surely, the fiend knew this too, Donnay considered, as he envisioned what kind of treachery the fiend might have arranged in advance for his pursuers to encounter.

By now, Donnay's men had joined him on the landing and could see and hear the fleeing murderer themselves. Verneuil immediately unstrapped his pistol and prepared to shoot, but Donnay grabbed his arm and barked at the dismayed *flic*, "I want him alive!" Then Donnay turned back to their quarry and shouted with all the volume he could muster, "Halt!"

Though reverberating loudly throughout the cavernous space, the demand had little effect on the fleeing man except for prompting a fleeting glance over his shoulder as he ran.

Donnay shouted once more: "In the name of the government and the people of France, I said HALT! Or we'll shoot." But the fiend paid him no heed, except, perhaps, to increase his running speed.

"Fire a round over his head," Donnay ordered the more-than-eager- Verneuil, who pointed his pistol and pulled the trigger.

The warning shot boomed deafeningly against the walls of the enclosed space, but failed to slow the fiend at all.

"Let's go!" Donnay thundered.

He and his men took off in pursuit.

The "Opera Ghost" reached the corner of the edifice and quickly darted round it, disappearing from view.

As he and his men drew near that same corner, Donnay abruptly signaled them to stop. His suspicious nature had once more kicked in and was screaming a warning. There was no telling what the fiend might attempt in order to free himself now that he was, in effect, *trapped* inside this hell like his fellow rats.

Responsible for four lives, including his own, Donnay knew he'd best be careful, and so he slowly edged forward and peered cautiously around the corner. What he saw stunned him.

There were no apparent booby-traps waiting to surprise them that he could see, no weapons trained against them. Just the theatrically robed "Opera Ghost" himself. He was standing upon a fallen slab beneath a cracked arch, his foot upon a large rock, his cape wide open, torch resting upon his hip, the broad brim of his hat casting his face in shadow. He looked for all the world like he was welcoming an opening night crowd, or making a curtain call. As best Donnay could tell, he was unarmed.

Donnay stepped out into the open, his men moving in closely behind him, their weapons trained on the malevolent *poseur*.

"So, Monsieur Prosecutor, we meet at long last face-to-face," the fiend taunted from his perch.

"Not quite face-to-face," Donnay threw back. "Yours is hidden in shadow."

The "Opera Ghost" cooperatively lifted his torch an inch or so and tilted his head slightly, eliminating the shadow, to reveal a face of yellowish white with most of the flesh and other tissue removed, including veins and musculature—a ghastly *living skull*.

There were small patches of skin around the nasal bone and the fiend's deeply set dark eyes, which bore into you. These patches had the texture of old parchment. There were myriad cuts and slash marks across the skull and his lips had been removed, leaving large scabs with a blackish tint that enabled him to enunciate.

Donnay wondered in horror and disgust: *What manner of man could have performed such grotesqueries on a fellow human being?*

And what manner of human being could possibly have merited such egregious punishment?

"*O, that this too, too solid flesh would melt,*" the fiend quoted *Hamlet* with a laugh that was not a laugh—for there were no facial features to help express one—but only an unnatural chortling sound that emanated from his throat, and was utterly mirthless. "But it did *not* melt," he went on. "It was brutally *scraped* away."

"Who did this to you?" Donnay asked aghast.

"The law," the fiend replied sharply.

"Whose law?" Donnay returned skeptically.

"Persian law," the fiend fired back. "But what's the difference? The *law* is the *law*."

Donnay thought he'd detected the trace of a Mediterranean or Mid-Eastern accent in the man's speech.

"So, now you see why I am not afraid of *your* law, nor of your puny little army of *flics*," the fiend went on, capping off his words with another mirthless, guttural "laugh."

Donnay advanced to the edge of the landing, his men following in unison. He heard a sharp intake of breath from each of them as they more clearly took in the "Opera Ghost's" hideous visage.

"Puny or not," Donnay said, "we are still going to take you into custody on behalf of the government and the people of—"

"Yes, yes, I heard all that before," the fiend interrupted impatiently. "On what charge?"

"On multiple charges," Donnay responded. "Murder, attempted murder, kidnapping, assault and there are others. We are authorized to take you in dead or alive. My preference is the latter. But the choice is up to you."

He advanced closer, stepping onto one of the large chunks of stone in the water. Behind him, Verneuil and the *flics* cocked their weapons.

"Stay where you are!" the "Opera Ghost" commanded.

Donnay did as he asked. "So, you have decided it's to be death?" he said with chagrin.

The fiend scoffed. "The choice was always death," he said. "Either by the guillotine, the hands of the authorities, *or by my own!*"

With that, he pulled the large hat from his head with his left hand, while maintaining the position of the torch in his right, and offered a long, sweeping, highly melodramatic bow to his audience.

"*Bon nuit*, Monsieur Prosecutor," he said with a grim flourish as he restored the hat to his head. "And *adieu!*"

The fiend lifted the torch to reveal a short fuse attached to several sticks of dynamite that had been inserted into a crack in the arch above his head.

The fuse ignited.

"Get back," Donnay shouted to his men, who had already bolted—except for Verneuil, who stood his ground and fired at the fiend as the sparking fuse reached the dynamite.

The explosion rocked the enclosed space with a roaring thunder as the arch collapsed. The shock wave tossed Donnay into the water, submerging his lantern, and threw Verneuil back against the foundation of the opera house though he managed to hold onto his pistol and his own lantern.

As the smoke and dust from fallen chunks of stone and other debris began to clear, Verneuil spotted the "Opera Ghost's" plumed headwear floating upside down in the still-swirling froth. He also made out part of the fiend's cape sticking out from

11

under a huge block of the collapsed arch. He could also see that there was a large spatter of blood on the dark fabric.

A look of deep satisfaction suddenly crossed Verneuil's astonished face, and he muttered with deep incredulity, "Oh my God—*I think I got him.*"

"*Help…me,*" came a strangled plea that broke Verneuil from his reverie. At first he believed it had come from the "Opera Ghost" himself, who was *not* dead, he thought with bitter disappointment but trapped under the debris. But then he heard the plea again, coming from near him, and he looked down to see Donnay struggling in the water.

Scrambling to get a grip on the landing to pull himself out, his bloody fingers kept slipping away. The lower half of his body was completely submerged and he was having increasingly great difficulty keeping his head above water. He realized he was caught on something.

Verneuil put down his lantern and started kneeling to help the man when he heard a loud *crack* from above. His head snapped up to see an old wooden support beam that had almost been split in two from the blast. Now it was swaying precariously, threatening to come loose and fall on them at any moment.

Instantly, Verneuil was on his feet and to Donnay's dismay and bewilderment the man was backing way.

What's wrong with him, Donnay wondered. *What's he doing?* "*Dammit, Verneuil, pull me out!*"

He twisted his body as best he could in order find out what had frightened Verneuil off, but he was too pinned by debris; the angle was too sharp for him to crane his neck; his agonized muscles gave out and his face slipped once more into the foul water.

He came up sputtering, then made another desperate attempt at grabbing hold of the landing. But the surface was so slick, the effort again proved futile. It was then that Donnay heard a splash next to him and then felt a strong pair of hands grasping his legs.

"Where are you caught?" came an unfamiliar voice. It did not belong to Verneuil. Had one of the other *flics* come back?

"My right leg," Donnay burbled as more rank water poured into his mouth. He spit it out as he felt the man's hands pushing at the debris around his leg. The pain was so excruciating, Donnay guessed the leg was broken.

"Give me a hand!" the *flic* shouted. At whom, Donnay could not suppose. Verneuil, perhaps? Or had the other *flics* returned as well?

Suddenly there came an even more frantic cry of *"Watch out!"*

It was followed by a cut-off gasp and an explosion of pain throughout Donnay's body such as he'd never known as a terrible weight fell upon him, forcing his head into the rising water. The *flic*'s hands had gone slack.

Donnay coughed as he involuntarily gulped water. He tasted the metallic sweetness of blood in his mouth and spewed it out with disgust, panicked that he might have been further injured by whatever had fallen on him. Or had the blood come solely from the *flic* himself?

Straining to lift his head to keep from swallowing more rancid water, Donnay attempted to cry out, but the water swiftly rose over his chin. He quickly sucked in a deep breath then snapped his mouth shut as the water poured over him.

Pierre Donnay struggled to hold his breath for as long as he could, praying that help would come in time.

Then, miraculously, he felt more hands pulling and prodding him.

Was it his imagination—brought on by the growing delirium of trying to keep from breathing—or was it real?

He could hold his breath no more. Air exploded from his aching lungs. And then the world went black in a cascade of bubbles.

TWO

La Sanatorium et hôpital Boldieu
Guyancourt, France
Eleven Years Later

"Bonjour, monsieur," Babette announced in her usual buoyant manner as she threw open the curtains in his room. Bright early-winter light poured into the previously gloomy interior, hurting his eyes.

He was sitting in a straight-backed chair beside his bed, which was made up; his packed suitcase lay open on top, along with his suit coat and wooden cane. He'd taken to carrying it recently when the cold bit into his legs.

As Babette turned away from the curtains and saw him sitting there, fully dressed, she let out a gasp of surprise. "Have you been there in the dark all this time, monsieur?" she asked with concern.

He shrugged. "Just an hour or so," he said. "Couldn't sleep."

The nurse's ebullience returned. "It's all the excitement of finally going home," she reassured him.

A portly black woman from the island of Martinique, Babette was the sunniest, most positive person Pierre Donnay had ever met. But she was no pushover. During his convalescence, she had demonstrated infinite patience with him, but also possessed a very hard nose. She never pushed him past his limit of endurance, but she would countenance no backsliding from him either. She was his ministering angel.

"In many ways, this place has become my home," he answered ruefully. It was true. He had spent the better part of the last decade of his life here at the sanatorium Boldieu.

The place had begun life in the 1850s as a facility for the wealthy. It had been converted to a hospital because of the war with Prussia in the 1870s. After the armistice, it was re-converted to a sanatorium again, albeit no longer just for the well-to-do.

During the recent so-called "Great War" with Germany and its allies from 1914 to 1918, it saw temporary duty again as a hospital for the tide of wounded soldiers coming from the battlefields and the trenches. Donnay had been a firsthand witness to this influx of patients while recovering from his own wounds—the two broken legs and injured spine he'd received during the closing moments of the "Opera Ghost" affair when the fiend's treachery had led to his almost being drowned.

The soldiers' wounds were in many cases so severe that these men were housed in a separate wing of the hospital away from the eyes of the general population. The hospital staff was prohibited from discussing the nature of their wounds with other patients. And the physical therapy of those few who possessed even a chance at recovery and rehabilitation was held at odd hours away from prying eyes. Donnay could sympathize. At times he'd found his own physical therapy and rehabilitation to be an often agonizing and humiliating experience.

Prior to his stay at the sanatorium, there were a few years spent in a Parisian hospital where he'd been in a coma from which the doctors believed he might not emerge. But then one day he just woke up, imagining that the events that claimed the life of a *flic* and almost killed him had occurred only hours before, not years ago. He learned that he had even stopped breathing at the scene but was miraculously resuscitated.

As those years he'd been in a coma went by, his leg fractures knitted and constant massage kept his muscles from atrophying. Surgery on his lower spine addressed the fortunately minor issues there, but doctors judged that all would be for naught if he didn't wake up soon. They considered that they might even have to break his legs again if the fractures failed to set properly, but things hadn't come to that. Nevertheless, he'd lost all those years of his life, years for which he still had no memory—a thought that continued to terrify him.

"Ah, this is no proper home," Babette replied bluntly. "This place is for the sick, the wounded, and the dying. You are none of these, monsieur, not anymore."

"Babette, what would I ever do without you," he said, rising from his chair. "I shall miss you."

She seemed embarrassed at first by the sentiment, but then, with a flirtatious curtsy, returned, "And I you, monsieur." There was a soupçon of sadness in her voice.

Donnay closed the suitcase containing his few belongings, most of which had been donated by the sanatorium, and snapped the locks. Everything else he possessed was being held for him in storage at his former lodging house in Paris' 9th arrondissement. At least he hoped it still was there.

Soon after he'd come out of the coma, he'd arranged for his solicitor to pay the concierge, Madame Delon, a small monthly stipend to put his belongings in storage, assuming she hadn't already done so.

As by then three years had passed, he figured his old apartment must have been cleaned out and rented anew. If so, he'd instructed his solicitor to pay Madame Delon anything that was owed her in arears. The money was to come out of his pension fund. As he'd not been made aware of any complaints, he took it for granted that everything had proceeded smoothly.

As he put on his suit coat, he turned and saw Babette admiring him. "You look *très chic*," she said approvingly. "Very dapper. Especially now with the walking stick." She bit on a thumbnail, thinking hard. "As a matter of fact you remind me of someone famous, but who…?"

"Max Linder?" he suggested.

"*Exactement!* The funny fellow in the picture shows." Suddenly her face turned beet red. "Not to say that you look funny, monsieur," she stammered in apology.

He smiled quickly. "Not to worry, Babette," he reassured her. "The comparison's been made before."

Just then the door opened and the director of the sanatorium walked in carrying a long wool overcoat. "The carriage has arrived to take you to the train station, monsieur Donnay," he said handing him the coat. "It's very cold outside. I thought you could use this."

The coat looked a little long for him, but Donnay accepted it gratefully. "I hope I'm not putting anyone out," he said.

"It's an old one of mine that I no longer wear," the director replied. He was a tall man, and slim. In fact, everything about him was slender, from his face, which was almost gaunt, to his fingers. With his copious white hair he looked more like an orchestra conductor than a hospital administrator. "Come," he said, picking up Donnay's suitcase.

Donnay slipped on the coat and found that it came to his heels. At least it would keep all of his backside warm, he thought with a smile. As he started following the director out of the room, he was stopped by a sudden shout:

18

"Oh, Max!"

He spun around to see Babette holding out his walking stick. "You almost forgot this," she said with a grin, tossing it to him.

He plucked it from the air, then blew her a kiss and walked out of the room, leaving her with a tear in her eye.

The director's eyebrows furrowed as he and Donnay strolled into the long hallway that led to the sanatorium entrance. *"Max?"* he said, looking perplexed. "What was *that* all about?"

Donnay laughed. "Just a private joke between Babette and me. She thinks I look like the comedian Max Linder."

The director studied him for a moment. "You know," he said with amazement, "I think she may be right."

Donnay laughed again. "Now don't you start, or I'll soon be signing autographs!"

The director chortled robustly. Then: "Oh, before I forget." He suddenly reached into the pocket of his white coat and pulled out a slip of paper. "Your train ticket to Paris," he explained, handing it to Donnay.

"I can't thank you enough," Donnay said, accepting the ticket gratefully and putting it in his coat pocket. "For *all* you've done."

"Think nothing of it, my boy. You did all the hard work yourself," the director replied. "Speaking of which, how have you been doing with those nightmares?"

"They've diminished in frequency," he assured the director. "Although I did have one last night," he added with chagrin. The director paused in his stride and looked concerned, but Donnay pulled him along breezily.

"It didn't last long," Donnay explained. "But as with the others, for a moment I was right back in that grimy underground lake again, struggling to breathe as the water rushed over me."

"Seems reasonable you'd experience a nightmare last night after not having had one for some time," the director reassured

19

him. "You're understandably anxious about returning to a world that in many ways will seem foreign to you," he suggested. "A lot has happened since you came to us, monsieur Donnay. And not all of it pleasant. Our returned veterans, for example, our 'walking wounded' as I call them, they serve as uncomfortable reminders of our new age with their missing arms and missing legs, and other, invisible injuries that can never be amputated.

"You must be very careful of the changes you will encounter out there, especially in your field of criminal detection, for they could precipitate a resumption of your nightmares and another bout of severe anxiety attacks," he cautioned.

"Yes, I guess firsthand experience won't be like reading about the world in *Le Figaro*, will it?" Donnay replied. "But, of course, the choice to return to the practice of criminal prosecution may not be entirely mine to make. I'm sure many changes will have occurred in the law as well and I may not be accepted back into the fold. They'll see me as too out-of-date, perhaps. A fossil."

"That turn of events I can't even imagine happening," the director returned with a vigorous shake of his long white hair. "Not to the hero of the 'Opera Ghost' affair!"

"Ancient history, my friend," Donnay responded.

The director shook his head again, suddenly furious with himself. "Ah, but here I am bringing up depressing things when you should be excited about what you will see," he said. "There have been some marvelous changes too," he went on almost without a breath.

"The motor car, for example. You won't believe how many of them there are now," he explained. "Some people complain of the smell, but I ask you, what are some gasoline fumes compared to the old, ever-present stench of horse apples in the street?"

They were each laughing as they reached the building's entrance. Suddenly, Donnay opened his overcoat and reached into the inside pocket of his suit. "I almost forgot this," he said, withdrawing a small book. "Thank you for lending it to me."

The director looked down at the plain blue, all-text wrapper:

Le Fantôme de l'Opéra
un romance gothique
par Gaston Leroux.

He held up his hands. "No, no, it's yours," he urged. "Please keep it. As a memento of your time here with us."

"I shall treasure it always," Donnay returned. "Thank you again."

"Given all you've been through, I had misgivings about even showing it to you," the director offered. "But your therapist, Dr. Sauvage, felt reading it might prove to be a catharsis."

Donnay smiled. "I'm not sure it was that," he said. "But it did provide me with a considerable amount of amusement as so little in it is factual. Perhaps monsieur Leroux had tired of simply reporting the facts of the case in *Le Matin*, and decided to spruce things up a bit in his novel. How else to explain so prestigious a journalist turning a true tale of kidnapping and murder into a gothic variation on beauty and the beast? But in reality, this beast had no kind soul. And rather than loving him, our beauty lived in abject fear of him, not only for her own life but for that of her lover's as well."

"Nevertheless, the reading public soaked it up," the director replied. "It's been a tremendous success both here and abroad and has made monsieur Leroux a very rich man."

Donnay smiled again as they walked. "Then perhaps I'm just jealous I'm not in it," he offered. "Except as a vague synthesis of all the 'authorities' muddling around in the background."

The director laughed wholeheartedly at the healed man's self-deprecating humor.

The director pulled open the entrance doors, revealing Donnay's horse-drawn carriage at the bottom of the sanatorium's marble steps.

"What, no motorcar?" Donnay remarked, feigning disappointment.

"Not until the next budget year," the director replied with an apologetic shrug.

As the dark-haired coachman shivered from the cold despite wearing a thick winter coat and hat and also being draped in a large gray blanket with red trim. His brown horse bristled at the reins, anxious to get going. Puffs of white vapor erupted from the animal's nostrils in the chill atmosphere. Donnay thought he could smell a coming snow storm.

The director extended his hand. "Now that you have successfully beaten back the worst, from here on I wish you nothing but the best," he said to the prosecutor. The two men shook hands warmly.

The director gave him his suitcase and Donnay started down the steps. As the heavy oak doors of the building began closing behind him, he suddenly heard the muted cries of the wounded coming from deep within the sanatorium's walls. Then the doors shut and the cries were gone.

As he climbed into the carriage, Donnay felt himself tremble briefly—not from the cold but from the memories such cries represented to him. For they had once been his.

Pierre Donnay cast a less than nostalgic look back at the dark, box-shaped figure of the Sanatorium Boldieu as it receded in the carriage's rear window.

He'd miss some of the people who'd cared for him, of course. But not the institution itself. To him it represented little more than a very bad memory full of pain and frustration. But that was the past. Now he was determined to set his sights on the future.

As if in response to that determination, he settled back in his seat and glanced out the side window where he could see part of that future already rushing upon him.

He wasn't exaggerating when he'd suggested to the director that his future with the Office of the Public Prosecutor was uncertain. He'd received a letter several years ago from the *Ministère Publc* inquiring about his recovery and assuring Donnay that his old position would be waiting for him when he came back. But nothing was sure in the highly politicized environment of the State. He would find out for certain how much the official's assurance meant only when he got there.

The distance to the train station in Versailles was only a few kilometers, but already the interior of the coach had become ice cold and his legs were aching. There was a thick wool blanket identical to the one the driver wore on the seat beside him. He quickly draped it over his legs and underneath him in an effort to generate some warmth.

As he shifted the blanket around him until he felt more comfortable, he thought back to his conversation with the director and hoped his criticism of *The Phantom of the Opera*, the book the man had given him, did not cause any offense. The truth is Donnay wasn't as blistering as he might have been given author Leroux's voluminous distortions and outright fabrications.

With an expression of pure scorn, he pulled the book from his coat and riffled through the pages, ruminating that years from now, should the affair of the "Opera Ghost" be remembered at all, the details of the affair will likely be cemented in the public's mind more from Leroux's fabulist romance than from all the factual contemporary newspaper reports put together. And that disturbed him. He'd almost lost his life in pursuit of the murderous fiend. And others had been killed or severely injured by him.

Even the "Opera Ghost's" own grisly end had been romanticized by the author. As Leroux described it, in a grand gesture of his enduring devotion to Christine Delfont—renamed Christine Daae in the book—the fiend had set her and her fiancé Alain (renamed Raoul by Leroux) free to marry and live the rest of their lives without fear of him. After which, he had died *somewhere, sometime* of a broken heart. What clap-trap!

Following the explosion set off by the fiend, which Leroux altogether omits, Donnay thought angrily, the authorities later searched through the rubble for a body, only to find a battered hat and torn fragments of a dark cape with some blood spots on it. The latter indicated that sergeant Verneuil might indeed have succeeded in putting a bullet, perhaps even a fatal one, into the devil just prior to the blast, as Verneuil had claimed.

Thereafter, these same authorities, Donnay had later read in the newspaper, conducted a manhunt for the vanished (and presumably wounded) "Opera Ghost" throughout the city. It proved futile until several weeks later when a body was found floating in the Seine that matched the fiend's description. The dark clothing it wore was blood-stained and hanging in fragments from weeks of exposure in the river. A single pass-through bullet wound was found in what had been the fleshy part of the deceased's right shoulder. No fingerprints could be taken as the corpse's hands were virtually raw from being chewed on by insects, fish, rats and the other denizens of the river.

The key to identifying the deceased as the late, unlamented "Opera Ghost" was the skull itself. What little flesh around the eyes and mouth the ghastly countenance had possessed was now gone, as were the eyes themselves, having been ravaged by the same hungry scavengers. But the skull belonged to *him* alright. The survivors of the blast, exempting Donnay himself, confirmed it. No one else alive or dead could possess a face like that!

Donnay slapped the book shut and stuffed it back in his coat pocket, turning his attention to the scenery passing serenely by his window.

Death from a broken heart indeed!

THREE

Train Station
Versailles, France

The Versailles-Chantiers railway station was built to bring sightseers and dignitaries around the world to the nearby historic Palace du Versailles. In 1918, for example, such dignitaries would have included the leaders of Europe and the United States, who had come for the purpose of signing the treaty that brought an end to the carnage of the Great War.

The station was a large edifice. Its slightly off-white color made the now gently falling snow a bit difficult to make out as Pierre Donnay's coach pulled up to the sidewalk fronting the wide, two-columned entrance.

The coachman narrowly avoided a collision with a red Citroen roadster boasting a white top that was pulling away at the same time. The motorcar's nose-in-the-air driver made a show of his annoyance with the horse-drawn conveyance by bearing down on his klaxon.

Using his cane to steady himself, Donnay climbed from the coach with his suitcase. The coachman was on retainer with the sanatorium and had already been paid, so Donnay gave him a generous tip, bidding him "merci" and "adieu."

He watched briefly as the coachman circled the vehicle around to head back to the sanatorium, maneuvering cautiously among the colorful array of motor cars—a silver and white Delahaye convertible (with top up), a garishly purple Bugatti Royale, an elegant and luxurious black Darracq. They looked every bit the symbol of a disappearing past—the move from horse flesh to horsepower. Donnay couldn't help wondering— and once more worrying—if he too had become an anachronism. Time would tell.

He turned toward the entrance to the train station, using the cane to keep from slipping on the wet sidewalk, which had become slick with snow in just the past few minutes. As he went in, he found himself already missing the sweet, clear air of Guyancourt. The aroma outside of gasoline was still so thick in his nostrils he was becoming nauseated.

The long and expansive interior ran the length of the terminus, culminating in a large sign marked "SORTIE" where passengers arriving from Paris and other parts of the country could exit onto the street.

The place was bustling with activity. The scene ranged from vendors selling flowers and souvenirs and cages of ticket sellers busily taking care of impatient travelers to manned kiosks offering coffee, croissants and newspapers to soothe the growling stomachs and idle brains of passengers departing on their respective journeys.

Restive passengers eager to board their trains, mixed with eager relatives and friends anticipating arrivals, clustered before a large board on the wall marked "TRAINS EN PARTANCE." It listed arrival and departure schedules for all incoming as well as outgoing trains, and if they were on time. It was updated every few minutes.

Donnay found his train to Paris right away. It was departing in fifteen minutes from the C platform to the rear of the building.

As Donnay elbowed his way through the crowds, he took notice for the first time of what the director had described as the "walking wounded." There were more than a few milling about. While Donnay had been prepared for the sight, he was shocked by it all the same. There were men in old, torn and dirty blue greatcoats propelling themselves along on crutches. Others were laden with packages or a suitcase they struggled to manage with just one arm.

Donnay found it difficult not to stare. Many of these men were quite young—in their early twenties, perhaps—but they all looked so much older with their graying hair. With all the years they had ahead of them, Donnay found it difficult to believe they would ever come to complete terms with their shattered bodies and not succumb to bitterness. They would have so much time to dwell on what might have been if not for the pointless brutality of the Great War.

Donnay's train was ready and waiting when he arrived on platform C, the Paris-Brest line, which would take him to his familiar destination, the Gare Montparnasse in the eastern part of the city—and do so in the remarkable time of just under an hour.

Given the number of people crowded inside the terminus, it surprised Donnay that so few were on the platform boarding the Paris-bound train. There were already some passengers seated inside, and more came in behind him. But on the whole, the car was fairly empty.

Twin rows of seats faced forward on both sides of the aisle. Each pair of seats had a large window, making the car nicely bright. But it was also quite chilly inside. Donnay quickly sat next to a window and slid his suitcase under the seat. He decided to keep his wool coat on until the air inside warmed up a bit.

There wasn't much to look at yet apart from the dirty platforms and the waiting trains exhaling steam. So, Donnay turned his attention to his immediate surroundings. Dark strips of some kind of adhesive lined the length of the aisle floor, presumably to keep people from slipping and injuring themselves when the train was moving.

The seats were of a light blue fabric and comfortable enough—for short journeys, Donnay decided. Luggage racks were conveniently mounted overhead. But Donnay's suitcase was small enough to have fit snugly beneath him for even quicker access.

As he continued looking around, a small boy of about five or six with wavy brown hair took the seat in front of him. The boy's mother, who looked to be around thirty-five, wore a green hat and a long gray coat, which she quickly shed before taking the seat beside him.

"Here, let me take this so you won't get too warm," she whispered, removing the boy's own coat and placing it on her lap.

Already, the boy was scrambling to his feet. He peered over the back of his seat, looking down at Donnay with an expressionless stare that made the latter feel ill at ease.

The mother tried pulling the boy into his seat with a stern, "Do you want to fall and hurt yourself when the train starts moving?" But the boy was having none of it and pulled away from the woman with a whiny "No, mama!"

She tried seating him several more times, but only met with increased resistance and finally gave up with a resigned, "Oh, all right, suit yourself, but hold onto the seat." This he agreeably did while never taking his eyes off Donnay, who shifted uneasily in his seat, hoping the recalcitrant child would eventually get bored and go to sleep.

As the last few passengers straggled aboard and settled in, the train whistle blew, the iron wheels beneath grinded slowly, gathering speed, and the locomotive lurched out of the station. Soon, the ugly station platforms and scenic village of Versailles itself were replaced by snow-flecked fields and trees shedding leaves in preparation for a long winter's hibernation.

Donnay turned away from the passing landscape to find that the boy was no longer staring at him. Instead, the child's gaze was fixed elsewhere—on the row directly opposite. Donnay followed the boy's eyes and saw immediately what had stolen the child's attention away from him.

The object of the boy's curiosity now was a hefty soldier in the aisle seat of the row opposite. His tattered sky-blue greatcoat, now a muddy gray from exposure to the elements, was bundled around him. The rounded steel helmet from the war years that graced his head was scratched and battered. But what undoubtedly captured the boy's interest, as it did Donnay's, was that the man was wearing a mask that covered the right side of his face from eyebrow to chin.

The mask appeared to be made of plaster, held on by an elastic band around the man's head. It was molded to fit the contours of the missing half of the man's face (eye, cheekbone, jaw), which had been painted onto the plaster to approximate his missing features by giving the mask a more realistic look. Where the man's right ear should have been, there was now only a dark hole surrounded by scarred flesh from what looked to be a severe burn.

Embarrassed that he too was now staring, Donnay turned away in time to see the boy lean to his mother and whisper excitedly, "Mama, look, that man back there has a doll's face!"

The woman twisted around and caught a glimpse of the disfigured veteran in the mask. Her face turned red and she quickly resumed trying to pull her son down into his seat.

"He's obviously suffered some terrible injury. Don't stare. It's impolite," she said harshly into the boy's ear in a rattled whisper. But the boy's curiosity was now so strongly piqued that he yanked himself away from her petulantly and fixed his eyes once more on the masked soldier, likely wondering just what kind of imagined monster lurked behind that weirdly painted doll's face.

Donnay understood the boy's fascination but was disgusted by his behavior all the same. Like many who have never been parents, he was sure he could control the boy better than his mother. He was deciding whether or not to intervene when suddenly the boy screamed and threw himself into his mother's arms, crying inconsolably and trembling with fear.

Donnay's eyes snapped back to the soldier just in time to see him readjusting his mask, and Donnay knew immediately what had transpired, and why. The veteran had apparently had enough of the boy's rude stare and given him something to really see—and remember: a glimpse of the hideously ruined face beneath. It would likely satisfy the boy's woeful inquisitiveness for a good long time to come.

FOUR

Gare Montparnasse
Paris, France

As the train rolled to a stop in the Gare Montparnasse, the central metro station serving the Left Bank, Donnay scooped up his suitcase and was fast out of his seat to join the exiting queue. He was anxious to take in the sights, sounds and smells of this "New Paris" he'd read so much about and was eager to experience.

As the line of departing passengers steadily moved off the train, Donnay caught a glimpse of the rude child sleeping in his mother's arms—where he'd been ever since the disfigured vet had frightened him into civility.

As for the vet himself, there was no sign. Apparently he'd been faster on his feet to get off the train than even Donnay, and was already gone.

The Versailles station he'd traveled from may have been bustling with activity, but the Gare Montparnasse was positively throbbing inside with life. The aroma of freshly made pastries and other sweets assaulted his nostrils pleasantly from a patisserie close by. Likewise, the aroma of baked bread fresh from the oven drifted on the air from a boulangerie across the terminus.

One could buy rings, bracelets and other items of jewelry from a glass-enclosed bijouterie near one of the exits to the street. Also, there were several newsstands offering the latest periodicals and newspapers from around the world, and an equal number of kiosks giving out information to tourists or selling flowers. Of course, there was also the requisite café—two of them, in fact, on opposite ends of the building—as well as the usual bank of ticket cages.

Donnay marveled at how in just a few years, the Gare Montparnasse had transformed into a city unto itself, a busy metropolis within a metropolis. He wondered: What must the Gare du Nord, Paris' main metro artery, be like?

He considered taking the metro to his old apartment in the 9th arrondissement, but decided that would probably take too long as there were so many stops along the way. Besides, even though it was a bit nippy outside, the sun was shining and the falling snow had so far remained in Versailles. The Boulevard des Capucines was only a short walk away, and from there it was a straight walk to his old apartment in the Rue Drouot. So, he decided to go by foot and sightsee.

As Donnay strolled along the tree-lined boulevard, he was beset by all the wonders of the "New Paris," some of which weren't so wonderful, he decided.

First of all there was the noise of the traffic. Never had he seen such an abundance of motorcars, including many makes and models with which he was totally unfamiliar—even with all his reading. And there wasn't just an influx of motorcars to contend with but a coterie of buses and trucks as well. Horse-drawn carriages and carts filled out the congestion, moving with a surprising efficiency among all the gas-powered vehicles.

Already, Donnay was missing the inviting aroma of those pastries in the Gare Montparnasse as the stench of gasoline again tormented his nose. Progress was indeed exciting, he thought as he sneezed, but it did not come without cost.

Given that the smell of gasoline was so pungent in the air, Donnay found it remarkable how many more outdoor cafés had sprung up along this route since last he'd been here. There were at least a dozen more scattered along the Boulevard, and all of them seemed to be doing a brisk business even on a very brisk afternoon.

There were elegant shops selling everything from lingerie to perfume and the latest fashions for both men and women. A fancy chocolatier called out to his sweet tooth but he resisted the invitation. He also came upon a theatre he'd never seen before—the Beaux-Arts. Its front was elaborately designed in the Baroque style. According to the marquee it was reserved for showing the "latest in moving picture entertainment."

A large placard and several smaller posters promoted the current offering titled *Simplette*. The stark illustrations on the placard indicated it was a drama, featuring Suzanne Graudais and Pierre Sailhan, names that were unknown to Donnay, who couldn't remember the last time he'd taken in a "moving picture." He wondered if the picture shows had gotten any more sophisticated in that time. The photos of scenes from *Simplette* that decorated the theatre suggested this might possibly be so.

He had only continued a few more blocks when over the sound of the passing traffic, he heard the shout of "Thief! Thief!" coming from somewhere a short distance behind him.

He spun around and saw a man in a long coat running toward him, knocking solo pedestrians and strolling couples out of the way, all the while clutching an object tightly to his chest.

Donnay heard a *flic* blow his whistle, and then he saw the *flic* himself in pursuit of the thief. The *flic* blew the whistle again, a signal for the thief to stop, which he clearly had no intention of doing.

As the thief drew nearer, Donnay realized that if he didn't move out of the way, he'd be knocked to the sidewalk too. So, he backed quickly against the window of a restaurant.

The thief actually seemed to pick up speed as he ran, the exertion showing on his already ruddy face under a black sailor's cap. It was the rugged face of a man who has experienced more than his share of hard times in this life, Donnay perceived quickly.

He looked back and saw the *flic* was still huffing and puffing in pursuit, but no longer blowing the whistle as he struggled to close the gap between himself and the thief. Without some help, Donnay realized, the *flic* was likely going to lose his man, and so as the thief flew by, the former prosecutor thrust out his cane.

The stick was almost ripped from his grasp as it tangled in the man's legs, and the thief quickly went down in a sprawl, sliding to a painful stop on the pavement, the stolen wallet aviating from his hand.

In a matter of seconds, the out-of-breath *flic* was already cuffing the dazed thief. The *flic* then snatched up the fallen wallet and pulled the protesting thief to his feet.

"That was already there when I fell because this man tripped me," the thief spewed angrily, and unconvincingly, as he eyed Donnay.

"But of course," the *flic* responded caustically, still huffing and puffing. "And I ran after you for the sheer exercise alone," he said, turning to Donnay. "Thank you, monsieur, for your timely assistance."

"Just doing my civic duty," Donnay assured him with a tip of his cane.

Suddenly they were joined by a dapper little man with a gray mustache. He was also out of breath from running — the wallet's owner, Donnay presumed. The man said he'd overheard Donnay's exchange with the *flic* and was quick to offer his thanks as well.

The *flic* held up the wallet. "Is this your billfold, monsieur?"

The dapper little man nodded, gesturing with his thumb to the thief. "This one snatched it as I was paying my bill at the café," he said. "Very embarrassing."

The *flic* inclined his head towards the little man. "Then if you will follow me to the nearest *poste de police*, we can take care of this matter and you and your wallet may be on your way."

"*Certainement*," the little man agreed.

As the three started to leave, the *flic* glanced back at Donnay, and said. "Thank you again, Monsieur, for..." He stopped suddenly, his words trailing off as he stared hard at Donnay. Then, looking very much agog, he hesitantly said, "Aren't...you...?"

Not again, Donnay thought with annoyance. He was ready to disabuse the poor *flic* of his mistake when, with amusement as well as a sudden sympathy for the harried man, he changed his mind, and decided: Why not let him enjoy telling his colleagues and friends how the celebrated comedian Max Linder helped him collar a criminal? What harm could it do?

He saluted with his cane. "My pleasure," he shouted as the trio walked away, the *flic* buzzing excitedly in the dapper little man's ear.

Grinning, Donnay tapped his cane on the sidewalk and with suitcase again in hand continued on his way, musing: *I've not been in the "New Paris" an hour and already crime has reached out to grab me.* He decided the highly quotable writer Karr was right when he said, "Plus ça change, plus c'est la même chose." *The more things change, the more they stay the same.*

The Rue Drouot was well known throughout the city as the "Opera Center" of Paris because of the many small opera houses in the area, which were topped off by the opulent Grand Garnier a stone's throw away on the Avenue de l'Opera.

If opera wasn't your cup of tea, there were many other theatrical venues in the vicinity to choose from as well for entertainment, ranging from vaudeville to cabaret, stage plays to several newly constructed or re-modeled moving picture houses—something to suit every taste.

And if you had real money to burn, the Rue Drouot was also known for its plentiful auction houses. They numbered some of the country's most prestigious, including the vast Hotel Drouot, several floors of which were devoted to auctioning everything from rare art to historical artifacts.

Farther on down the street were several apartment houses, including Donnay's own former lodging house at number 74. He stood before the door now. He took out his pocket watch and checked the time. It was a little after three thirty, the time when the concierge, Madame Delon, customarily had her afternoon tea, so she should be in.

He turned the knob, pushed open the door and stepped into the enclosed entrance that led a few steps into a sunlit courtyard around which the apartment building had been built. His old apartment was on the third floor, a long way up given that the only way to get there was by stairway.

Madame Delon's office-cum-living quarters were located at the courtyard level—fortunately for him as his legs were a bit tired from all the walking he'd done. He put down the suitcase and quickly rang the bell.

Following what seemed like several minutes of no response, but which was likely only a few seconds, he grew impatient and rang the bell again, leaning into it harder. This time there came an irritated shout from inside: "Alright, alright, hold on!"

A lock clicked and the door opened to reveal the face of an older women with rust-colored hair now streaked with gray, her customary Gauloises cigarette dangling from her lips in a cheap holder of gold leaf. "Yes, can I help you?" she asked, sizing him up through squinty eyes for a thief or potential customer. Perhaps because he was too well-dressed for a thief, she decided the latter and opened the door wider.

"Please forgive the intrusion, Madame Delon," he began politely, "but I wish to inquire whether you have any apartments to let."

She shook her head. "No, monsieur. I'm sorry. We're full up."

He looked crestfallen. "Could I arrange then to have the things being stored for me re-located to my new lodging house once I obtain it?"

She looked perplexed. "But I have nothing of yours stored here…" She paused, eying him quizzically as the long ash from her cigarette dropped unnoticed onto her dark work dress. Then the light of recognition came into her eyes and her face broadened into a smile. "*Oh, my word,*" she said. "*Monsieur Donnay, is that really you?*"

He grinned back. "Oui, madame. C'est moi."

"I was wondering how you knew me by name," she said. "You shouldn't tease an old lady."

"My apologies, madame, but I saw no old lady here."

"Flatterer," she scoffed. "Please, come in." She widened the door more and he stepped inside with his suitcase.

She dropped the cigarette holder in an ash tray and led him through the kitchen into the parlor where she invited him to sit down. He chose a large armchair with thick brown cushions.

Putting her fingers to her lips, she studied him with deep concentration. "I know it's you, but you look different somehow," she said.

"That's because I am ten years older than when we last saw each other," he responded breezily. "Which is more than I can say for you, madame Delon. You haven't aged a bit," he fibbed. "What's your secret?"

"Oh, monsieur, now you *are* joking," she gushed, knowing full well he was pulling her leg but still pleased by the blandishment just the same. "But why didn't you alert me that you were coming?" she asked. "I could have prepared —"

"No worries," he reassured her. "I didn't know myself that I was being released from hospital until fairly recently."

"You are completely recovered then?"

"I don't know about 'completely,'" he replied. "But I'm sufficiently healed in body and mind to resume making a living. That's why I was hoping to get my old apartment back."

"I am sorry, monsieur, but that one is indeed occupied," she apologized. "By a musician at the Grand Garnier as it happens."

He acknowledged the coincidence with a fatalistic shrug.

"I'm forgetting my manners," she said after an awkward silence. "I was about to make some tea. Would you like some?"

"That would be very nice," he said and she returned to the kitchen, where momentarily he could hear the running of water in the sink and the clinking of cups and saucers.

He was amused by the woman's unchanged predictability. In addition to chain-smoking Gauloises like they were going out of fashion, she had always taken a break for tea at around four o'clock, which is what his pocket watch told him the time was now. One would almost think she were English.

While she was gone, he made a quick survey of the room, which he'd never been in. His dealings with her had always taken place in the kitchen. The room spilled over with mismatching styles of furniture and was cluttered with knick-knacks, though everything was neat and orderly, clean and well attended, making the place feel quite homey.

He spotted what appeared to be a thick scrapbook on the table beside him. Family pictures, he assumed, and was about to satisfy his curiosity when madame Delon returned with the tea service. She set the tray down on the table beside him, pushing the scrapbook aside.

"I've brought milk and sugar if you take it," she said, handing him his steaming cup. "As for me, I like it straight up."

"Me too," he said, taking a sip and savoring the liquid warmth.

Donnay regretted that the apartment building was fully occupied. The location was convenient to the Palais de Justice where he had once worked and where he hoped to work again, as well as to the rest of the hub of Paris. When he remarked as much to the concierge and inquired if she knew of any available lodgings in the area, she waved off his query with one hand while lighting up another of her Gauloises with the other.

"Forgive me, monsieur, but I was just being lazy because I mistook you for a stranger," she said. "You see, a married couple moved out of the second floor apartment just yesterday, and, well, I just hadn't been inclined to tidy it up yet. But if you want it, it's yours."

"Perfect," Donnay exclaimed. "Then I can move in right away?"

"It's not as big as your old apartment," she explained. "But the couple was quite neat and clean, so it shouldn't take me more than a couple of hours to make it ready for you," she said.

"It's settled then," he said lightheartedly. They agreed on the monthly rent, which saw only a small increase from what he had been paying earlier.

He was overjoyed at his luck at practically getting his old rooms back—and with one less floor to climb as well! He asked how much she would need to pay the movers, and she fell silent, nervously lighting a fresh Gauloises with the tip of her old one. Donnay marveled at how deeply she breathed in the smoke, how slowly she let it out, and all without coughing. He had been a smoker too—until his years in coma broke him of the habit—and had practically coughed up a lung each morning with his first puff.

She spoke suddenly. "Monsieur Donnay, I have a confession to make to you," she said, her voice a little shaky. "I hope you will not be too offended by what I'm about to tell you." She took another long draw of her cigarette as if needing the time to summon the courage to go on.

He couldn't imagine what she might have done that would "offend" him, but she was obviously quite nervous, embarrassed, or both about what she wanted to tell him. He was all ears and gently pressed her to go on.

"When I read that you had almost been killed by the 'Opera Ghost' and that your prognosis was unknown, I knew right away that the management company owning this building would tell me to put your apartment on the market," she said, hesitantly at first but gaining confidence and momentum as she pushed on.

"So, before they could come to me, I went to them first with a proposition," she continued, adding a little drama to her delivery. "I suggested keeping things as they were—at least until we knew more about your condition—and use the time to promote the building as the home of the hero of the 'Opera Ghost' affair. I could even give tours, letting visitors see where you put your feet up and relaxed while contemplating your next move to bring the monster to justice. Then, to top off the tour, I could show them the compilation I've put together of all the newspaper clippings about the case, which I had planned to eventually give to you."

She pointed to the thick scrapbook he had noticed earlier. He picked it up and began leafing through it. She was right about its thoroughness. It contained every conceivable newspaper and magazine article about the affair from every Parisian journal he could think of and was truly impressive. He said so, which prompted her to squirm with delight.

The pages boasted such sensational headlines as:

"Hideous 'Ghost' Panics Patrons of Paris landmark"
"Stagehand Slain in Opera House"
"Manhunt for Kidnapper of Opera Star"
"Monster Perishes in Subterranean Blast"

As the apartment building wasn't fully rented at the time, the tours, she maintained, could bring in a lot of visitors. "And I was right," she added with great satisfaction. "Once my idea was accepted and put into action, before long we had every apartment rented. I even suggested charging a little something for the tours for more income, and that worked too. Nobody objected to paying and I even got tips!"

Donnay understood why she was uneasy about telling him all this. He wasn't sure how he felt about this invasion of his private space and the exploitation of his name even though he believed the concierge's motive was to try to hold onto his apartment for him as long as possible. And he was grateful in spite of his misgivings about the scheme itself.

As if reading his thoughts, madame Delon said, "I want to assure you, monsieur Donnay, that I never once in all that time let anyone look through your apartment. I stopped them all at the door so they could just see inside. I didn't want anything touched or broken—of worse, stolen. And that's how things worked out. I hope you are not too put off.

"Of course, once management learned of your prolonged convalescence, renting the place finally happened anyway," she went on, sounding disheartened.

He was moved by the sincerity of her impulses. Previously, he had thought of her only as his landlady. But she was more than that, a true friend. "It was the good fortune that monsieur Leroux's book was such a success that kept my idea working for as long as it did," she concluded.

As he flipped to the back of the scrapbook, he came upon another series of clippings under the headline:

"Reporter's Book on Notorious Case International Success"

"Yes, I can imagine its effect," he said somewhat dourly. "Have you read the book, madame?"

"Yes," she answered. "I thought it was thrilling!"

Donnay cleared his throat. "Something like a fairy tale from the pen of the Brothers Grimm—and just as truthful," he responded with caustic humor. He closed the scrapbook and slapped the cover with his palm. "Fortunately we have this record of yours to set things straight. You are to be commended, madame. I for one am in your debt. Thank you for your diligence and your generosity in giving this scrapbook to me."

"I have something else for you," she said hastily in an effort to conceal her blushing.

She doused her cigarette in the ashtray stand by her chair and hurried into the kitchen where she noisily moved around some crockery. When she returned, Donnay saw that her hand was clenched tightly to conceal what she held. He was intrigued.

"When your solicitor began paying the back rent and the storage fees," she began, sitting down again, "I felt that in a way we were robbing you by charging for the tours so I decided to hold onto my share of what we made.

"This is for you," she said, "minus my tips, of course." She opened her hand, revealing a wad of bills. "There's 500 francs here—not much for more than three years of effort—but I felt it was due you." She was full of surprises.

Donnay was genuinely touched by the woman's openness and honesty; she need not have told him any of this, let alone given him any money. For a moment he was lost for words. Then, with a bit of emotion in his voice, he said: "I'm inclined to give this back to you. You've earned it."

She shook her head vigorously. "I won't take it."

He smiled. "Very well then, I accept. With my deepest gratitude. You are indeed a treasure, madame Delon." Now she was really blushing.

Donnay got up from his chair. "Matter of fact, I think I'll use a few centimes to buy some dinner." He yawned deeply. "It's been a long and busy day. And will be even busier tomorrow when I see about getting my old job back. Is there any chance of my moving into the new apartment tonight? I don't mind sleeping on the floor."

"Oh, we can do better than that," she said, brushing aside the suggestion. "I'll get some of your cushions and blankets out of storage downstairs. You can sleep on them. Then we can get the rest of your things moved in over the next couple of days. How's that sound?"

"Perfect," he said.

"As I said, all your things are stored downstairs, clean and up off the floor so they wouldn't get damaged by any flooding from the heavy rains," she said.

He extended his hand. "Like I said before, you *are* a treasure." They shook hands heartily as she turned her deepest shade of pink yet.

FIVE

Pierre Donnay had planned on getting an early start that morning to the Palais de Justice. But instead of going to sleep at a reasonable hour, he had sat up until the wee hours reading the scrapbook madame Delon had given him.

The primary focus of his reading was the clippings she'd scrupulously collected covering details of the case that had occurred during his long convalescence. These began with eyewitness accounts of the explosion in the subterranean lake and hospital reports of Donnay's injuries and recuperation. The clippings then went on to update readers on the fates of the "Opera Ghost" affair's other dramatis personae. Donnay learned much.

For example, it was reported that opera star Christine Delfont had herself identified the remains of the fiend found floating in the Seine. After that, she and her then-fiancé (and presumably now husband), Alain, had disappeared entirely from all journalistic view. The only news of them since was that Christine announced giving up her career so that she and Alain could live out the rest of their lives in "blissful serenity and anonymity." Reading between the lines, Donnay construed that she must have decided to disappear from public view because she was still in lingering fear of the "Opera Ghost" and what he'd wrought upon her, even though he was dead and could trouble her no more. So, she had just vanished in order to escape the spotlight.

Moving on, Donnay read of the appointment of the new at the Palais de Justice named M. Severin to replace his old boss, Jacques Chislain, who had decided to retire. Donnay knew nothing of the new man or where he'd come from, but it was Chislain who had written to Donnay after he'd emerged from his coma offering him his old job back when the time came. That time was now, but Chislain unfortunately was gone. If that would make any difference, Donnay did not know. But at least he still had Chislain's pledge in writing, and he trusted the new chief would honor it.

Speaking of appointments to new positions, Donnay learned also of the promotion of his former detective Etienne Verneuil to the position of Chief of Detectives at 36 Quai des Orfèvres, Paris' central police headquarters. Donnay read that Verneuil had avoided conscription into the armed services to fight in the Great War due to a hearing impairment he'd incurred from the blast that traumatic day.

Donnay vividly recalled and, until recently, all too often relived, those moments after the explosion when he was in danger of drowning and had seen Verneuil suddenly back away from helping him, resulting in the death of another officer.

Verneuil's timely intervention might have made all the difference, but he'd stepped away, and frozen, at a critical stage.

Perhaps since then, Verneuil had added some stiffness to his backbone and also succeeded in being able to control his temper and ambition. He would need to in his new leadership position at the busiest police station in all of France. In any event, even if he remained the same old Verneuil, it wouldn't really matter that much to Donnay. As second grade public prosecutor in line for Chief someday, he would still have authority over Verneuil should they ever be thrown together on a case.

Lastly, Donnay learned something from the scrapbook about the esteemed author himself, monsieur Gaston Leroux. Surprisingly (to Donnay at any rate), journalist Leroux had simultaneously been covering the "Opera Ghost" affair for *Le Matin* while fictionalizing the same events in serial form for the monthly newspaper *La Gaulois*. Madame Delon had faithfully clipped and pasted each installment into the scrapbook.

The serial concluded in the December 1909 edition of the newspaper and was published in book form several months later in the spring of 1910. The appearance in *La Gaulois* of the final installment approximately a month before the case itself was bloodily resolved in the waters beneath the Grand Garnier was very likely, Donnay surmised, the reason why Leroux's serial ended in such a heavily romanticized and fanciful manner. The author simply had no reality to draw upon in time to meet his deadline. Nevertheless, the journalistic side of him was able to conclude his coverage of the actual affair for *Le Matin* with the facts.

Donnay was impressed with the man. Leroux was clearly someone who could spot a good opportunity when it came calling and then dared to seize it. As a result, he'd successfully managed to have it both ways—as a reporter *and* as an author— at the same time. Donnay couldn't help but view him as a very clever man indeed.

Donnay had a quick breakfast consisting of coffee and a roll at a patisserie near his apartment before heading to the metro station. From there he traveled to the exit for Île de la Cité—literally an island in the Seine in the middle of Paris. It was here that the imposing Palais de Justice, built during Napoleon's time, was situated.

Since that time it had sprouted several new wings. Altogether they housed all the courtrooms in which Paris' criminal and civil cases were heard and appealed, as well as the offices of all first and second grade prosecutors and the Chief Prosecutor—plus their aides, Palais functionaries and staff. It also housed the temporary offices of all currently participating defense teams and their personnel. All High Court cases determining the laws of France were heard and decided at the Palais too.

Also on the Île were such essential spots for sightseers as the cathedral of Notre Dame immortalized by Victor Hugo, which was situated at the foot of the island. And conveniently located around the corner of the sprawling Palais complex was 36 Quai des Orfèvres, which received its share of sightseers as well.

To his shame, Donnay had to admit he'd never visited Notre Dame in all the years he'd worked at the Palais, although he'd been to police headquarters (or the "Three-Six" as it was more familiarly known) many times.

It was a bit past ten when Donnay arrived at the Palais—sufficiently late enough, he believed, for the Chief Prosecutor to have comfortably settled in for a day's work, but still early enough (he hoped) that the chief would not yet have become too swamped with work to see him.

As always, Donnay paused before the steps leading up to the grand edifice to marvel at this powerful symbol of the court system of justice in his native land. It was here that anyone, high or low, could expect due process—and to receive justice impartially under the law. However imperfectly that justice could sometimes be meted out and seemingly unfair the result might be, perfect justice was always the ideal sought from the beginning. It was that goal of perfect justice that continued to hold Donnay in awe of the majesty of the law.

As he entered the Palais, Donnay was greeted by the familiar hubbub he remembered from his years of working there. He was not so full of himself as to expect everyone with whom he came in contact to recognize him immediately with a welcoming slap on the back and a "Great to see you!" But it was dispiriting that no one among the employees he encountered acknowledged him. Nor, it must also be said, had he recognized them. Surely there couldn't have been that much turnover in the time he'd been away, he thought. Or had the Great War gutted the ranks of the Palais de Justice as mercilessly as it had the rest of France?

As his mind contemplated that unpleasant thought, he found his way to the Chief Prosecutor's chambers. He stood before the desk of the aide out front, who offered a brisk, "May I help you?" without looking up from the paper he was writing on.

"Yes, I'd like to see the Chief Prosecutor please," Donnay responded firmly to the youthful aide whose thick sandy-colored sideburns and full goatee were obviously aimed at giving him an older, more authoritative look.

"Do you have an appointment?" the aide asked, reaching for another piece of paper with a list of names on it.

"No, I'm sorry," Donnay responded pleasantly. "But I'm sure he'll want to see me as I was once a public prosecutor here. Still am, I guess. The name's Donnay. Pierre Donnay. I've been away recuperating from my injuries in the 'Opera Ghost' case."

The aide squinted quizzically. "'Opera Ghost' case?" he repeated with a lift of an eyebrow, as if trying to remember. "I don't—oh, wait, do you mean the old 'Phantom of the Opera' affair?"

"'Ghost, Phantom,' whichever you prefer," Donnay said with a nod, trying to conceal his irritation with this imbecile.

Just then the chief's door opened and he stuck his head out. At least that's who Donnay assumed he was as he had never met the man.

"Oh, sorry, I hadn't realized you were with someone," the chief said to his aide without a note of genuine apology in his voice.

"This gentleman has asked to see you," the aide responded with deference as he turned to face his boss. "He tells me he was a prosecutor here."

"Oh?" the chief said with curiosity, sticking his head out farther.

"Name's Pierre Donnay," the aide continued. "Said he was injured in the case of the maniac who terrorized the Grand Garnier some years back."

"Oh?" the chief said again, this time with even greater curiosity. Still, Donnay noted with concern the chief's apparent lack of familiarity with his name.

"I can only give you a few minutes," the chief said to Donnay, his vocabulary suddenly expanding.

"Thank you. That's all I promise to take up," Donnay assured him.

"Then please come in, monsieur," the chief said, widening the door for Donnay to enter. There was a buoyancy to Donnay's step now that wasn't there before; he felt things were looking up.

"Did you want me for something, sir?" the aide called from outside.

"It'll wait," the chief answered brusquely as he closed the door.

"Thank you for taking the time to see me," Donnay said politely as he took a seat before the chief's polished desk.

"For a colleague, always," the chief replied with a wave of the hand that said it was nothing. He did not introduce himself to Donnay nor offer his name, but the plate on his desk read "M. Severin."

He was a smallish man, impeccably dressed, with the pale face of someone who did not see much sun. His dark hair was parted in the middle; along with his authoritative manner he seemed more Prussian than French.

"Nevertheless, I remain grateful, especially as I am a colleague not under your watch," Donnay returned.

"I know who you are, monsieur Donnay, and your record too," Severin responded very business-like. "Furthermore, I'm quite familiar with the 'Opera Ghost' case and how much you have suffered in its wake." He offered a quick smile. "Unlike my aide, not all of us here were born yesterday. So tell me, what is it you wish to see me about?"

Donnay reached into the inside pocket of his coat and withdrew an envelope. "I have here a letter from your predecessor. It was sent to me some years ago before I was sufficiently healed to take advantage of it," he said, passing it to Severin. "It is in the way of a commitment that I trust will still be honored."

The chief read carefully, without reaction. When he'd finished, he put the letter back in the envelope and returned it to Donnay.

Donnay put the letter in his pocket and waited out the uneasy silence that followed as Severin put his thoughts together. Finally, he spoke.

"If this letter were more timely, I would have little hesitation honoring my predecessor's pledge," he began slowly. "But during the long period you have been away, through no fault of your own, much has happened, including a so-called 'war to end all wars' as some optimists would have it. We lost many people including a number of your colleagues in this office, all of whom had to be replaced as quickly as possible due to a soaring crime rate that has arisen from the ashes of the war.

"I'm not talking about petty crimes either like vagrancy or burglary," he continued, "but uncommonly bizarre and vicious crimes like those horror plays they put on at the Théâtre du Grand-Guignol where hands are lopped off and throats slashed to astonish audiences."

Donnay was familiar with the theatre although he had never been. It was located in Pigalle, one of the seedier districts of the city, and known for its sensationalist dramas and realistically bloody effects presented on stage. He was surprised it was still in business in these troubled times. He would have thought the public's appetite for macabre and ghoulish entertainment had been sated by the horrors of the war. But from what the chief described, it had only been whetted.

"And then, of course there are the crimes of real-life monsters like monsieur Henri Landru," the chief was saying. "Are you familiar with his case?"

As with the "Opera Ghost" affair, newspapers were full of sensational stories of the meek-mannered furniture and antiques dealer who'd been arrested in April of last year on suspicion of multiple murder. Donnay had followed them with great interest. The case was still being investigated as Landru, continuing to proclaim his innocence, awaited trial without bail. The press called him "Bluebeard" because his victims were mostly women, whom he'd swindled out of their money before making them "disappear."

Donnay confirmed his knowledge of the case with a nod. Then he steeled himself as best he could for what he anticipated was coming next.

"For a variety of reasons, some of which I've just explained, I cannot restore you to your former position," Severin went on. "Quite simply, it is currently filled. As are all other positions here in the prosecutor's office. I'm sure you would not approve of having someone else displaced to make room for you."

Donnay shook his head solemnly. "No, of course not."

"But all is not lost," the chief prosecutor suddenly continued brightly. "If it is work you seek, I may have a lead for you over at the Three-Six. It would allow you to keep your hand in so to speak."

"Police work, you mean?"

"No, not exactly. The position is for an assistant archivist."

"A file clerk in other words," Donnay remarked, feeling deflated.

"Yes, in a manner of speaking. The filing of all records, police reports, and case notes from this office and the Three-Six. It's an important job, and from what I'm told the chief archivist is getting a bit long in the tooth and may soon be retiring. So there could be an opportunity for advancement right away," Severin explained, still trying to sound positive.

Advancement to what? *Chief* File Clerk? Donnay thought sourly, suppressing a mirthless laugh.

He'd half expected getting his former position back was a 50-50 proposition—at best. But he was trying hard not to let his disappointment show. He didn't want to come across as insulted nor resentful. It was in his best interest to keep the chief prosecutor on his side.

"Given your experience and celebrity as the vanquisher of the 'Opera Ghost,' I recognize this solution is not ideal," the chief prosecutor said as if reading Donnay's thoughts. "But it's only temporary until an opening here comes up."

Yes, there is that side to it, Donnay contemplated somewhat optimistically, recognizing that he had few other immediate options.

"So, are you interested in the position, monsieur Donnay? Or not?" Severin inquired abruptly, breaking the silence.

"Yes, thank you, monsieur Chief Prosecutor, I should like to look into it. I am most grateful," Donnay responded, making his decision. He couldn't afford a bruised ego and added the last remark as a touch of flattery.

"Very good then," Severin replied with satisfaction. He picked up a pen and scribbled something on a piece of paper, handing it to Donnay. "Here's the person to see at Three-Six."

For a very long time Donnay had considered it was hit and miss whether he'd ever work again let alone as a public prosecutor. But he now had his health back and that's what he should focus on. He accepted the note with the contact's name and rose to leave, offering his hand. "Thank you again, monsieur."

"Good day and good luck to you, Donnay," the chief prosecutor said, shaking his hand.

As Donnay left the room, he glanced down at the paper in his hand and felt the impact and supreme irony of the name written on it as if it were a body blow. It was that of the man who had almost cost him his life.

Etienne Verneuil.

PART TWO

HOLLYWOOD
1921–1923

SIX

Hollywood Hills
Los Angeles County, California

Ever since being a part-time cub reporter for his hometown newspaper—the Egerton, Nebraska *Courier-Ledger*—Ted Alexander had a thirst to see his proud byline on a Major Scoop.

Rather than go on to higher education after graduating school, as his parents had wished, he'd taken a job as a reporter full-time at the *Ledger* for the, to him, astonishing salary of eight dollars a week. Of course, he was the weekly newspaper's *only* full-time reporter so that may have accounted for the publisher's largesse.

Even a newcomer like him knew that his chances of landing that Major Scoop in Egerton were few and far between. The most scandalous story he'd covered during his entire time there involved the falsification of grades by some of the teachers at Egerton High under school board pressure to give the sons and daughters of some of the town's wealthier citizens a leg up in acceptance at ivy-league colleges. But even that scandal was greeted by a collective ho-hum from the citizenry who apparently believed, "What else is new?"

No, the only legitimate opportunity for landing that Major Scoop, Ted realized, lay elsewhere in a big city like New York or Chicago where the most important newspapers of the day were located. So that's where he had focused his ambition.

But getting out of Egerton wasn't as easy as he thought it would be. Judging by the number of rejections for employment he'd received from all the papers in those big cities—and there were plenty of them—the competition was just too fierce.

And so, he had set his sights on the growing west coast instead, specifically Los Angeles. It was a newspaper-friendly town with a dozen or more dailies, weeklies and bi-weeklies, ranging from top-tier publications like the *L.A. Times* to lowly sensation-seekers like the *L.A. Crier*. Ted figured he stood a better chance at getting hired by one of these papers instead.

Los Angeles was the land of opportunity where America's hottest new industry—the moving picture—had firmly taken hold of the public's imagination and spending money across the country. Big-time scandals and major exposés were only to increase, he anticipated.

And so he had decided not to bother sending out query letters of employment to the L.A. papers. Believing it was harder to say no to an eager-beaver like him face-to-face than it was to a letter, he determined to pitch each paper in person.

First though, he would need a car. He'd been told that unlike New York and Chicago where reporters could easily travel anywhere on public transportation, L.A. County was still the Wild West, topographically at least. There were some bus and streetcar lines serving the more populated areas. But if you were a newshound whose job was to sniff everywhere, you had to own or have access to a car.

Thereafter, Ted began putting aside a small amount each week from what he now realized was a meagre, no longer generous, salary to purchase a Ford touring car, otherwise known as a Model T or "Tin Lizzie."

It had taken him two whole years of hard saving and austere living, but by Christmas 1920, he'd accumulated the money he needed to purchase the latest model off the Ford assembly line. It was a beauty too with a dark tan convertible top, wood lining and cotton interior. He even got a spare tire thrown in for a few extra bucks, bringing the total for everything to $365.

That night he'd begun packing for his getaway. The next morning he filled up the gas tank under the car's front seat, and was on his way west.

The route to California took him through Colorado and Utah and consumed five solid days of dawn-to-dusk driving. Along the way he'd had to stop over at enough prairie dog towns to serve him a lifetime. The muscles in his lower back still ached from all the rough roads he'd bounced over during his trek.

Mercifully, he'd experienced just one blowout the entire way when he'd hit a sharp rock on a long, dusty road in Utah. Just in case, he'd fortuitously brought along a wrench to put on the spare and was able to get the flat fixed in the next dirt water town. It took him another half day to reach the outskirts of Los Angeles, but the closer he got, the better the roads became. Some were even paved!

Once there, he rented a cheap furnished apartment on Malcolm Street in Santa Monica. It was near enough to the ocean that he could hear the waves rolling in. The landlord had given him a tough time at first, constantly shouting "No movies. No movies" at him in a foreign accent Ted couldn't place.

Eventually the meaning of the landlord's words became clear. In this case "no movies" meant no here-today-gone-tomorrow tenants like those looking for work in moving pictures. In other words, no lease-breaking itinerants. But Ted was able to convince the man that he was a gainfully employed newspaper reporter in the job for the long haul. Fortunately, the landlord had apparently not run into any other reporters as tenants or he would have known that they were among the most itinerant lease-breakers of all.

After a few days of resting up and doing some sightseeing, Ted then had begun his search for the gainful employment he'd already assured the landlord he possessed. The quest took him to newspapers on both sides of the not-quite-a-mountain-but-more-than-a-hill that divided the sprawling county of Los Angeles. He'd gotten nowhere fast as one by one each turned him down.

Finally, he'd gotten "lucky" and was hired by the *L.A. Crier*, whose small, dark offices were at least conveniently located on his side of the divide in what was euphemistically called downtown Los Angeles where many of the movie people lived, but, more importantly, *played*.

Now he was officially a representative of the L.A. press—albeit a lowly one at a publication of equal stature.

Several months later he was on the scent of what he believed to be the biggest scandal of the moving picture era so far and his Major Scoop.

He'd had to cajole the publicity department at Universal to land an interview with the subject of his investigation. It was under the pretext of doing an updated profile in conjunction with the release of the interviewee's next picture for the company, a swashbuckler titled *Prince of Pirates*, that he'd gotten the plum assignment. In hopes of digging up some high-quality dirt, he was on his way to the interview now at the Hollywood Hills home of his subject, the celebrated actor and "man of mystery" Sebastian Vane.

Not bad for a wet-behind-the-ears cub reporter from Egerton, Nebraska.

Sebastian Vane Residence
Hollywood Hills, California

Sebastian Vane lived in a re-developed area of the Hollywood Hills called Whitley Heights. An earlier attempt at developing the area had gone up in flames a few years back when some say a brush fire and others say arson raged out of control, reducing every semi-built structure, pepper tree, and all the lush landscaping to cinders.

The restoration and rebuilding of the Heights were resumed about a year ago. Homes were expensive, catering mostly to the nouveau riche who had climbed to the top in the young but lucrative business of moving pictures.

Ted Alexander pulled into the lighted courtyard of Vane's opulent, two-story Spanish Colonial Revival complete with stucco walls, low-pitched clay tile roof and large, arched windows. He turned off the engine, filling his nostrils with the pungent aroma of citrus floating up to him from the orchards in the San Fernando Valley.

He stepped enthusiastically onto the gravel drive and straightened his tie. He seldom wore one nor the light brown suit that went with it, which matched the color of his hair. But tonight was special and he wanted to make a good impression with the actor who was known to be a bit off-putting. He'd even polished up "Lizzie" so that she sparkled like new again after her long, trying journey.

He now girded his loins for the interview to come. Having rehearsed it in his mind over and over again, he felt comfortable that he would be able to steer Vane into confirming the dramatic revelations Ted knew in his bones to be true even though he had little actual proof.

That was the big question, of course. Would Vane admit to the sensational charges? But just in case he remained tight-lipped, Alexander had planned for that too—by giving Vane a whiff the star would quickly pick up on of the potential "squeeze" he wouldn't otherwise be able to avoid.

He pulled on the door chime and heard a muffled ringing inside. Momentarily, the door was opened by one of the most imposing figures Ted had ever encountered. It wasn't Vane but his manservant-cum-bodyguard of whom Ted had heard but never seen, until now.

At five feet eleven inches tall, Ted Alexander didn't consider himself to be a small man. But the manservant had a good four to five inches on him and appeared even taller with the thick, dark blue turban that graced his head. His deeply lined, swarthy face and blank expression worn over a black shirt, loose-fitting black pants and a long, flowing robe of red and black made him look scary as hell. So much so that Ted was now wondering if perhaps he had miscalculated and should just turn away with an, "Oops, sorry. Wrong house!"

But then he heard a voice shout from within: "Let him in, Bahram. I know who he is. I'm expecting him."

The manservant stepped aside, widening the door, and Ted stepped in, the door thudding behind him. It was too late to run now.

The stoic Bahram led him down several steps into a sunken living room where Vane awaited in a plush armchair beside a large, open fireplace of clay, a Southern California design tradition. The embers glowed a soft orange, giving off a gentle heat.

Vane rose slightly to extend his hand. Alexander accepted the iron grip with a subtle wince.

"We'll talk here," Vane said, sinking into the armchair again. "Please have a seat. Would you like some refreshment? Wine, beer, or perhaps something stronger?"

"No, thank you, I'm fine," Ted said, taking a plush chair opposite his host. He continued rubbing the circulation back into his hand.

Bahram moved behind Vane's chair and stood there silently as a statue.

"Not much of a conversationalist is he," Ted said, eyeing the giant. "I take it he only speaks when spoken to?"

"Not even then," Vane replied. "You see, Bahram has no tongue."

Shocked and embarrassed, Ted made his apologies to both of them and took a minute to regain his reporter's composure.

Without the false mustaches, beards, and wigs he typically wore in his pictures, Sebastian Vane was an extremely handsome man with dark olive skin and a smooth, unlined face characteristic of a man in his mid-to-late twenties rather than one in the thirty-five to forty range that Vane's studio biography stated. He wore a scarlet ascot with a light-colored sport coat.

Ted knew from articles he'd read about Vane that the actor preferred character rather than leading man roles just like his only competitor in the "man of mystery" category, Lon Chaney. But unlike the rough-featured Chaney, Vane had the matinee idol looks to play both. Which made Alexander wonder why studio executives would let Vane hide those looks under wigs and behind mounds of crepe hair. Perhaps the studio just went along because his pictures always pulled in the crowds, male and female.

"So, you've come to ask about the new picture I'm starting—*Prince of Pirates*?" Vane asked in a deep, mellifluous voice.

Ted took out a pad and pencil. "That and some other things," he replied.

Vane lifted an eyebrow. "Other things? Such as what, for instance?"

Ted cleared his throat. "Your background, for example."

"You can get that from the publicity department or almost any back issue of *Photoplay*," Vane responded.

"Yes, but they deliver only the frosting," Ted replied. "What I want is the cake."

Vane's eyebrow rose again. "You have an interesting way of putting things," he said.

"I guess that's why I'm a reporter," Ted replied with his eager-beaver grin.

"OK, so what is the cake in my background that you wish to be served?" Vane asked after a pause.

"You were born on the Mediterranean island of Corsica. Correct?" Ted queried.

"Yes. Me and Napoleon. As everybody already knows."

"Why did you leave Corsica?" the reporter asked.

"Because there were no opportunities for me unless I wanted to be a shopkeeper, a fishmonger, a member of organized crime, or, perhaps, a future emperor," Vane said with some sarcasm. "None of which appealed to me."

"So you went to Italy to try and get into pictures."

"Yes, they were producing many spectacles there for which they required background players," he said. "I thought that might be a way in for me. And it was. I was consumed by lava from the erupting Mount Vesuvius in *The Last Days of Pompeii*; consumed by fire from the burning of Rome in *Quo Vadis?*; and

66

consumed yet again by lava from another erupting volcano in *Cabiria*.

"Going up in flames grew a bit monotonous so I arranged passage on a steamer out of Sardinia bound for California. We disembarked in San Diego and from there I made my way up to Hollywood with the goal of finding more satisfying work in the pictures being made there. Is that enough cake for you?"

Alexander smiled. "Not nearly enough," he said. "Is it true you were discovered by D.W. Griffith?"

"No. Not 'discovered,'" Vane corrected him. "I'd heard Mr. Griffith was making a picture called *The Mother and the Law*," he explained. "Part of it was to be a spectacle similar in size and scope to the pictures I'd made in Italy. When I arrived in Hollywood, they were already putting up the great hall of Babylon for the picture, which had been re-titled *Intolerance*. It was the most colossal set I'd ever seen, even including those in the Italian epics." He paused for a second to cross his legs and take a sip of the drink by his chair.

"My hair was a bit long and shaggy after so long at sea," he continued, "and so I shaped the sides into ringlets befitting an ancient warrior, pasted on a convincing beard to look fearsome and sought a job as an extra for one of the picture's battle scenes. It was during shooting that I met the director, Mr. Griffith, who took a shine to me and had me kill or be killed in more than one scene. As a result I was paid a little more than the box lunch most extras got."

"But you only made the one picture for him."

"So far," Vane responded with a chuckle. "I hope we have at least a few more years left between us to get together again."

"Why do you think he took a shine to you particularly?" Alexander asked pointedly.

"I don't 'think.' I *know*," Vane replied. "He was very interested in the pictures I'd made in Italy. Asked me all sorts of questions about them—how this effect was done and that one. He wanted to outdo them, you see. And he did. Marvelous man. Generous too. He helped me get parts in some western two-reelers over at Universal and that led to my getting a big part as the villain in *The Prairie Schooner*."

"Your big break."

Vane nodded. "Yes. It was another epic about the pioneers crossing the Oregon Trail and settling the West. It was Universal's biggest picture of the year. A Universal 'Jewel' they advertised it. Made the company a fortune."

"And that led to your starring in *The Prisoner of the King*."

Vane nodded. Then he laughed. "Universal didn't like to pay a lot for properties," He said. "So for that one they went back to the classics, which are available for free to anyone. They got a writer to contrive a mixture of *The Man in the Iron Mask* and *The Count of Monte Cristo*." He laughed again. "I wore a trim mustache and small goatee as the hero. Worked out quite well, I thought."

Ted shifted position and flipped a page in his notepad. Here goes, he said to himself anxiously. "There's something about your chronology of events that I find a bit puzzling," he offered provocatively.

Vane visibly stiffened, as did his manservant, Ted noticed. His question had put both of them on guard.

"And what's that?" Vane asked, impatient as to where this was going.

"You said you left for Italy right after finishing school. Is that correct?" Ted queried.

"Not immediately, no," Vane replied. "But within a few years, more or less."

"When you were nineteen or twenty, perhaps?"

"That sounds about right."

"And the pictures you made in Italy were first released for exhibition to the public in 1913, is that also correct?"

"Yes…," Vane let out warily. "You seem to have something on your mind, Mr. Alexander. Why not come right out and ask it?"

Ted smiled mischievously. "OK, I will. How did you support yourself all those years in between?"

"Really, what possible interest would your readers have in that?" Vane scoffed.

"Oh, I think they would be very interested in how a major star such as yourself made ends meet before catching a break," Ted said. "Shows persistence."

After a long pause, Vane answered. "I did a lot of menial work. Odd jobs. Things like that. Is that enough persistence for you?"

Alexander looked skeptical. "Menial work for more than a decade? A sharp cookie like you?" He shook his head.

Anger flashed across Vane's face, and that of his otherwise impassive bodyguard's as well. Ted knew he had hit a nerve.

Vane eyed him suspiciously. "What are you getting at?"

The reporter let the man cool off a bit—and then sprung his trap. "Are you familiar with the name Earle Kincaid?" he asked.

Vane took a moment as if trying to recall—or making it seem that way. "He was a stunt player on *The Prairie Schooner*, I believe. Yes, I knew him slightly."

"If I'm not mistaken, you knew him well enough to attend his funeral," Ted put in.

"Yes, he was injured on that picture and never quite recovered."

"Broke his back in a wagon fall, wasn't that it?"

Vane nodded.

Ted flipped through his pad. "Actually, my notes say he did recover—although he'd been in a lot of pain while convalescing, for which his doctors prescribed morphine."

"I believe that's true, yes."

"But the pain stayed with him," Ted pressed on. "And so did the morphine, although no one knew where he got it—and he died of his addiction."

"That was a rumor spread by vicious gossipers," Vane said loudly.

"Among them his widow?" Ted replied calmly. "Was she a vicious gossiper too?"

"What are you suggesting?"

Ted closed his notepad. "What I'm suggesting is that you supplied Kincaid with the illegal morphine."

"That's outrageous!" Vane thundered.

"Furthermore, I suggest that you've been supplying illegal drugs to the rich and powerful in this town ever since you got here," Ted added. "Just as you did in Italy all those years you were 'making ends meet'—while creating a pipeline for illegal drug smuggling on behalf of your benefactors, the Corsican mob."

Vane exploded out of his chair. "That's enough!" he shouted. "This interview is over and I want you gone. *Now!*"

Vane's mighty manservant started moving ominously from behind his master's chair.

"Down boy," Ted quipped at the giant while rising to leave. "I can see I've worn out my welcome."

"You print one ugly word of those accusations in your tawdry rag and you'll be hit with the biggest lawsuit your publisher has ever seen," Vane fulminated, shaking his fist.

"Message received," the brash reporter quipped once more. "Meanwhile, I want to thank you for taking the time to talk to me."

"*GO!*"

Holding his breath that he would make it outside, Ted moved quickly for the door, the sound of Bahram's heavy boots echoing behind him on the tile flooring.

The reporter almost tripped making his exit, but once he was safely out the door, he could breathe again. It was cooler at night in the hills and he sucked in the fresh air greedily. Behind him the door closed and was locked.

The interview with Sebastian Vane had gone even better than he had hoped. The actor was full of righteous indignation and moral outrage at the charges the reporter had leveled. *But he hadn't denied them.* Which indicated that Vane would think twice about bringing a suit against the newspaper for slander. Bluster works both ways and Vane would be fearful of not knowing how much actual evidence the reporter possessed. This was known in journalistic parlance as the "squeeze" — a way to draw more information from your subject as well as the proof you didn't really have. Besides, it wasn't Vane the reporter wanted to take down anyway. It was the ringleaders of the Corsican mob behind the operation that he wanted to expose, and Vane was his route to them.

"Lizzie, take me back to the office," Ted Alexander said excitedly to his waiting automobile. "I think we're finally in business."

SEVEN

Coal Springs, Wyoming

Ever since she experienced her first moving picture, Leslie Pagano knew exactly what she wanted to do with her life—become a star of the "flickers." And from then on she was determined to make that happen. She was ten.

Coal Springs, Wyoming's only movie house was located, like practically everything else in the one-horse town, on Main Street. It was given the highborn name the Regal even though it was built over what had once been an old livery stable.

A weathered sign tacked to the front of the ticket booth for the longest time proclaimed the name of theatre itself and its specialty: "2 BIG Features Daily Mon. thru Sat." The sign disappeared when the ticket booth was torn down in 1920 and replaced with a more elegantly shaped structure called a "box office."

The Regal changed programs three times a week and Leslie went to every Friday or Saturday show. The theatre was closed on Sunday because the religious folks ("blue noses," Leslie and everyone else called them) wanted everyone's eyeballs fixed only on God on the Sabbath. But that was okay with Leslie because the schedule gave her time to get most of her chores done for the upcoming week and leave plenty of space weekdays to complete school work, thus keeping her folks off her back.

By tenth grade, Leslie got permission from her folks to see the Monday-Tuesday and Wednesday-Thursday programs as well. As long as she was home weeknights by nine thirty, they never complained. They may not have been happy about their daughter's pastime, and things did get a bit dicey when her teacher called to express concern over the schoolgirl's near-obsession with "the pictures," (as she called them disdainfully), but as long as Leslie didn't fall behind in her chores or her grades, her folks reluctantly continued to give her their support.

Of course, all this picture-going cut substantially into the time she was able to devote to her after-school dramatics class. She and her close friend Aggie Coates had been taking the class together ever since eighth grade when the activity was first offered.

Aggie's real name was Agnes, but Leslie (and everyone else) called her Aggie for short. Aggie used Leslie for short and long because "Les" sounded too much like a boy's nickname.

Even though they tried out for every school play and talent show together, Leslie was always chosen—not just because of her acting and singing skills, Aggie always insisted, but because of her beauty and poise, as well. Whereas whenever Aggie was chosen, she, who was a bit on the plump side but also had talent to burn, believed it was because she was Leslie's friend. That was typically Aggie, always selling herself short. Whereas Leslie never sold herself short. She knew she would have a lot to learn to make it as an actress, especially as the profession was so frowned upon in much of the country and especially in her native Midwest as "shameful."

But Leslie had the ability, which was often commented upon in the town newspaper's reviews of her school shows, and she had the drive; she was going to make the most of them. Leslie's involvement in dramatics had given her the bug for performing, but it was her omnivorous picture-going habit that nurtured the bug into a passionate goal.

Leslie's favorite stars of the screen among the men were dapper but funny Lew Cody, athletic Tom Mix (though he appealed mostly to the boys), charismatic and commanding Sebastian Vane, and the heartthrob of every girl in her class, Wallace Reid.

But it was the female stars who captivated her most. She could imagine dressing in the latest fashions like they did and being one with them up there on the screen. Her favorites were the stunning "Biograph Girl" Florence Lawrence, pixie-like Mary Pickford, saucy Blanche Sweet, the elegant Gloria Swanson, and golden-curled ingénue Mary Miles Minter whom Leslie's friends said she most resembled — except for the color of Leslie's hair, which unlike Minter's was long and Mediterranean dark.

To subsidize her passion — again with her parents' consent — and before she turned seventeen, Leslie managed to get a part-time job after school. The town's biggest employers were the coal mining industry and the railroad, for which she was totally unqualified. But she finally lucked out and was hired by a general store on Main Street not far from the Regal itself.

She didn't make much money in the job, which mostly involved sweeping up and keeping the shelves stocked, but enough that together with her meagre allowance, she was able to afford seeing the three weekly programs at the Regal as well as indulge her new hobby — reading about the actual making of the pictures she saw in the monthly magazines *Photoplay,*

Picture-Play and *Motion Picture,* which cost her between five and fifteen cents each issue.

Leslie also began making plans for getting out of Coal Springs once and for all to realize her dreams in Hollywood. As soon as she graduated from high school and saved enough to pay her train fare, she would be on her way.

To her surprise and delight, Aggie asked to come along and started saving up too. Now they could become screen stars together! Aggie realized that her own appearance was rather drab and that might work against her. But she knew she had talent and it was worth a try. "Not everybody out there's a raving beauty," she would exclaim. "Look at Zasu Pitts!"

Her friend welcomed Aggie's company because as determined as Leslie was, the prospect of being so far away from home for the first time, and on her own besides, made her downright anxious. But with Aggie along, the adventure would be fun and not as scary. In fact, Aggie's request to accompany her also sat well with Leslie's folks who had otherwise strongly opposed their willful daughter's plans. Her mom wanted her to go to the newly built college up in Laramie County because it wasn't so far away. Whereas her dad believed higher education was wasted on girls unless they were to become teachers or nurses. He wanted her home until she was married.

Additionally, Leslie's mom was of the conviction that while her daughter was indeed exquisitely pretty, looks like hers were probably the norm in Hollywood. So she was fearful that Leslie's dreams could be crushed by all that competition, and her spirit along with them.

In spite of all their misgivings, Leslie's folks would offer their blessing under one condition. Her dad had a cousin who owned and operated a poultry farm in the San Fernando Valley. If the cousin and his wife agreed that Leslie and Aggie could stay with them, her folks would no longer object to the girls' big adventure.

"It'll be like having a piece of home there with you and being away won't be as intimidating," her mom said. And safer too from all the human wolves she was convinced roamed around out there, which remained unsaid.

And so the arrangements were made to board the two girls with the cousin and his wife, who were childless and therefore welcomed the idea with considerable favor, saying there was more than enough room for the girls to stay there for as long as they liked.

Come the day of departure, however, Leslie waited and waited for her friend to show up at the train depot. But Aggie never did. Was she in an accident? Had her folks at the last minute decided she couldn't go? Leslie wouldn't know for months what had happened to her companion when, now settled in California, she received a letter of apology from Aggie.

"In the end I had to face up to the fact that my dreams weren't as strong as yours, and my jitters were a lot greater," the girl wrote. "The idea of going so far away and being such a total stranger in so different a place than I'd ever known just became too overwhelming for me to handle. I at least should have shown up and told you in person that I wasn't going," the girl added, asking for forgiveness. "What can I say but that I'm a coward?

"You're totally different," the letter concluded. "Our graduation yearbook says it all. You *are* most likely to succeed. And I'll be rooting for you every step of the way. Love, Aggie."

They never saw each other again.

EIGHT

Universal Studios
Universal City, California

Victor Reilly had it made.

From common laborer in tattered clothes on a chicken ranch under the blistering sun to casting director and talent scout in a tailored dark blue suit at a major studio in the new mecca known as Hollywood—all in less than a decade, from 1914 to 1923.

He almost had to pinch himself.

If his folks back in Pennsylvania coal country knew of his good fortune—which they didn't and never would if he had anything to say about it—they'd be here faster than a gold seeker with their hands out, begging for deliverance from their hardscrabble existence. But the only things his folks ever delivered to him was life itself, followed thereafter by an endless stream of whippings and demands to get this and that. He'd been nothing to his folks but a punching bag and a servant. Now they were nothing to him.

As soon as he was grown—he'd shot up to six feet by age sixteen—he'd hopped a series of trains headed west to seek his fortune. He never expected to find it on a sprawling ranch fixing chicken coops, but damn if that's not where it finally showed up.

On a hot July day in 1914, Reilly had been fencing in a coop he'd reconstructed like a fortress to keep out coyotes and other poultry-stealing riff raff when a green Scripps-Booth Rocket convertible pulled off the dirt road in front of the ranch. It quickly got stuck in the mud from one of the chicken coop run-offs that had soaked the parched earth.

The driver, an older man in a three-piece gray suit and camel-colored felt homburg, tried rolling the vehicle back and forth to free it, but the mud held the wheel in a tight grip and wouldn't let go.

Finally, he called over to Reilly. He spoke in a thick German accent that Reilly had little trouble deciphering given the large population of German immigrants in his Pennsylvania hometown.

"Excuse, please, can you help me? Mein auto ist kaput," the man shouted.

Reilly smiled as he strolled over. "It ain't kaput, mister. Tire's just mired in mud," he returned pleasantly.

"Can you *un-mire* it?"

"Well, let me see now," Reilly said as he stepped in front of the car. Then he reached down and wrapped his fingers around the iron bars beneath the grille, and with several warm-up shrugs of his broad shoulders, lifted the car's front section from the mud and set it on dry land.

"There you go," he said, wiping sweat from his face. Except for the bigger models, all these *lizzies* weigh just about nothing, he smirked.

The older man looked at Reilly agape. "I haff neffer seen any-ting like that," he exclaimed in his thick accent.

"Work on a ranch awhile and you'll be able to do it, too," Reilly said.

"No, tank you," the man replied. Then he asked if the ranch was just for raising chickens.

"No, no," Reilly replied. "It's more than a couple hundred acres of land so there's plenty of cows, steers and other livestock, horses, the whole lot. Why, you interested in gettin' into ranchin'?" The thought amused him for he couldn't see the dapper gentlemen, who appeared to be in his fifties, ordering around a bunch of cowpunchers.

The man explained that he was interested in buying a ranch, not running it. This location perfectly suited his needs. "I run a moofing picture studio and vant to expand," he said, thrusting out his hand. "I'm Carl Laemmle," he offered. The two of them shook hands.

"Victor Reilly," he replied. He was surprised by the man's grip. It was quite strong.

"I vill need big men like you to build mein studio, Mr. Reilly," Laemmle said. "Vould you like to come vork for me?"

Reilly couldn't believe what he was hearing. A real, live opportunity was coming his way out of the blue—from an apparent big shot in the picture business. He was going to seize it with both hands. "I sure would," he said, then added uncertainly: "You ain't just playin' with me, are you?"

Laemmle smiled broadly, revealing a stained set of smoker's teeth, and took Reilly's hand again, shaking it vigorously. "I'm qvite serious," he said.

"Me, too," Reilly said and the two men shared a smile of mutual good fortune.

Laemmle got out of his car and lit a cigar. Reilly was surprised by how tiny the man was—just a tad over five feet, if that—and how big the cigar seemed by contrast. He felt ill at ease towering over Laemmle. The balance seemed wrong somehow. But for a big muckety-muck the old gent was awful down to earth and friendly.

"Tell me about yourself," Laemmle said chomping on his cigar.

Reilly gave him a watered down version of his upbringing, revealing that his mother's side of the family was German also, named Thiele from a place called Bavaria.

Laemmle whipped out his cigar and beamed with excitement. "Ve are almost relatives!" he shouted exuberantly.

Only later did Reilly learn that most of the employees at Laemmle's studio—Universal Pictures—were relatives of their employer if not in fact at least in nationality. That's why everyone called him "Uncle Carl." Reilly did too after a time. It was like one big happy family.

Laemmle was as good as his word. Within a few weeks he had negotiated a deal to buy the entire Taylor Ranch. And almost as soon as the papers were signed, the earth movers were called in to demolish all buildings and flatten the landscape to make way for the studio complex.

Hedging his financial bets, Laemmle insisted on keeping a small parcel of that land, however, to be maintained as a working chicken ranch. "People may get tired uf pictures, but they'll never get tired uf eating chicken," he would say.

Reilly had set up the chicken ranch for him and run it until construction began on the studio. It hadn't happened soon enough for him.

One day an obstinate chicken pecked him on the face when he'd tried moving it, breaking the skin and drawing blood. Furiously, Reilly had grabbed it by its scrawny neck and ripped its head off like some crazy geek in a carny show. Stupid creatures. He was sick of the sight of them.

But once again, Laemmle was as good as his word. He hired someone else to take care of the chickens and put Reilly to work building the first of the new "open stages" — so-called because they had no roof; a roll of muslin was used instead to pull over them in order to control the intensity of the sun for lighting the set, and also to keep out the rain.

By the early Twenties, the "open stages" were torn down and replaced by "dark stages." These were lit wholly by artificial means. Cameramen had become such wizards at simulating every lighting scheme offered by the sun that the sun itself was no longer required.

In addition the number of stages grew to more than eighteen and eventually to twenty-eight. Also, there were separate buildings for executive offices, wardrobe, props, carpentry, a writer's building and a commissary that had to be constructed as well. Reilly was among many laborers who had worked on "Laemmle's Folly" as the press called it early on. They were wrong, and Reilly was kept very busy indeed, earning a regular paycheck week in and week out for quite a few years until fortune smiled on him again.

As soon as each stage went up, it was put into use. As a result, Reilly had enjoyed a front row seat to how pictures were made. Even more to his liking was the close-up view it gave him of the seemingly endless array of beautiful girls it apparently required to make them — from voluptuous stars to up-and-coming starlets to wannabe extras.

"Uncle Carl" had a lot of women on his payroll, not just in front of the camera but behind it in technical, creative and even supervisory positions, as well. He had just one rule that he demanded of his co-ed workforce: *No funny business!* The rule was enforced, too. If word of any hanky-panky reached Laemmle's ears, the miscreants would be summarily put on suspension or fired. Nothing was to interfere with the harmonious functioning of Universal Pictures, he insisted; not a whiff of scandal would be tolerated.

But Reilly had his own set of rules. His co-workers might imagine all they wanted to of his acquaintanceship with numerous starlets and extras, but they never had any hard evidence of misbehavior on his part to bring to anyone's attention. That's because Reilly's rules were: (1) Never at the studio and (2) always be discreet.

Many of the women he bedded didn't even require plying with liquor or drugs to be seduced. They were all too willing because of his assurances that he would put in a good word for them to the right people, one that might lead to bigger parts or a desired screen test. They knew it was in their best interest not to talk about their dalliances with him—and he, a gentleman, of course, *never* talked, Reilly smiled to himself. Nobody ever caught on, or if they did they kept it to themselves. And Reilly reaped the rewards with continued gratitude from the women and impunity from above.

He had also reaped another even more important reward. After a time it was noticed by Universal executives and by Laemmle himself that not only was Reilly a good worker, but he had an eye for spotting talent, too. Several extras he'd recommended for screen tests to executives and picture directors he was friendly with around the lot had indeed demonstrated great screen presence and were summarily placed under contract. He'd also kept his word to those starlets he thought had real potential by letting them know when an appropriate role was in the offing and boosting them to the right people. Two of these starlets had already risen to star status.

As a result, "Uncle Carl" had asked Reilly as a personal favor to take the job of casting director and chief talent scout, an offer the flabbergasted Reilly had accepted at once. He couldn't believe his good fortune. An executive at a major Hollywood studio and he was just twenty-six! Only the youthful Irving Thalberg had risen as fast, but he was no longer at Universal, having just moved over to Metro as vice-president in charge of production.

Reilly stepped from his office and strolled toward the studio's main gate where today's collection of flotsam and jetsam was already gathering in hope of securing employment as extras for five dollars a day and a box lunch with a chicken sandwich and an apple. Some had bigger dreams, but for most that's all they could expect.

Quite a few were even dressed in costume—gowns, top hat and tails, or as cowboys, dance hall girls, Indian maidens, and ferocious-looking thugs. This effort to separate themselves from their competition and be noticed could work if there was a society comedy, a western or a crime picture currently before the cameras. But most of the time it didn't because more and more of these hopefuls showed up dressed in the same type of costume.

A rotund man named Nick with a clipboard in his hand was dispensing the good or bad news to the eager throng on the other side of the gate. Two studio guards were on hand to open the gate to the lucky few and force it shut on the unlucky many. Most of the studios operated this way in hiring extras, who would travel to each studio at the crack of dawn five days a week.

Reilly made his way over to Nick, who greeted him with a nod then turned his attention back to the hopefuls at the gate.

"Anything for me?" one of the men in cowboy garb shouted at Nick.

Nick glanced at his clipboard. "Let him in," he told the guards. Then he surveyed some of the other men in cowboy costume and said, "You, you and you." They each slipped through the gate excitedly and Nick handed them individual passes. "Report to Stage 14," he said as the gate once more was closed.

Reilly eyed the women dressed in costume or in street clothes, assessing their potential on screen and off like a hungry wolf. His gaze quickly fell on a particularly striking young woman in a frilly red dress who was being squeezed against the gate. She had green eyes, long, dark hair and was no more than twenty or twenty-one, he guessed. She looked virginal but was pleasingly buxom up top—an ideal mixture for pictures, and for him.

Pushing back with a temper at the surging crowd crushing her, she waved at Nick and called out, "I've been here since six; what have you got for me?"

"Sorry, nothing today," he responded without looking up from his clipboard.

Crestfallen, she started to move away when Reilly whispered something in Nick's ear and the rotund man quickly shouted for her to stop. "Unless you don't mind shedding some clothes," he queried.

"How many clothes?" she asked warily. Reilly liked that. She was no pushover.

"Not many," Nick said, rolling his eyes. "It's a family picture. You in or out?"

"*In!*" she whooped and was let inside the gate.

Nick handed her a pass, told her where to report and pointed in the direction. As she walked away with a spring in her step, he made a note on his clipboard, then looked at Reilly with a lopsided grin. "Happy now?" he said.

"You've made my day, Nick. Hers too, I'll bet, if the director isn't blind," Reilly said. "Who is the director?"

Nick looked at his clipboard. "Cabanne," he said.

Reilly nodded approvingly. "I think I'll mosey down there after a while," he said. "See how she makes out."

Reilly walked away, letting Nick get back to work. There was a spring in his step now too. "Yes, Vic old boy, you've surely got it made," he said to himself.

Then he spotted the headline of a copy of that week's *L.A. Crier* an idle stagehand was reading.

"DRUG RING INFILTRATES MOVIE COLONY"

The headline stopped him in his tracks.

NINE

Pagano Chicken Farm
Canoga Park, California

Dear Mama and Papa,

I have wonderful news! I've been cast in a moving picture. It's not a big part, more of an extra in the background, but it's a big, expensive picture out next year. The title is Prince of Pirates and it stars Sebastian Vane and Marie Prevost. I haven't met Miss Prevost yet but I did meet Mr. Vane. He was very down to earth, warm and considerate toward me, as were all the other extras and crew, especially the director, Mr. Cabanne, who is quite handsome and could be a movie star himself. I'm still walking on air. I play one of several aristocratic British women captured by pirates and held for ransom in the hold of their ship. Miss Prevost is the wealthy young wife of a plantation owner also being ransomed who falls under the spell of the title character played by Mr. Vane. He looks ferocious in his makeup with a large black moustache and a small but ugly scar.

Leslie Pagano relaxed her pen for a moment to consider what she'd written. She was still overcome by the amazing turn in her life that had occurred today. After a year of showing up weekly at the front gates of all the major studios (and some minor ones too), she had finally been called as an extra and taken her fledgling steps onto a big studio lot for the first time. She hoped she wasn't coming across to her folks as too giddy.

Arno and Elena Pagano, the cousins on her father's side of the family who had taken her in, had been wonderful to her throughout, giving her all the space she needed to pursue her dream without asking anything of her in return. But she had insisted on helping out with the chores and was assigned to feeding the chickens early in the morning before grabbing the bus or streetcar to one of the studios, and at night before going to bed. Only just now had she finished and begun writing at the kitchen table. Her cousins had already gone to bed and the house was quiet, a perfect time for corresponding.

Leslie had been writing to her folks regularly and in previous letters had strived to keep from showing them how low she had come to feel about her prospects of making any headway through the infernal studio gates. She wasn't alone in this, of course. Most of the people seeking work as extras remained anchored in the same boat. But that hadn't made her feel any better, especially as it was difficult if not impossible to make friends out here.

The women extras in particular were a fierce bunch. They saw her and others like her only as competitors. And so it had been a very lonely and disheartening existence for her almost from day one. Many a time she had been on the verge of quitting in tears and moving back home.

Until today.

Leslie picked up her pen and started writing where she'd left off:

> *My first time on an actual shooting stage was magical. All those big, powerful lights on the rigging above. The actors springing into their roles as the director called "Action!" The extras milling about in the background employing bits of business to fill out the scene. The cameraman, his hat turned around so the brim was in back, capturing the action with a steady crank of the camera. It was a thrilling adventure and I was now part of it! After being introduced to Mr. Cabanne, I was whisked into a side room and applied with white pancake makeup as I was supposed to look like someone hidden away from the sun. All that time outside on the farm and at the studio gates had given me quite a tan. Then I was put into my costume of a tattered dress, torn in all the right places, and whisked back to the studio to begin work. Mr. Vane was in the scene too and fully costumed, his wig a combination of long, stringy hair and dreadlocks under a Tricolor hat.*

What happened next, she did not write about for fear of worrying her folks. Mr. Cabanne was instructing the extras what he wanted them to do in the scene when one of the crew suddenly shouted, *"Look out!"*

Not knowing what to look out for or where, Leslie had just stood frozen, her eyes darting every which-way, when she felt someone grab her and pull her aside as one of the big studio lights crashed on the spot where she'd been standing, the fixture shattering into pieces. It was later determined that a clamp holding the light to the rigging was defective and had given way. She might have been killed.

In a soft and reassuring but authoritative voice, Sebastian Vane asked if she was all right. She nodded although she was still shaken up. It was he who had pulled her to safety.

Vane turned to Cabanne and suggested a short break. The director agreed and called out, "Take fifteen, everybody!"

Vane tapped the shoulder of one of the departing stagehands and said, "Take Miss Pagano to my bungalow, please." Then to Leslie: "I'll be with you in a minute." He looked darkly serious as he added, "But first I want a word with the gaffers[1]."

As Leslie was ushered from the set, she overheard the star harangue the gaffers in a booming voice for their incompetence. She hoped they wouldn't hold Mr. Vane's brutal reprimand against her. After all, however serious it might have turned out for her, it was an accident that could have happened to anyone on the set at any time.

Sebastian Vane's bungalow was on wheels so that it could be moved to whatever stage the star was working on. The stagehand helped Leslie up the steps and let her inside, leaving her alone until Vane got there.

The interior possessed a style that, except for an antique American grandfather clock standing against the wall near the entrance, was Mediterranean or perhaps even Arabic with thick multi-shaded rugs, fluffy floor cushions, and a riot of colorful patterns. The style reminded her of Vane himself, who looked a bit dark-skinned in his makeup and spoke with a slight, unidentifiable accent.

She was clearly in awe of him, a major star who played his status to the hilt, but without offensiveness. He was not at all overbearing, at least not toward her. In fact, when he arrived at

---

[1]Movie parlance for those heavy-lifters who, among other duties, rig the giant overhead lights on the set.

the bungalow he was still solicitous of her nerves and offered her a drink from his well-stocked hideaway bar to help steady them. She declined but he poured one for himself, the early hour and Prohibition be damned.

"Please sit," he said, stirring the drink.

She didn't dare try one of the comfortable looking cushions for fear of not being able to pull herself from it again, and so she took a chair instead. He sat in a rocking chair opposite her and sipped his drink.

"So, you're going to be an actress," he inquired.

"Not to sound conceited, but I already think of myself as an actress," she answered. "I want to be a better one."

"And you believe moving pictures can do that for you?" he asked.

"They're so glamorous and challenging, I just had to give them a try," she responded earnestly.

"And your first day almost became your last."

"Forgive me for not having already said so, but thank you for intervening on my behalf," she said sheepishly, looking down into her lap. "I don't know why but suddenly I just couldn't move."

"Fear does that," he said.

"I guess I've never experienced that kind of fear before," she said. "And hope to never again."

"You're from the Midwest," he said, changing the subject. "I can tell by your accent."

She smiled. "I didn't know I had one."

"In this business, we all come from somewhere else," he said, finishing his drink and putting the glass aside.

"I hear the trace of an accent in your speech, too. But I can't place it."

"Quasi-French," he confessed easily. "From an island in the Mediterranean. I come from a long line of thieves and bandits, architects and builders—on both sides of the family. But no actors. I'm the first."

She grinned. "Me, too," she said.

"I've been acting all my life, really," he said contemplatively.

There was a great solitude about this man, Leslie sensed; she believed that he was lonely. Perhaps that was why he had befriended her. Or maybe he was just flirting with her, though she ultimately decided against that alternative. Sebastian Vane didn't strike her as the kind of man who flirted, but rather as one who took what he wanted when he saw it and had the power to do so.

"When did you come to Hollywood?" she asked.

"A few years ago," he said. "I've been lucky."

"I hope some of that luck rubs off on me," she said, showing her fingers crossed.

Vane glanced at the grandfather clock. "Look at the time; we'd better be going before Christy develops an ulcer."

She stood up quickly. "Yes, I don't want to be late on top of everything else."

"Don't give it a thought. You were with me," he reassured her. "Now let's show 'em what you can do."

At the kitchen table, Leslie reflected upon her continuing good fortune, which carried over after the break onto the set where the director was preparing an action sequence. Again she put pen to paper, wrapping up the letter by describing to her folks what happened next:

> *Mr. Cabanne arranged us captives in position in the pirate ship's hold, a separate set built in a corner of the huge stage. As he called "Action," the door to the hold slid open and several disheveled members of the crew*

stumbled into the room to have their way with us, all of them drunk on rum. At the director's instructions, we all cringed in fear as they moved closer to us with lust in their eyes. At this point, Mr. Vane's character was supposed to burst into the hold and rescue us from "a fate worse than death" by fighting off each of the men and beating them to a pulp. But suddenly I felt a supreme indignation over the cowardly way my character was acting and rather than continue to shrink like a violet from these drunken sots, I grabbed a prop iron candle holder and leaped at them, waving it about threateningly. Rather than get mad and yell "Cut," Mr. Cabanne waited until the men froze in their tracks and only then signaled Mr. Vane to make his entrance. But instead of rescuing us with a dramatic fight, he grabbed the men collectively by the scruff of their necks and booted them out the door. I still don't know what made me get so feisty—actor's instinct, I guess. But it turned the scene around, converting it from a typical action piece to a comic finish, and there was a round of applause after it was over. Mr. Cabanne loved what I'd done and Mr. Vane said with equal enthusiasm that my improvisation had inspired him to improvise as well. Mr. Vane had a lot of input with the director on story. Together they expanded my part with other bits to do and by the end of the day, they told me I was no longer an unnamed extra but would receive billing in the picture's credits with the promise of bigger and better parts to come. Can you believe it? Dreams really can come true. From here on it's the life of a screen actress for me!

Your loving daughter,
Leslie

TEN

Offices of the *L.A. Crier*
Los Angeles, California

It was raining—and had been, practically non-stop, ever since three o'clock that afternoon. In otherwise sun-soaked Los Angeles, this was an anomaly except in rainy season, and it wasn't rainy season yet. But Ted Alexander didn't care. He had nowhere to be at this time of night except at his desk, which was where he was now with his feet up, reading—or rather re-reading for the umpteenth time—his bylined exposé of drug trafficking in the moving picture community.

Ted liked seeing his byline, especially on something as substantial as this—his first crack at some serious investigative journalism since he'd joined the *Crier* months and months ago; hell, in his entire professional life, which admittedly was not all that long. But Ted was impatient and he wasn't going to let a little gloomy weather spoil his triumph.

The newspaper's telephones hadn't stopped ringing since the week's edition hit the streets. Already the newspaper's editor/publisher, Mr. Swain, as well as his team of lawyers, had fielded furious accusations of journalistic impropriety from all the studio heads in town *and their lawyers.*

The studios' publicity people had also called, threatening to blackball the *Crier* from ever getting another interview from any of their respective organization's major or up-and-coming stars. Likewise, the studios fulminated about pulling their advertising from the *Crier*—not that they spent that much.

His exposé had definitely struck a nerve. For the first time in the *Crier*'s history, it had gone back to press three times already. Ted had no idea what circulation was up to now, but he believed it was sufficiently high to fill any advertising shortfall in the weeks to come.

Mr. Swain was delighted and not at all worried about any potential lawsuits. Ted had assured him and the lawyers that the facts supporting his exposé were unassailable. He had the goods. And Part Two, which was scheduled for publication in a few weeks, promised to be even more explosive.

He'd already sketched the piece out but hadn't started writing it yet as he had plenty of time until his deadline. But given the reaction Part One had caused, he imagined Part Two would cause twice the furor. In it, he would be naming names — most names anyway. Even in his zealousness to report all he knew, he wasn't about to be stupid.

The telephone rang on his desk and he snatched it up, anticipating another earful. He wasn't wrong.

"Ted Alexander," he announced proudly.

The caller identified himself in a furious bluster as Universal's publicity chief, Victor Reilly.

"Hey, Vic," Ted shouted jovially.

"Sure, spread it all over the office why don't you that I'm one of your sources," Reilly snarled.

Ted looked quickly around him and saw no one in the office but Adela Grant, the middle-aged woman who wrote the industry news, lovelorn columns and sob sister stories. She was way across the room and at work on one of her pieces, smoke enveloping her head from the cigarette dangling perpetually from her lips, dropping ash onto the typewriter keys. She seemed oblivious to the world around her. Nevertheless, Ted lowered his voice.

"There's no one here but me," he told Reilly. "What's up? You sound sore."

"Sore ain't the half of it," Reilly sputtered. "Why did you include the story of that dead doper Earle Kincaid? I thought we agreed it was off the record."

"Nothing was off the record," Ted corrected him. "I said I wouldn't use your name, and I didn't."

"You might as well have," Reilly fumed. "Only three people know that story and one of them can't speak."

Ted began whispering, not knowing how much Adela *could* hear over the rain even if she were not actually listening.

"That can't be true, Vic. This town leaks like a sieve, you know that," he said. "You think you and Vane are the only middle men pushing dope around here? Everybody knew Kincaid was an addict. His wife certainly did. She went on that crusade about addiction and the availability of illegal drugs, remember?"

"Yeah, but she never said where her husband got 'em from," Reilly shot back unconvinced. "You think she would have kept that to herself if she knew? I'm a dead man, Ted, and *you* put the mark on me!"

"I'm sure you're blowing things way out of proportion," Ted replied, still trying to calm the man down. "Have you seen Vane or talked to him since the paper came out?"

"Couple o' times at the studio," Reilly said.

"And how did he react?"

"Well he wasn't about to do anything to me there on the studio lot," Reilly scoffed.

"What I meant was did he treat you any differently, even in subtle ways, that you picked up on?"

Reilly thought for a moment, then offered a chuckle. "No. He treated me like I wasn't there, as always."

Ted could hear the man's anger softening.

"Of course, maybe he hadn't read your article yet," Reilly added.

In the wake of the last few tense minutes of his interview with Vane, Ted doubted that was likely. "I'm sure he had his eyes peeled for it," the reporter replied. "Face it, Vic, you're in the clear," he reassured Reilly. "Relax."

"From now on you get nothing more from me. Understood?" With that, Reilly hung up.

Slowly Ted Alexander replaced the receiver and set the telephone back on his desk. A smile crossed his lips. "That's okay, Vic," he thought, "I've got everything from you I need." The file and his notes were stored safely away.

He switched off the desk lamp, grabbed his raincoat, and headed for the exit, the rain still slapping at the office windows. It hadn't let up.

"Night, Adela," he called out above the din, giving her a little wave.

Still engulfed in cigarette smoke, she waved back without looking up from her typewriter as he went out the door.

Ted almost felt like whistling as he thought again of all the phone calls, including Reilly's, since his story broke.

Yessir, he sure had struck a nerve.

Pulling the collar of his raincoat up over his head to keep dry, Ted Alexander exited the *Crier* offices at Broadway and 3rd and walked briskly to his car at the curbside.

He was glad he'd had the presence of mind earlier that day to put the top up on his convertible at the first sign of threatening skies, and to roll the windows up tight as well. He climbed quickly inside, straightened his raincoat, and keyed the electric starter. "Lizzie" sputtered to noisy life.

The interior was nice and dry although a bit chilly. But that would change as soon as the engine warmed up and started throwing off heat.

On a night like this he knew the better, safer itinerary was to stay at a hotel in town rather than drive to his apartment in Santa Monica, a challenge even in the best of weather. The exhilaration of the past few days had finally caught up with him. He was bone weary and wanted to sleep in his own bed that night. Besides, his job hadn't made him flush enough yet to start renting hotel rooms.

The route wasn't at all welcoming except for the main streets in the series of small towns that dotted the way to the Pacific coast. The out-of-town roads consisted of mud-soaked flats when it rained, perilous curves, and steep hills. Plans were already underway to build a paved straightaway from downtown L.A. to Santa Monica and the already-under-construction Pacific Coast Highway that would bypass those roads until they too could be made safe. But completion was as yet some way off.

Ted pulled away from the curb and headed west, the headlights of the car cutting through the downpour as the wiper blades jerkily swept the water away.

Once more his thoughts returned to the reaction his exposé had generated around town. He had to laugh at the threats of the studio heads to cancel all future interviews and advertising. The moving picture business needed the *Crier* to keep stirring the public interest in its product as much as the *Crier* needed the material to stay afloat. The relationship was symbiotic. All that was required of the studios to keep scandal from their doors was to keep their employees' noses clean—literally as well as figuratively.

Ted laughed loudly at the pun he had made, then let out a deep yawn. He was more than bone weary now; he could feel his mind starting to drift. He rubbed the sleepiness from his eyes and put all his effort into keeping them fixed on the road ahead.

The hypnotic *whoosh* of the tires on wet pavement suddenly turned to a rocky *slurp* as muddy earth pulled at the wheel.

What Ted did not know was that his drowsiness wasn't entirely due to exhaustion. But he soon realized that something was off when he smelled an odd odor emanating from the vehicle's instrument panel.

The odor came from a tube of non-lethal knockout gas placed under the hood earlier. It was triggered to dissolve when the car started and the engine heated up, filling the interior of the vehicle with fumes as the car accelerated.

Ted was soon unable to fight off the sleep-inducing effects of the gas as it grabbed hold of his brain; he found himself unable to focus on driving and even struggling to breathe.

As the car bounced over rougher terrain, the steering wheel jerked from his grip.

He pulled it back under control spastically as he felt a numbing of his hands. He was beginning to lose feeling in his legs and didn't know whether his foot was easing up on the gas pedal to slow down or pressing hard on it to speed up.

The wiper blades couldn't keep up with the downpour and he could no longer see clearly. Before long his eyes started to close.

A tall, thick tree materialized suddenly in the center of the road. But that was impossible, he thought. He'd driven this route many times and had never encountered a tree growing in the middle of…

Then he realized he was on a curve and swerved the car just in time to miss the tree, which was actually on the side of the road, and avoid a collision.

The darkness that surrounded him got even darker as his closing eyes shut and he felt sleep descending.

Even the loud crunch as the car ricocheted off another tree, crashed through a fence and rolled down an embankment into a ravine swollen with rain failed to revive him.

Nor did the brief but terrible pain from a jagged piece of mangled steering wheel that pierced his sternum.

Within minutes, Ted Alexander was dead.

By morning, all remnants of the knockout gas had dissipated and when an autopsy was later performed, Ted was found to have perished in part from the severe wound in his chest, but mostly from drowning. His death was ruled an accident due to inclement weather.

Adela Grant wrote the glowing obituary in the *Crier*. Condolences poured into the paper from every level of the industry—actors, actresses and directors to studio heads.

Part One of Ted's exposé was soon usurped in notoriety by another now-long-forgotten Hollywood scandal. The notes to Part Two languished safely somewhere no one knew about but the dead man.

Until Adela Grant found them.

PART THREE

PARIS
1923-1924

ELEVEN

36 Quai des Orfèvres

Pierre Donnay was surprised by how much he had come to enjoy his work as assistant archivist.

No, it wasn't as challenging as being a public prosecutor—far from it. But reviewing and putting into order all the old case files had its own rewards, like keeping his brain active and alive.

That first day on the job two years ago had been a tough one. He and his new position seemed at first a poor mix—not because of the job itself but because of his new boss, the man he now had to report to rather than the other way around: Etienne Verneuil.

Many years had gone by since they had last seen each other in the watery netherworld of the Grand Garnier when the man's cowardice had almost cost Donnay his life.

Verneuil still had his sandy-colored hair but there was less of it now. And while Donnay had managed to remain trim, largely through the rigor of regaining his health and strength in hospital, the once-slim Verneuil had fleshed out considerably. In fact, he was now on the plump side and heading quickly towards fat. Donnay considered this was due to Verneuil's now being rooted to a desk as chief of detectives rather getting regular exercise moving about the streets of Paris solving crimes.

Or maybe it was all that crow he now had to eat and political asses he had to kiss to remain where he was, Donnay pictured with amusement.

Their first encounter after so long had been predictably polite but uncomfortable. Verneuil had invited Donnay to his office several flights upstairs in the "Three-Six" building for a welcoming chit-chat.

Over and over Verneuil had expressed his regret that the position was not up to Donnay's particular talents, but "a job is a job, after all," he'd concluded as if offering a comforting pearl of wisdom. Then he had launched into a description of just what the job entailed, which was not much considering that Donnay would be working with another man.

When that uneasy moment had passed there followed an equally uneasy silence, which Verneuil ended with a summary of the "Opera Ghost" case "as you weren't with us to share in the triumph," he said somewhat guiltily, or so Donnay imagined.

Donnay already knew most of what Verneuil reported but a few details got filled in here and there. "After a painstaking but fruitless search of the rubble for the devil's body, every surface he might conceivably have touched in his lair within the Garnier was fingerprinted for future comparison," he'd said. "But, alas, when the body we believed to be his was found floating in the Seine, it was so badly decomposed and otherwise mutilated that there were no fingerprints to be obtained. So, comparison was out of the question. We opted instead for a visual identification as much as that was possible. Christine Delfont took a look at the still-intact skull and she identified it right away as belonging to the 'Opera Ghost.' Case closed." He slapped the desk emphatically.

"And we were able to shut the file on the most difficult and controversial investigation in our history," he'd added. "One that had given the police and the public prosecutor's office such a black eye from the press and scorn from the public for so long." Then, leaning back in his chair, he'd smiled with satisfaction. "For all involved, it was time to turn the page and to move on. Don't you agree?"

Donnay had simply nodded.

"Then welcome," Verneuil had replied as if relieved. He held out his hand.

Donnay had accepted the flabby grip with feigned gratitude and then departed, taking the lengthy stairs down to the basement where hundreds upon hundreds of case files awaited his attention in their watertight boxes.

In the two years since, Donnay and Verneuil had seen little of each other except in passing—in mornings on their way in or going home at night. On each occasion, Verneuil had acknowledged Donnay with a casual glance that seemed to sum up the ex-prosecutor's reduced status in the eyes of his former underling. They seldom spoke.

Donnay had always returned these glances with a pleasant nod. There seemed little point in doing otherwise as Verneuil held the power of employment over him. And there were still no openings in the public prosecutor's office, as Donnay continued to be told.

The bulbous-nosed (from drinking) Michel Blier, his amiable sexagenarian co-worker in the archives, believed otherwise, although there was no evidence to the contrary. Blier accepted *nothing* on its face or preached as gospel by anyone.

He would often go into a coughing fit when he got worked up because like Donnay's landlady, Madame Delon, he smoked like a chimney. Donnay didn't pursue asking why he was such a skeptic for fear the old man might choke. He just attributed his skepticism to Blier's overall crustiness and left it that. He enjoyed the old iconoclast's company and liked working with him.

In terms of requiring careful weeding and structural attention, the oldest files were clearly in the worst shape. They were a mess—a veritable grab-bag of catch-as-catch-can.

Since working together he and Blier had made a good-sized dent in organizing the huge volume of case files stored in the basement of the Three-Six. Still, there was a long, long way to go. Many of these files dated back decades before Donnay or even his elderly co-worker were born. And more files were coming down all the time, some of them new, others just recently located after being misplaced in someone's desk drawer or lost behind a file cabinet.

For example, Donnay had just finished going through the recently discovered file on the mass killer Henri Landru whom the chief prosecutor had told him about. Following his arrest in 1919, Landru had been convicted on eleven counts of first degree murder and executed by guillotine in 1922. The file had languished somewhere in the halls of justice for two more years! But such instances were infrequent. Most files were where they were supposed to be if one looked hard enough.

Donnay found many of the older cases to be mesmerizing. A well-organized case file should ideally tell a story, he believed, one that moved progressively from offering a clear picture of the crime itself through laying out all the details of the investigation to presenting an incisive report on the conclusion of the case if there was one and the sentence of the accused if found guilty. Unsolved cases were simply filed "open until resolved."

Constructing that story out of the sometimes overflowing amount of typescripts, notes, scribbles and other scraps of paper stuffed willy-nilly into each file and then cataloguing all that information was a tall order. Laborious too. But it had to be done so that future researchers, prosecutors and other officials could access and review these files without tearing out their hair in frustration.

Donnay leaned in closely and made a few notes, then shut the latest file he'd been reading. It was the 1809 file on forger, thief and prison escape artist Eugène Vidocq. He added it to the stack of other files on the investigation and prosecution of Vidocq's numerous offenses dating as far back as the 1770s. They were absorbing, especially this last one, which marked Vidocq's final brush with the law before undergoing a miraculous conversion from incorrigible felon to dedicated *flic*—ultimately to become the father of French criminology. Who better to have such a title? Donnay considered. Sometimes it does take a thief to catch a thief.

He rubbed his tired eyes. Going through file after file and making sense out of them with appropriate cross-references was giving him a headache in the smoke-filled, airless room. His chain-smoking colleague didn't suffer from the smoke of his excessive cigarettes nor the lack of fresh air—nor from eyestrain. Blier too had spent the morning reading through files. He was now relaxed over his lunch of sausage, cheese and red wine perusing the day's newspaper.

Suddenly he sat up straight. "Listen, Pierre," he announced. "You'll find this of interest."

Donnay lifted his head while continuing to rub his eyes as Blier read aloud: *"Leroux's tale of 'Phantom of the Opera' to be filmed in America."*

Donnay perked up.

"Gaston Leroux's popular chronicle of the real-life exploits of the fiend who stalked Paris' legendary Grand Garnier more than a decade ago has been purchased for the screen by Universal Pictures president Carl Laemmle," Blier continued reading aloud.

"The deal was struck on a visit here several years ago by the producer while on a European holiday. No performers have yet been named to play the hideous Phantom and his love interest, the beautiful opera star Christine, but it is rumored that chameleon actor Lon Chaney is strongly in the running to play the Phantom. Meanwhile a widespread search is underway for a newcomer to play the female lead.

"'No expense is being spared on this production,' Laemmle said recently. 'We've built a special stage—the largest in our history—to accommodate a full-scale replica of the spectacular lobby of opera house and auditorium with its centerpiece chandelier.'

"The adaptation is set to go before the cameras this year with worldwide distribution scheduled for early to mid-1925."

Blier closed the paper and looked over at Donnay. "Well, what do you think of that?" he asked, popping a slice of cheese into his mouth.

"Not much," Donnay responded with dismay as he saw his misgivings over Leroux's romanticized fiction beginning to bear fruit. Between the author's popular novel and the potential reach of the upcoming moving picture version, the truth of the "Opera Ghost" affair would soon be lost forever in the dusty files of the "Three-Six" and in newspaper morgues across France.

"I wonder who'll play you," Blier said cutting off a hunk of sausage.

"Nobody. The police don't figure much in the novel," Donnay replied dismissively. He could feel his headache overtaking him and decided to call it a day. "I need some air," he said. "After that I think I'll go home and relax."

"Well, don't get too relaxed," Blier said between mouthfuls. "We've still got hundreds more files ahead of us and I'm not getting any younger."

"And here I was under impression that we were making progress," Donnay teased back.

"We *are* making progress. We're into the 19th century," Blier returned with a twinkle.

"I feel better already," Donnay countered. He put on his coat. "Goodnight, Michel."

"Goodnight, Pierre," his friend replied.

Donnay headed up the stairs to the exit of the "Three-Six," listening to the man light another cigarette to enjoy with his sausage and cheese.

TWELVE

Rue Drouot
9 Arrondissement

With his headache and irritability, Donnay didn't feel much like walking from the "Three-Six" to his apartment, and so he took the Metro to his stop. It was not an especially long route, but time-consuming given the number of other stops along the way. The remaining short stroll to his lodgings in the Rue Drouot was just enough to clear his nose of the suffocating smell of Blier's filthy cigarettes. He could feel his headache already going away.

As for his irritability, that was another story. As he walked, his thoughts turned again to the item his colleague had read about the Hollywood production of *The Phantom of the Opera* which he'd found to be so discouraging.

He had his emotions under better control now as he adopted a healthier *comme ci, comme ça* attitude toward the news. After all, what did it really matter whether history knew the truth of the "Opera Ghost" affair or believed the fiction? In time, both would become faded memories, and, perhaps, not even that.

Nevertheless, he hoped Madame Delon hadn't yet seen the same item and was not now eagerly awaiting his return to show it to him for inclusion in the scrapbook she'd made. He was in luck. She was out when he arrived, perhaps to do some shopping. Maybe if he ducked in and out quickly before she got back, he could put off her ambushing him with the news to another day.

While walking, he'd passed by the Beaux Arts theatre and seen posters being put up for the new Max Linder comedy, *The King of the Circus*. He decided to have an early supper somewhere close by and then take it in.

During his time back in Paris, he'd gone to see revivals of a number of Linder pictures and the new ones, too. He'd found them to be inventive and funny—a perfect evening's entertainment—and became a major fan. As a result, he no longer thought it amusing to go along with those who mistook him for the comedian. He had shaved his mustache and thrown away his cane, both hallmarks of Linder's persona, to go unnoticed. It worked. He hadn't been mistaken for the actor in some time.

The last Linder comedy he'd seen was a couple of years ago, he now recalled. It was *The Three Musketeers*, a parody of the American picture of the same name featuring acrobatic star Douglas Fairbanks, which he had not seen. Both were based on the same historical novel by Alexandre Dumas.

He'd almost passed on the Linder version too, figuring that, as it was a spoof of a film he did not know, he wouldn't get most of what was being parodied. But by that time he'd become a dedicated fan of the comedian and decided to go anyway. Years later now, a smile still came to his lips as he recalled Linder's hilarious antics as a bumbling and totally inept (but lucky) incarnation of D'Artagnan.

Perhaps *The King of the Circus* would lift his spirits and leave him in stitches too, Donnay thought.

With still no sign of Madame Delon, Donnay slipped out after changing his clothes and had a light supper at a nearby bistro. Then he set out for the Beaux Arts.

What he encountered when he got there was a major disappointment. All the posters for the new Max Linder comedy bore a red banner in big black letters that read "Coming!" He had misinterpreted the posters that were going up that afternoon as signaling the comedy was opening tonight.

But the bill of fare currently playing its final engagements was quite different—a swashbuckler titled *Prince of Pirates* that he had little interest in seeing.

On the other hand he reasoned that if he went home now the chances were good that Madame Delon would have returned, and be ready to ambush him with the "thrilling news" that *Phantom* was being made into a moving picture. Unable to counter her inevitable enthusiasm for the project as she already loved the novel, he wanted to delay the encounter for as long as possible. And so he stepped up to the box office and paid his money for the preferred alternative.

The lights were already dimming as he went into the theatre but he could see the pianist loosening up his fingers to accompany the picture on the screen above him.

The lights went all the way down as Donnay took his seat. Almost immediately the pianist let loose with a dramatic flourish of mighty sound as the screen above him filled with the picture's title and performers.

Donnay settled into his seat hoping at best to be absorbed and at least entertained by the derring-do of Sebastian Vane's pirate prince and his band of cutthroats who plagued the

Atlantic and the Caribbean in search of wealthy hostages and loot.

Ninety minutes later as the film came to an end he was sitting straight in his seat stunned by the climax he had just witnessed.

The lights went up and the audience started to file out to make room for the next showing. But Donnay could not move. He just sat there shaken by the picture's final moments, *an almost identical recreation of the very incident that had nearly taken his life!*

Pursued below deck into the captain's cabin of the pirate ship by the king's men, Sebastian Vane's hero-villain in long, hair and bushy mustache—colored a sanguinary red, as described by one of the title cards—finds himself cornered in the stern. With nothing to defend himself but his flintlock pistol, he is far outnumbered.

As the king's men close in on the trapped pirate, he suddenly stands proudly erect and removes his plumed tricolor hat. He sweeps it before him in a long, flamboyant bow, then raises the pistol to a space above him, a corner of the stern where two sticks of dynamite, linked together by a short fuse, are revealed in close-up.

In a final mocking gesture capped off by a triumphant grin, the pirate fires the pistol into the fuse. The king's men draw back quickly as the fuse reaches the dynamite. It explodes, blowing part of the stern out to sea in a cloud of billowing smoke and a shower of flaming timbers.

As the smoke clears, the king's men move cautiously through the debris but find nothing of their quarry but a tattered tricolor hat with a splotch of blood on its brim.

The picture goes to black then irises in again on a shot of a long boat and the tattered, but very much alive, pirate prince in the arms of his hostage-turned-lover played by Marie Prevost. They kiss. The End.

Donnay found himself still holding his breath from the jolt he'd received by these final scenes. He now gasped for air. Was it his imagination or had he just witnessed an almost-exact re-enactment of his final confrontation with the "Opera Ghost"? A re-enactment complete with that steely-eyed look of scorn on the quarry's face as he sets off the dynamite. It is a look only two people on earth would have known about, and allegedly one of them was killed in the actual blast.

Or was he?

THIRTEEN

Archives
36 Quai des Orfèvres

The next morning, Pierre Donnay had a quick breakfast of a croissant and coffee at a kiosk across from the entrance to the Metro station, then travelled straight to the "Three-Six."

When he arrived, he was surprised but not alarmed to find himself alone. Usually Blier was there before him and already busily at work. He saw nothing potentially alarming in this. At least he hoped not. Blier was an old man. He deserved to indulge himself now and then.

In a way, Donnay was grateful not to be greeted by the man's good cheer first thing, for he had not slept well that night. He'd tossed and turned in bed the whole time, his restive mind on fire with the images he'd seen at the Beaux Arts.

For the first time since leaving the sanatorium, he'd experienced the familiar nightmare of those final moments in the debris-filled water beneath the opera house after the explosion by which the "Opera Ghost" chose to end his life and his pursuer's.

This nightmare was different, however, in that images from the finale of the pirate picture mixed with his memories of the confrontation with the "Opera Ghost" and that triumphant last look in the eyes of the fiend that Sebastian Vane's pirate captain so closely mirrored.

Donnay had awakened with a start, covered in sweat and feeling as if he were suffocating from drowning until he drew fresh morning air into his lungs.

He was unable to shake the belief that the "Opera Ghost" was alive. The evidence was there on the screen.

Or was it?

Could he be losing his mind?

The fiend *couldn't* be alive. His body was found and identified by a victim of his crimes who would have recognized him well!

Donnay slumped into his desk chair and put his head in his hands.

"It can't be as bad as all that, can it?" came a voice from the stairs.

Donnay's head snapped up to see Blier coming into the room. He too looked weary, but managed to be his ebullient self.

"Bad night. Couldn't sleep," Donnay explained.

"Me neither," Blier replied. "Even coffee hasn't put life into these old bones."

"What kept you awake? Counting case files instead of sheep?" Donnay quipped.

"Something like that," Blier replied enigmatically. Looking serious, he pulled off his coat, slipped it over the back of his chair and sat down at his desk. "How about you?"

Donnay thought for a moment about sharing the events of the past evening with the old man. Would Blier scoff at his suppositions and also think him to be going obsessively mad?

He didn't believe so and decided to chance it anyway—if only to help relieve some of the pressure by getting it off his chest.

"You may think I'm going crazy," he began hesitantly. "But last night I'm sure I saw a ghost—the 'Opera Ghost,' in fact."

Over the next few minutes, Donnay recounted the events of last night. When he finished describing the film's almost mirror image demise of the "Opera Ghost," his forehead was beaded with sweat. He wiped it away with a handkerchief and then looked over at his friend, fully expecting to see a look of deep concern on the man's face that said, "I think you need some time off, my friend." But the look wasn't there.

"Think I'm getting addled?" Donnay remarked.

"Yesterday I might have said yes," Blier responded. "But not after what I discovered last night."

He leaned forward pensively and whispered. "Not long after you left, I decided to call it a day myself. I'd gotten my coat and was heading for the stairs when I remembered that item I read to you from the newspaper. I'd clipped it out and thought that before it got lost I'd better slip it in the Phantom case file. I had to look up the file's whereabouts in the master log." He looked perplexed. "My initials and the date were right next to where I'd logged it in," he went on. "But there was this other notation next to it—don't know who made it, wasn't me—that said 'sealed from public view.' I thought that was odd because I'd never seen such a notation before. And I've been here a long time.

"Well, I told myself that as an employee I wasn't exactly a member of the public, so it would be all right for me to unseal it long enough to slip in this clipping then seal it back up again and put it back. I located the box the file was supposed to be in according to the master log, but guess what? It wasn't there."

Blier harrumphed. *"Wasn't anywhere!* Thought it might have gotten misfiled, so I looked around in box after box. Nothing. I was here to almost nine."

"It could have been misplaced like the Landru file," Donnay suggested.

Blier shook his head of thick gray hair. "No. Because after it was logged in, there was no record of anyone signing it out. It just vanished."

"Who would have access?" Donnay wondered aloud.

"Practically anybody in the office of the chief prosecutor or the office of the chief of detectives," Blier responded. "But I've got the only set of keys."

"Anybody can pick a lock. Especially around here," Donnay suggested. "The bigger question is why it was taken. The answer to that would tell us who."

Blier snapped his fingers suddenly. "Maybe it was you!" he said.

Donnay looked astonished. "Me?"

Blier shushed him. "You coming back here, I mean. I never told you this before because I thought you had enough to work through, but I found out that your friend Verneuil and the new chief prosecutor go back a long way. Every piece of paper generated around here eventually makes its way to the archives, and I see it. Everybody thinks I'm just an old paper pusher who never reads what he files, but I often do, and I learned that those two are pretty close. They've helped each other a lot over the years to reach their current positions."

"What has all that got to do with me?" Donnay asked impatiently.

"Keep your pantaloons on, I'm coming to that," Blier said with feigned irritation. "Now, you and Verneuil aren't exactly friends."

"That's not news," Donnay put in.

"No, but he and the chief prosecutor *are* friends. They watch each other's backs. And the chief prosecutor doesn't apparently much like you either or he wouldn't have offered you this shitty job instead of giving you your old one back," Blier said. "So, what's at the root of all this hostility? What do the three of you have in common?"

Donnay could see now where Blier was going with this. "The 'Opera Ghost,'" Donnay said. "Except that Severin wasn't chief prosecutor then."

"No, but he inherited the case, even though it was closed, and everything in the file that may have been damaging," Blier returned.

"Like a description of Verneuil's cowardly behavior that killed a *flic* and almost me," Donnay said.

"*Exactement!*" Blier retorted. "Its exposure would reflect badly not only on Verneuil but also on Severin, who was in on selecting him for his current post."

"And there may be other reasons we don't know about," Donnay said.

Blier nodded. "My guess is that either on orders from Severin or on his own, Verneuil took the file shortly before or after you returned here and started work, just in case you tried to take a peek."

Donnay and Blier spent the rest of the morning discussing alternative locations where the "Opera Ghost" case file might be hidden. They both agreed that Verneuil was the likely thief.

Donnay described his former underling as aggressive without being very imaginative, who did his job by rote until he could pull a gun. In all probability, Donnay suggested, the man would not stash the file in a bank vault somewhere; that would be too creative. Besides, he would likely want it close by—

literally as well as figuratively—in case he had to get his hands on it quickly.

Destroying the file outright would be a criminal offense. Therefore, the obvious place to hide it was somewhere in his office to which he had sole access—in a locked file cabinet or drawer, perhaps, where no one but him would chance upon it.

Once this was agreed to, Donnay raised the issue of breaking into Verneuil's office. Blier revealed *how* would be easy as he had a passkey for most offices in the building. Janitorial work had been one of his responsibilities early on in his tenure there, he admitted with a grin. What they had to decide was *when*?

As the central hub of the metropolitan police, the "Three-Six" was busy at all hours of the day and night, but there was a lull in traffic in and out of the building during the late hours. It was then that the chances of moving about unnoticed were best.

Also, unless a major high-profile case had broken that required his round-the-clock attention, Verneuil would be out of his office during the late hours. Knock wood, there were no high-profile cases being investigated at this time.

Tuesday nights were traditionally when arrests were the fewest and overall activity was the lightest at the "Three-Six" so they decided late next Tuesday they would make their move.

At this point, Donnay proposed that as he was the younger man, he alone should take on the responsibility for the search and the chance of being discovered. But Blier would have none of that. He wanted in on the action. He knew the layout of the building better than Donnay if it came to quickly finding a hiding spot. And as far as the search itself was concerned, four eyes were better than two, he said adamantly.

Donnay couldn't counter either argument, so it was settled. They would both break in and take their chances.

FOURTEEN

Tuesday Night
36 Quai des Orfèvres

They waited until eight p.m. By then, darkness had completely fallen and they could hear that foot traffic on the first floor above them had slackened considerably.

Blier had locked the entrance to the archive at the top of the stairs and turned on the overnight security lights around six p.m. to make it seem the two of them had quit for the day.

It was time to move.

They each carried a small candle to help in the search of Verneuil's office on the second floor. Blier dropped the key ring in his coat pocket. He no longer remembered which key opened Verneuil's office so it would be trial and error for a time. This meant they would be exposed for the duration, but nothing could be done about it except to cross their fingers and pray the time was short.

They quietly ascended the stairs. Once at the top, Blier unlocked the archive door and opened it a crack to peer out. The hallway was empty. The stairway to the second floor and above was across from them. They listened for the footsteps of anyone coming down the stairs. There were none so Blier quickly closed and locked the archive door behind him.

They scurried across to the stairs and climbed cautiously to the second floor. This time Donnay looked out into the hall, glancing back and forth to see, but no one was about.

Verneuil's office was several doors down to the left. When they reached it, Blier put his ear to the wood to hear if Verneuil or anyone else was moving about inside. Nothing. Quickly he started trying the keys.

Sweat broke out on each of their faces as Blier tried one key after another. He pulled the next one out of the lock. No luck. He wiped his forehead.

Donnay glanced up and down the hall again and could hear no one coming, but it was only a matter of time. "Try faster," he whispered urgently to his colleague.

"I'm going as fast as I can," Blier hissed back as he tried and failed with the next key.

Then they both heard the sound. Footsteps. Coming their way from down the hall.

Blier pointed to an alcove across from them. "Hide there while I try another key, then I'll join you," he whispered to Donnay, who nodded and darted to the alcove, concealing himself as the footsteps grew louder.

Blier inserted the next key and gave it a turn. He felt something move and turned harder and the lock clicked open. He was in.

Motioning for Donnay to stay where he was, Blier slipped inside and closed the door. He squatted there listening as the footsteps passed the door and receded. He had no idea who they'd belonged to; perhaps Donnay had seen.

He eased the door open and looked out both ways, then signaled Donnay to come across. Blier held the door open as

Donnay hurried inside the dark room, then he closed and locked it again.

"I didn't see who it was," Donnay said, breathing rapidly. "I was too busy keeping my head down."

"No matter," Blier said. "Let's get to work."

They each lit their candles.

Early on, they had agreed that Blier would go through the file cabinets while Donnay searched the desk and any other places of possible concealment.

Anticipating the cabinets and desk drawers would likely be locked, Blier brought along a lock pick he'd confiscated from one of the "Three-Six" evidence rooms. "Always thought it might come in handy someday," he'd told Donnay, who had smiled indulgently but was inwardly grateful for the man's sticky fingers.

There were three file cabinets, all of them wood, and each stacked atop the other. To Blier's surprise, none of them was locked. He didn't need the lock pick after all.

Donnay discovered the same was mostly true of the desk. Only the bottom left and top right drawers were secured.

"Seems pointless going through these cabinets," Blier whispered. "Who'd steal something and then hide it in an insecure spot?"

"Unless he was lazy," Donnay suggested.

"Or bold as brass," the older man returned.

"Trust me, Verneuil's not bold," Donnay said knowingly. "Long as we're here we might as well go through them. Hand me the lock pick."

Blier handed it over and Donnay started on the right hand drawer of the desk. Trouble was, he really didn't know how to use the pick except by trial and error and he was getting nowhere fast. His job had been to prosecute burglars not learn their trade. All the same, he wished now that he had picked up some tips.

Blier finished going through the bottom cabinet. He looked over. "Nothing here but copies of old police reports in duplicate and triplicate. How're you coming?"

"Not too well, I'm afraid," Donnay answered. "It's all a lot of poking and prodding to me. I just don't have the knack."

"Here, let me," Blier said holding out his hand and moving to the desk.

Donnay gave him the pick and Blier went to work.

Momentarily there was a soft *click* and he pulled the drawer open. "Worked for a locksmith when I was younger," Blier said, covering a grin. Donnay said nothing but nodded skeptically.

Together they went through the drawer, which was largely filled with copies of requisition forms, invoices and other bureaucratic work product. There were also a fresh, unopened pack of Gaulioses cigarettes, and, most peculiarly, a ball of red yarn.

Donnay picked up the yarn. "What on earth do you suppose he does with this?"

"Maybe he's taken up knitting," Blier said deadpan.

"Wonder if he keeps the needles locked in the other drawer," Donnay said deadpan as well.

"Maybe he doesn't know you need 'em and that's why the ball is so full," Blier returned with a straight face.

Donnay started to laugh then quickly covered his mouth as they heard a loud *clatter* from the hallway outside, followed by a muted "*Merde!*"

They continued listening as whoever it was outside grunted several times as if stooping over to pick something up. This was followed by the sloshing of water in a bucket.

"One of the cleaning staff," Blier whispered. "I didn't think they'd reach this floor so fast."

A key was noisily inserted in the door of the office next to them and the door swung open. As the janitor wheeled the mop bucket inside, Donnay whispered urgently, "We're probably next. We'd better get a move on."

Donnay quickly straightened the contents of the drawer they'd just looked through and closed it up again while Blier went to work with the pick on the other locked drawer.

As soon as he'd opened it, they switched positions and Donnay peered into the drawer as Blier re-locked the other one.

Donnay looked crestfallen. There was only one item in the drawer: Verneuil's holstered pistol, a Modele 1892 revolver.

Blier glanced into the drawer and looked dejected as well.

They were both startled by some noisy bangs from the office next door as the janitor moved things about to clean.

"We're running out of time," Blier said as he started to close the drawer, but Donnay quickly stayed his hand.

"Wait a minute!" Donnay said as he once more looked inside the drawer. Then he scrutinized the outside of the drawer and quickly began probing the interior with his fingers.

"Look how shallow the inside is compared to the outside," he whispered to Blier breathlessly. "I think it's got a false bottom."

He handed Blier the pistol then reached into the drawer again, feverishly working the edges with his fingers. He felt the bottom move and glanced at Blier with excitement as he pulled the bottom up, revealing a hidden compartment.

Blier took the false bottom from Donnay as the latter removed what had been hidden inside: several sheets of blank paper and a thick case file.

"That's it!" Blier beamed as Donnay touched the red seal with the words beneath that said: *"Not for Public View!"*

Donnay's flat
Rue Drouot,
9th Arrondissement

After Blier had closed up the file cabinets and Donnay had locked the two desk drawers, leaving the scene as they found it, the two of them stole from Verneuil's office and out of the "Three-Six" without being seen.

Forty-five minutes later they were in Donnay's apartment, settling in for a long night of going through the errant "Opera Ghost" case file.

As both of them were hungry after an already long day and no supper, Donnay put together a platter of Blier's favorite foods for them to dine on as they worked: sausage and camembert cheese, topped off with some grapes and an inexpensive bottle of red wine.

Blier took the first half of the file as it roughly covered the period Donnay was the prosecutor on the case. The latter took the other half that covered the period of his recovery and would be all-new to him.

Blier had already found many reports, letters and memoranda signed by Donnay, but then came across a deposition with which Donnay would be unfamiliar.

"Here's something that might interest you," he announced, popping a grape into his mouth. Donnay looked up from the papers in his lap with intrigue.

"It's the transcript of a deposition from a Jacques Delair, one of the *flics* that pulled you and the dead man from the water that day," Blier went on, then reading:

Question: Where was Detective-Sergeant Verneuil at this time?
Answer: On the landing.

Question: Doing what exactly—shouting instructions to you?
Answer: No, sir. He was just standing there looking sort of frozen. It was only when we got the two men out of the water that he started giving orders for us to be careful with the bodies.

Question: He used the word 'bodies'?

Answer: Yes, sir.

Question: Did you think from his use of that word that he believed both men to be dead?

Answer: Yes, sir. I did at the time.

Blier looked up from the transcript. "Not a very flattering portrait of Monsieur Verneuil's backbone that day," he observed.

"No, but accurate, and then I lost consciousness," Donnay said. "I think Delair was right. Verneuil did believe I was dead, or dying. And he saw an opportunity to increase his role in the high-profile case. Either that or he really was frozen with fear."

"Or both," Blier said.

Donnay nodded. "Worked out for him though, didn't it?" he added solemnly.

Blier was silent for a moment. Then: "What've you got there?" he asked. Referring to a thin collection of papers Donnay held in his hand.

"Reports from cooperating police departments in Europe and the Middle East in response to queries I sent them about any criminals they may have crossed paths with similar to our 'Opera Ghost,'" he explained. "Most of them came in after I was in hospital. They make for some interesting reading."

He pulled out the report he'd just gone through. "Here's one from the police in Monaco," he said and started reading aloud. "*Description similar to an escaped prisoner from a Persian jail named*

Arik Cassell, born on the island of Corsica to a French-Norwegian father and Corsican mother. Rumored to be a drug smuggler for the Union Corse."

Donnay looked up from the report. "That's Corsica's homegrown version of the Italian mafia," he said to Blier.

"Heard of 'em," the older man returned.

Donnay continued reading. *"Under the name 'Arik, Man of Mystery,' subject travelled the continent and parts of mid-East with a solo magic show, a front for the drug operation."*

Donnay drew another report from the pile. "That's all for that one," he said. "But here's another. From the Egyptian police. *Subject Arik Cassell arrested in Tehran for drug dealing, an activity frowned upon as blasphemous in Persian society. Sentenced to life in prison after confession under extreme torture, in which he was terribly disfigured—allegedly. No details provided. Escaped from jail with co-conspirator named Darrass about whom little is known other than that his tongue was cut out by his jailers. The pair is rumored to have made their way to France where Cassell holds dual citizenship, then disappeared."*

Donnay pulled one more report from the file. "And here's another interesting tidbit, from the police in Marseilles," he said. "According to their information, the elder Cassell worked as a builder in France before re-locating to Corsica. And guess what? One of the structures he'd worked on was the Grand Opera House Garnier!"

Blier slapped his thigh. "That's it! This Arik Cassell is definitely our man!"

"Or very likely *was* our man," Donnay pointed out. "The only evidence we have that he's still alive is what I saw on that movie screen, which would never hold up in a courtroom. And remember that Christine Delfont identified his body. I haven't come upon her deposition yet."

"This Darrass fellow, I wonder whatever happened to him?" Blier muttered.

Donnay shrugged. "Don't know. But there was some speculation among investigators on the case, myself included, that the 'Opera Ghost' may have had help executing some of his more *miraculous* vanishing acts and with bringing down the Garnier chandelier, which almost certainly required two people."

"What about Christine's deposition. Did she say anything about an assistant?"

"I have to find it."

"Well, what's keeping you?" Blier *harrumphed*. "This is a better mystery than Leroux's book and I'm dying to know the ending."

Donnay smiled at his colleague's excitement and began skimming through the case file until he came to a thick transcript. It was the deposition of Christine Delfont. He opened it and started reading.

At least half the transcript was taken up by questions and answers about Christine's kidnapping and captivity by the "Opera Ghost." But it was the latter part dealing with her escape and subsequent identification of the body that really drew his interest:

Question: How did you and your fiancé manage to escape?

Answer: Contrary to what I initially told the police, we did not actually escape. He let us go.

Question: After all that time? Just like that?

Answer: Yes, I think he was already planning to escape and considered us a burden. So, he gave us our freedom in exchange for our silence.

Question: Silence about what?

Answer: What he was planning, I think, although he didn't let us in on any of the details. He was feeling cornered and rushed to get us out of the way.

Question: Why do you think he didn't just kill you?

Answer: I don't know. He did threaten to come back and kill us though if we talked too much.

Question: About what? His escape plans?

Answer: No, as I said he kept them secret from us, except to say that the police were closing in and he had to make a final disappearance.

Question: Do you know if he had help? Someone to assist him in his escape or at any other time throughout your ordeal?

Answer: We never saw anyone.

Question: Switching to your identification of the body—

Answer (interrupts): I never identified the body as his. What I said was that it could have been. I wasn't sure.

Question: What was the nature of your misgivings? Surely one isn't asked to identify a recently deceased cadaver with a skull-like face every day.

Answer: His was a "living skull" not the skeletal head of a corpse with much of its flesh eaten away.

Question: Did you voice your reservations to police at the time? Their report says you nodded in the affirmative when asked if it was the body of your kidnapper.

Answer: I was in shock and the "Opera Ghost" seemed so much "bigger" to me.

Question: Bigger in what way? Height? Weight?

Answer: In his overall presence. It was authoritative. Dominating. Threatening. That body on the slab seemed so much less imposing.

Question: Death does diminish us all.

Answer: That may have been it, yes. So, maybe it was him after all."

"Here, read this," Donnay said, holding out the transcript to his friend. His finger marked where Blier should begin. "It's Christine Delfont's deposition. Read from here to the end of the transcript and tell me what you think."

As Blier began reading, Donnay flipped through his portion of the case file until he came to what he was looking for—the autopsy report on the fiend. He'd only glanced at it earlier. Now, he studied it carefully.

Blier finished with the section of the transcript Donnay had specified and sat back in his chair, letting out another long, loud *harrumph.*

Donnay looked up from the autopsy report. "Well, what's your reaction?" he asked.

"I have two," Blier responded thoughtfully. "The first is the 'Opera Ghost' was quite a manipulator, wasn't he? He seems to have enjoyed toying with people."

"And the other?"

"Christine's identification is hardly what I'd call rock solid," Blier said. "In fact, she described the 'Ghost' as being bigger."

"*Exactement!*" Donnay responded excitedly. "Now look at the autopsy report." He handed it over. "The medical examiner describes the remains as being between five foot nine and five foot ten in height. But the 'Ghost' I confronted that day was bigger like Christine said—over six feet at least."

"Which means the body in the morgue couldn't have been his—unless it shrunk after weeks in the water."

"But a body submerged in water doesn't shrink, especially in a few weeks," Donnay responded. "If anything, it gets larger because it *bloats.*"

"Then whose body is it?" Blier wondered aloud. "Darrass?"

"No, the medical examiner would have discovered the removal of the tongue during the autopsy and noted it in his report," Donnay replied. "My guess is it belongs to some derelict who was killed prior to or after the explosion to be used as a plant. The face was skinned, a bullet fired through his shoulder, then he was dressed in the 'Ghost's' tattered clothing and set adrift in the Seine to be discovered later." He looked disgusted. "The whole escape was pre-planned and staged for us—like some magic trick."

"As I said. A manipulator who likes deceiving people," Blier remarked again.

"And only days after the autopsy and Christine's deposition, the case was prematurely marked closed, signed and dated by the chief prosecutor at the time—Monsieur Chislain—and the file was sealed."

"So, what are you saying?" Blier asked. "That Chislain went along with closing the case prematurely?"

"It's possible, of course," Donnay answered, but then he shook his head. "No, I worked for Chislain and always found him to be straightforward and trustworthy. In fact, he said he'd hold my job for me until I'd recovered completely. But then he was replaced."

Donnay took a sip from his wine glass as he continued thinking aloud. "The pressure was on to bring the 'Opera Ghost' fiasco to a close," he said. "My guess is that in my absence, Chislain relied heavily on Verneuil for input and just went along with his advice, which, after Christine's deposition and the autopsy report, as inconclusive as they were, was to close the case. Then to seal it from further inquiry. The new chief prosecutor—Verneuil's friend Severin—has continued the masquerade. And since there have been no more incidents at the opera house, they appear to be right."

"Then how do we persuade these people, many of them, like Verneuil, now in positions of power to re-open the case?" Blier asked. "Go to the press?"

"We still don't have enough evidence," Donnay said emphatically. "We'd probably be up on charges ourselves of breaking and entering and possession of stolen government documents."

Suddenly he slapped the arm of his chair in frustration. "Damn it, I *know* where he is—Hollywood, an ideal place for him to hide—and who he is: Sebastian Vane. If I only had the money to go there and prove it!"

"How much would you need?" Blier asked.

"To book passage plus living expenses for however long my stay, a lot more than I can come up with, that's for sure," Donnay replied dispiritedly.

"I have a little of my own I could give you, but it probably still won't be enough."

Donnay looked at his friend with affection and warmly said, "You're a good man, Michel."

"Too bad I'm not a rich one, as well," Blier quipped. "What you need is a patron."

Donnay's eyes lit up with a thought and suddenly he was alive again, snapping his fingers.

"You are absolutely right, Michel," he shouted. "And I know just the person to ask!"

FIFTEEN

The Ritz Paris
15 Pl. Vendôme

He was the roundest man Donnay had ever seen, but so finely tailored that he wore his weight well. He didn't *seem* fat. A small pince-nez graced the bridge of his nose.

His dark, curly hair was flecked with gray and his annular face was wrapped ear to ear in a beard the color of sunburned lawn.

Gaston Leroux looked every inch the distinguished French gentleman and man of letters, Donnay thought. And rich besides.

Leroux was staying at the Ritz off the Rue Cambon in the Place Vendôme, an easy walk from Donnay's apartment. His appointment was for one p.m.

Donnay wasn't half way through the door of Leroux's suite when the writer was shaking his hand vigorously.

"My dear *procureur* Donnay, I *knew* we should meet someday," he said with genuine pleasure. "You, the man who finally ran the phantom of the opera to ground. And me, the monster's chronicler."

134

"*Esteemed* chronicler," Donnay corrected him with a smile while not disabusing Leroux of the impression that he was still part of the public prosecutor's office.

"Scarcely *esteemed*," Leroux returned self-deprecatingly. "You apparently didn't read the reviews." He laughed heartily and Donnay felt the floor shake. "But not a poor first effort if I do say so myself. Please, sit down."

Donnay seated himself in an ornate chair next to an ornate table with an ornate lamp on top. He set the "Opera Ghost" case file he'd brought on the table.

"This suite is quite…ornate," he said admiringly. In fact, the entire hotel—or what he'd seen of it—was a study in Louis the XIV opulence. Ah, the French character, he mused; we behead our monarchs, but venerate their style.

"I stay here at the Ritz whenever I'm in Paris," Leroux remarked, taking a chair that groaned miserably under his weight. "My home is in Nice. By the way, have you had your lunch?"

"Yes, before I came, thank you," Donnay replied.

"Damn, I could do with another." He grinned broadly. "A brandy, then?"

"No, thanks. It's a bit early for me."

"A hot coffee, perhaps? Or tea?"

"I'm fine, really."

Leroux almost looked forlorn. "There is *nothing* I can offer you?"

"I wouldn't say that exactly,' Donnay replied with an amused shake of the head. "I have a proposition, but it will take some time to explain."

"I'm intrigued," Leroux responded. "You have my undivided attention for as long as it takes." He clasped his hands together over his huge stomach.

Donnay leaned forward eagerly. "Monsieur Leroux, have you ever considered writing a follow-up to your most famous novel?"

"Considered it?" Leroux laughed again. "I've begun it several times, but have always given it up. How many opera houses can one phantom terrorize, after all, before the public—and the writer—gets bored?"

Donnay turned serious. "That's because the story you want to write is, I believe, being written right now thousands of miles away as we speak," he said. "Not by a fellow author, but by the 'Opera Ghost' himself under a different identity. You see, monsieur Leroux, I have evidence that he is *not* dead. Nor has he disappeared from public view."

Leroux looked astounded as Donnay snatched up the file.

"This is the evidentiary case file to the 'Opera Ghost' affair," Donnay said. "In it is the proof, contrary to the official story, that he did not perish in the explosion that day, but carefully planned his 'demise' by substituting another body to throw authorities off. But what he was unable to leave behind is precisely what will bring him down for good in the end if you will help me. *His ego.*"

For the next hour, Donnay poured convincingly through the evidence for the "Opera Ghost's" resurrection—recounting everything from Christine's contradictory identification of the body in her deposition to the autopsy of a much-smaller-sized man found floating in the Seine. Furthermore, Donnay explained, the credibility of her belief the body in the morgue was not that of the "Opera Ghost" is reinforced by her disappearance with her lover into obscurity so as not to be found.

Donnay went on to discuss the foreign police agency reports of the fugitive drug dealer and escape artist known as Arik

Cassell and his compatriot, the mysterious Darrass. And he culminated with a description of the scene in *Prince of Pirates* where the "Opera Ghost's" escape from Donnay and his men beneath the Grand Garnier was re-enacted down to the smallest detail, including the fiend's final flourish to distract from his vanishing act and also to jeer at his thwarted captors.

By the end of the presentation, Leroux also was persuaded the "Opera Ghost" was still alive and his new identity could very well be that of Sebastian Vane.

"And to think that all he did here in Paris to disguise his identity was simply to substitute an 'E' for an 'A' in his name. You're right, the man does have a sizable ego," Leroux remarked, almost admiringly. "And from what you say his story is *not* over."

"No, but I hope to make his second act be his last," Donnay said determinedly. "The moving picture they are making of your novel is something, I am convinced, that his considerable ego will not permit him to ignore."

"You suggested earlier that you came with a proposition. What is it?" Leroux asked.

"Monsieur Leroux, I hate to make your acquaintance with hat in hand, but I must as I have nowhere else to turn," Donnay admitted with humility. "I need financial backing to go through with my investigation into this man, Sebastian Vane, which of necessity must be kept secret from officials here. But that is to our mutual advantage."

"How so?" Leroux inquired.

"I won't be muzzled or constantly second-guessed by a resistant chain-of-command, but will have a free hand to pursue leads wherever they may take me, including California itself to get a close up look at this Mr. Sebastian Vane," Donnay explained.

"And the advantage to me?" Leroux said with a wry smile.

"You get your follow-up novel with the story I give you first hand, exclusively," Donnay replied.

Leroux unclasped his hands from around his enormous belly and there followed a moment of silence. Then he spoke with deep seriousness. "As both a reporter and an author, I have one rule," he began, "which is never to pay for information in advance if I don't know how accurate it will be."

Donnay could feel the air go out of his stomach, his hopes slipping away.

"But you appear to be an honest man," Leroux went on.

Donnay could feel his hopes returning.

"And as I see it," Leroux continued, "what you will be doing is gathering primary research that I cannot gather myself." He smiled. "How much 'financial backing' do you think you will need?"

Donnay could breathe freely again. "About 5,000 francs," he said. "To cover round-trip passage by ship and train and an approximately three month stay. If I haven't run the 'Opera Ghost' to ground by then, I never will," he added excitedly.

"You're that sure?" Leroux said.

"As sure as I'm sitting here now," Donnay replied confidently.

"Very well then, if you're willing to take the chance of throwing away your career — you do realize that's what you'll be doing, don't you, whichever way this turns out?"

Donnay nodded pensively.

"Then I guess I'm willing to take a chance on you with a little amount of my money," Leroux said agreeably.

"It's not a little amount to me," Donnay offered humbly.

Leroux grinned broadly as he took out his checkbook. "Think nothing of it, my boy," he said. "It's not as if I earned it from hard labor. I had the good fortune of inheriting well." He laughed heartily. And Donnay laughed gratefully with him.

Blier's flat
11th Arrondissement

With the key element—the financing—now in place, Donnay mapped out the rest of his plan over a glass of Beaujolais at Blier's apartment.

The first step would be to inform his landlady that he was going out of town for an extended trip and advance her three months' rent to hold his apartment. He will not tell her where he is going or what he is up to. Should anyone inquire into his whereabouts, she can truthfully say she doesn't know. With that, he would give her a goodbye kiss on the cheek.

Step two: the only item from the "Opera Ghost" case file that he shall take with him is the fiend's fingerprints, which had been lifted directly from his lair in the Grand Garnier. Blier will then re-seal the case file and return it to its appropriate spot in the archives. Should Verneuil discover it missing from his desk drawer and come snooping for it, Blier can direct him to its proper location, and, if probed, consult his records, which show that it had not been signed out since the day it was archived, leaving Verneuil guessing.

Third, Donnay will cable Blier from the U.S. periodically on the progress he is making. For security purposes the cable will be sent to Blier's home address. Blier will then relay these updates to Gaston Leroux confidentially by mail to his home in Nice. This way Leroux will hopefully be assured that Donnay is not just using his money to take a vacation but that he is working hard to give Leroux his money's worth.

Finally, for several days, Blier will not alert his superiors of Donnay's absence from work unless someone, such as Verneuil, comes looking for him. This will give Donnay a solid head start. Blier will then complain that Donnay has apparently skipped out on the job. "Not that he did much of it anyway; he left most of it to me," Blier will *harrumph*. "No, I don't know where he went or where he lives. We weren't exactly pals, you know. It's good riddance, I say."

With all of this covered, there was nothing more for Donnay to do but pack, then travel from Paris to Southampton, England to board one of the White Star Line's enormous vessels bound for New York. From there, he would board the 20th Century Limited to Chicago and from there the *Superchief* for the final leg of his cross-country journey to Los Angeles.

Should it be of help to his investigation, Leroux had given Donnay a letter of introduction to Carl Laemmle, suggesting Donnay could be useful to the production as technical advisor on all matters French.

Donnay felt himself to be an avenger going on a choppy sea to a distant land in pursuit of final justice—for himself and all those others whose lives the "Opera Ghost/Phantom of the Opera" had infernally touched.

He couldn't wait to start.

PART FOUR

HOLLYWOOD
1924

SIXTEEN

Sebastian Vane Residence
Hollywood Hills, California

"UNIVERSAL LAVISHES $1M BUDGET ON 'PHANTOM'"

Arik Cassell read the *Variety* headline aloud once more, quaking with rage. "Carl Laemmle never lavished a million dollars on *any* picture, including mine, the old skin flint," he thundered. "As expensive as it was even *Hunchback* didn't come near that figure, and that picture was more Thalberg than Laemmle anyway. Now the company's making this *fiction*, of *my* story, *my* life!" He threw the *Variety* to the floor.

From his seat on the living room sofa where he was flipping through the pages of a recent issue of *Photoplay*, Darrass, Cassell's friend and co-conspirator, thought but could not say, "And making it without your participation, that's what's got you really mad." He simply grunted.

Cassell looked over at him, glowering. "You know, there are times when I really wish you could talk."

"There are times when I wish it myself," Darrass thought but again could not say.

He'd seen Arik in rages like this before. But he'd always been able to calm him down before they exploded into acts of impetuosity that might have threatened their freedom. Now, he would have to do so again.

They'd been together for more than a dozen years now, ever since being thrown into that Persian hell hole from which they had escaped.

Their common bond was the circus.

Darrass was an acrobat who had played throughout Europe and parts of the Middle East, lastly including Persia. Arik was a talented magician and skillful ventriloquist who used those performing abilities as a front for his more lucrative drug-smuggling activities on behalf of the Corse. He'd been caught with a cache of heroin and cocaine in his belongings and thrown into a Persian prison for life where he'd been tortured and horribly disfigured.

Strangely, this disfigurement did not destroy him. It made him more determined than ever to get out. They had escaped one night together, employing a combination of their respective circus skills to overcome their guards.

In Paris, what now drove his friend grew clearer. It was the need for absolute control over his own future and anyone who might impact that future, whether opera singer, police or the Unione Corse.

Like a super-criminal, he would sometimes get so carried away manipulating the owners, patrons, and performers of the Grand Garnier, as well as the authorities, into doing his bidding that Darrass would have to help him engineer an ingenious disappearance or miraculous escape to avoid entrapment.

It was an exciting life with lucrative fringe benefits for them both as Arik had continued his drug-pushing activities throughout the city—albeit with a better arrangement with his paymasters that gave him more control. But it was not as comfortable a life with so much opportunity as they enjoyed now.

Darrass knew his man inside and out, which is why he realized what was truly behind Arik's anger now. It wasn't so much that they were making a film version of *The Phantom of the Opera* as it was that Lon Chaney was playing the lead role.

Arik despised Chaney because he was the only real competition Arik had in the movies' leading-man-as-character-actor category. Both men depended heavily on makeup to achieve their screen personas—Chaney by making his facial features ugly and even inhuman, a symbol of "otherness"; Arik by concealing his real-life "otherness" behind the veil of the average man.

Arik deeply *hated* the very idea that Chaney was to play his haunted and haunting phantom of the Grand Garnier.

"We must stop them!" Arik erupted, smashing a fist into his palm. "Let the past stay buried rather than be vandalized."

Indeed, Darrass was well ahead of him. He had anticipated his friend's anguish over the production and was already laying the groundwork to cripple it.

Hollywood was the most luxurious and comfortable berth the pair had yet experienced and there was no way Darrass was going to risk losing it due to his friend's emotional outbursts of displeasure.

Pagano Chicken Farm
Canoga Park, California

> *Dear Mama and Papa,*
> *I have wonderful news!! I have been given the lead*

female role of Christine in Universal's super-production of The Phantom of the Opera, which is now filming. I play an ingénue at the Paris Opera who is kidnapped by the title character to mold her into becoming the star attraction. A disfigured monster, he falls hopelessly in love with her.

Appearing with me are Norman Kerry as my fiancée and Lon Chaney as the Phantom. I have met both men and they are very nice to me, the newcomer, and treat me with respect. Behind the scenes, Mr. Kerry is a prankster with a great sense of humor. But something happens to him when he goes before the camera; he loses all personality and becomes stiff as a board. Don't tell him I said so. Ha! Ha!

Mr. Chaney is quite friendly—when he speaks to you, which is not often. He's very aloof. But I guess that comes from getting so deeply into his roles. He is such a great actor. None of us has gotten a peek yet of his makeup as the Phantom, but knowing Mr. Chaney's reputation, it promises to be quite scary. In my scenes with him so far, he wears a plaster mask with a strip of cloth covering his mouth. The mask looks like the ones worn by returned veterans with facial injuries. The eyes and nose are painted on, somewhat like a doll. Very creepy.

Our director is Rupert Julian, a New Zealander. He and Mr. Chaney don't get along at all. Mr. Julian keeps trying to get Mr. Chaney to give the Phantom some highborn airs like a fallen upper class gentleman. But Mr. Chaney will have none of it. He sees the Phantom as a commoner, a ruined man of the people, in criminal disguise, and he plays him as such. The two of them barely speak to each other except through a go-between, our cameraman. It's really funny, but the tension in the air is often pretty high.

The truth be told, Mr. Julian doesn't get along with most people on the set, crew or cast, including yours truly. He's very strict about what he wants from us. He had desired a Universal contract player with more leading lady experience for the part of Christine. But the casting director, Mr. Reilly, pushed very hard for me and won out, which didn't sit well with Mr. Julian. He thinks I'm too confrontational in some of my scenes with the Phantom and that I should swoon more like some Victorian damsel in distress. But he's the only one complaining so far. He looks like one of those old-fashioned picture directors in photos of the early days of the movies, always dressed in riding britches and polished Jodhpur boots. The only thing he's missing to complete the image is a riding crop for cracking cast and crew into shape. Instead, he wears a long, flowing, colorful scarf around his neck. Today's color was bright red.

The picture is due out early next year—if finished on time. There have been some serious slowdowns because of items suddenly disappearing like my main costume and some important props. From what I hear, replacing them is costly in time and money, putting us behind schedule, over budget and Mr. Julian in a very bad temper indeed. But what else is new?

Your loving daughter,

Leslie

P.S. I almost forgot to tell you. The studio has given me a name change. I am now Leslie Paige. Hope you don't mind. I sort of did at first, but they said it would look better on a marquee. I'm getting used to it.

Leslie put her pen down on the kitchen table. She folded the letter and slipped it into an envelope. She'd mail it tomorrow at the studio, which had its own post office.

For the moment, she hesitated to seal the envelope. Something was troubling her and she needed advice, but she was unsure if her folks were the right source for that advice. She didn't want to worry them. As far as her folks were concerned, things were going great for their daughter out here in Hollywood. And they *were* going great, she admitted. But lately she couldn't help wondering if she had made a big mistake.

It all had to do with Victor Reilly and her contract with him. Most newcomers like her who catch the eye of the studio brass typically sign a seven-year contract if it is offered to them. This contract doesn't guarantee steady work, just a salary, nor does it grant any say in what projects their talents are used.

Prior to her being cast in *Phantom*, Leslie had been offered such a contract—by Mr. Laemmle himself. But the studio's casting director and head talent scout, Reilly, had persuaded her to turn it down and sign exclusively with him instead. He said he'd been planning to leave Universal and open his own talent agency and wanted Leslie to be his first client.

At first she was reluctant to sign with him, fearful she might anger Mr. Laemmle. But Reilly assured her that wouldn't happen. He explained that he and "Uncle Carl" were tight. "We go back to before there even was a studio," he told her. "He knows I want to branch out with an agency of my own and is all for it as long as I don't leave him in the lurch. So I told him I'd stay on as casting director for as long as it took to find a suitable replacement, and that I'd do it without pay. And you know what he said? 'Effryone dat vorks for me gets paid a liffing vage.' That's what kind of a guy, he is."

Reilly's arguments for the advantages of going with him rather than signing with the studio were convincing to her. For example, she would earn more from the start and her salary would grow into bigger pay days with each successful picture she made. Furthermore, she would have her choice of pictures and roles rather than be committed to take whatever the studio offered. And if she was unhappy with their arrangement, she could leave Reilly at any time rather than be bound up in virtual servitude for seven years.

So, she had signed with Reilly. The result was the role of Christine in *Phantom* at $300 a week for fifteen weeks, plus overages—more money than she'd ever see in a lifetime of working at the general store in Coal Springs, Wyoming.

Reilly had done practically everything to groom her image as a star. She had accompanied him to several premieres, including a memorable night for Mary Pickford's new picture, *Dorothy Vernon of Haddon Hall*, at Grauman's exotic Million Dollar Theatre. Everyone who was anyone in Hollywood was there. The number of spotlights turned the area bright as day.

She and Reilly had gone dancing at the Blossom Ballroom in the Hollywood Roosevelt Hotel where the elite also gathered. And they'd dined several times for lunch and for dinner at the Musso & Frank Grill, a favorite eating spot for many studio heads and important directors, as well as moving picture stars.

Reilly insisted that all of these high-profile appearances were to show her off to the people who counted and to generate big-time publicity. Unfortunately, their conspicuous togetherness had generated some unwanted publicity and innuendo, as well.

For example, in her *Guessing Games* column for the *L.A. Crier*, gossip reporter Adela Grant had tagged them as a couple.

"*Guess which rising star can thank her well-placed boyfriend for landing her the most coveted female role of the year?*" one of Grant's columns asked, making it seem as though Leslie had sunk her hooks into Reilly for career-boosting purposes when the truth was opposite.

And in the same column, Grant had fanned even more unwanted flames of speculation by asking, "*Can wedding bells be far off for this pair?*"

Reilly had been a total gentleman as he squired her around town. Nevertheless, she could hear the whispers their combined presence generated wherever they went. The speculation that she was nothing but a pretty gold hunter with a modicum of talent seemed to gain strength from the fact that she was still Reilly's only client. It bothered her that he had yet to sign nor even to look at other candidates for representation as far as she knew.

It also troubled her that he kept pressing her to "get out of Hicksville," as he called her cousins' farm where she was staying, and rent a bungalow "near the action in L.A." Over and over again, he'd insisted. "You can afford it now."

With all of these concerns weighing on her, she wasn't sure now that she'd made the right move. It was her first real business decision, made entirely on her own. Perhaps that was what was giving her misgivings.

She needed the advice of someone who *knew* the business, knew her dreams and aspirations, and could give her that advice in a non-self-serving, impartial way.

Her cousins couldn't do any more than her folks could. They didn't know the business of this strange land called Hollywood.

Ah, but there was one possibility she now considered and the idea filled her with enthusiasm. Should she dare impose on him?

Why not? After all, Sebastian Vane was both her benefactor and protector her first day on the job.

He wasn't currently making a picture so she'd call him at his home tomorrow from the studio.

With that decided, she sealed the letter to her folks, ready for mailing the next day.

SEVENTEEN

Offices of the *L.A. Crier*
Los Angeles, California

[From Adela Grant's Guessing Games:]

> *"Guess which top male movie star plays 'Mr. Feel-Good' to his paying friends and associates in want of illicit party favors? He is certainly making hay while the sun shines in sunny L.A., no matter which way the legal winds blow."*

Adela Grant surveyed her latest column with approval. That should shake the bastard up a bit, she thought with satisfaction, even though she hadn't identified him by name, albeit subtly. Winds blow. Weather *vane*. Get it?

She popped another cigarette into her mouth and lit it with the still-smoldering butt of her last one.

Grant had to be circumspect in her reporting of the drug influx into the film colony because there was little proof who was behind it all that would hold up in court. But she was sure she had her man: Sebastian Vane—even though no one had yet gone on the record other than Victor Reilly, however obscurely. He had admitted to her late colleague Ted Alexander that he had a pricey habit and was into his nameless supplier for a hefty amount. The notes had revealed as much. Unfortunately, that's about all they revealed. Alexander just didn't have the proof for part two of his exposé as he said he had.

Grant found that out when she'd discovered his notes. She'd been given the assignment by her boss, Mr. Swain, the editor-in-chief, after Alexander's accident and untimely death. He told her: "The kid still owes me a second installment. You write it!"

Lucky her.

She began her search for the notes by going through the deceased reporter's desk. She'd made a thorough job of it, but no dice. She'd gone through his locker and every potential hidey-hole she could find around the office, too. Again, no dice.

Access to his apartment was no longer restricted by the police. They never considered it a crime scene in the first place. She paid the landlord a couple of bucks to let her go through it. By then the apartment was mostly cleared out of his stuff. The landlord had packed it all up ready for shipment to wherever as soon as the folks at the other end of wherever paid him upfront. He was not a sentimental man.

She assumed the police had given Alexander's things the once-over and found nothing. So she'd turned her attention to the apartment itself. The place was barely furnished except for a couple of chairs and a table plus a cast-iron bed frame and a mattress.

She started by looking under the bed where she quickly found a loose floorboard. She pried it up but found nothing except the outline in dust of a small box that had once been there. She figured the police had already gone through the box, found nothing of any importance, and put it with the rest of

Alexander's belongings. She'd take a peek later if she had the time.

But while she was on the floor, something caught her eye that was not as conspicuous as the loose floorboard. There was a crack in the baseboard along the wall. In fact there were *two* cracks in the baseboard about a foot apart. As she looked closer she could see they were two *cuts*, not cracks at all.

Using her fingernails, she grabbed hold of the top and bottom of the cut piece and gave it a pull. It came away with some difficulty because the fit was so snug. But once she had it out, she could see something inside the space Alexander had made. It looked like the edge of a sheaf of papers.

She pulled them out and went through them quickly with her reporter's eye. They were indeed Ted Alexander's notes and other jottings on the "Mr. Feel-Good Affair" (her words, not his.) In spite of Alexander's pronouncements that they would deliver the goods and name names, they hadn't.

Yes, they made a convincing case for Sebastian Vane's guilt but without much, if any, corroborating evidence, other than a few reports from the relatively new Interpol organization, a group of cooperating police agencies throughout the world. They vaguely identified the drug supply as being shipped up to California through Mexico by associates of Corsican organized crime.

Grant knew there was little to write up from these notes that would not just repeat what Alexander had already published. So she'd drawn on her gossiper's instincts and gone at the story in a way that wouldn't generate any lawsuits, but would very probably unsettle the targets all the same—people who were unlikely to come forward with their lawyers to admit, "Hey, that's *me* you're defaming!"

Better to keep hammering away in her columns with gossip and innuendo, and let the public, including the police, draw their own conclusions. So that's what she'd done, firing shot after shot across her targets' respective bows, hoping to push them into making a mistake.

Mr. Swain had approved the strategy. And so would her late colleague Ted Alexander, she felt sure.

EIGHTEEN

Universal Studios
Universal City, California

Under the hot studio lights, it had been a grueling day for Leslie and everyone else before and behind the cameras. But apart from the heat, the difficulties were mostly due to their director, Rupert Julian, who couldn't seem to make up his mind about *anything*—from the placement of the camera to the movement of the actors.

Lon Chaney was not on call today or things might have gone a lot smoother. He had a way of making Rupert Julian's mind up for him. Norman Kerry got so riled at the director that at one point he shouted loud enough for everyone on the stage to hear: "He replaced Von Stroheim on his last picture. Now he thinks he *is* Von Stroheim. I was there. *He isn't!*" Now the two were not speaking.

As for Leslie, she'd almost died under the heavy costumes she'd worn. The temperature for this time of year (early October) was unbearably hot everyone said. It was certainly hotter than last year at this time, she thought. In the studio the heat index must have hit 100 degrees today.

She was so exhausted that the last thing she felt like doing was walking to the trolley stop to begin her journey to her aunt and uncle's chicken ranch. So when she heard a shouted "Want a lift?" from behind her, she swung around with a resounding, "Yes!"

But then she saw who had made the generous offer and hesitated.

Victor Reilly looked as warm as she felt in his sporty, convertible. He had tossed his suit coat in the back seat and loosened his tie, which hung in the air like a limp rag. He'd rolled the sleeves of his white shirt up past his elbows to keep cool. But it was a losing battle; his shirt was stained with sweat.

"Well, jump in," he shouted again, pulling up next to her. She wanted the ride but not with him. Another sighting of the two of them together was bound to make more tongues wag. She'd spoken to Sebastian Vane several days ago about the problem. He had assured her he'd give it some thought and see what he could do. Apparently either not enough time had gone by or he could do nothing, she thought with discouragement.

"Look, I'm not going to wait here all night," he shouted again over the car's noisy engine. "Do you want a ride or don't you?"

Against her better judgment, Leslie climbed into the car. "Thanks," she said, closing the door. "I really wasn't fancying the trolley or walking," she added.

"That's what I figured," Reilly said with a smile as he shoved the gear into drive and the car all but leaped forward away from the studio gate.

The wind felt good on her long, flowing dark hair, as did the breeze on her skin, she ruminated as they drove. The temperature outside was still in the eighties, so it was plenty hot. But at least the air was moving.

"I couldn't decide whether to have this shirt washed or just burn it," Reilly said with a grin. "Mind if I make a brief stop at my house and put on a fresh one?" he asked as he drove. "It's on the way."

What else could she say? "OK."

Victor Reilly Residence
Woodland Hills, California

Reilly lived in a Moorish-style model home in the otherwise undeveloped area of Woodland Hills. He'd bought it, he told her, as an investment in the San Fernando Valley's future *and* in his own.

All stucco and wood with a minaret on top, the place looked peculiar to Leslie—not so much because of its unique architectural style as its solitude; surrounded by eucalyptus trees, it was the only house around. Additional lots had been marked off, as if waiting for construction to begin. But so far it hadn't.

Reilly pulled into the driveway, got out, and opened the car door for her. "Come in and have a look," he said.

Leslie didn't want to. She was eager for him to change so they could get moving again. But she remained polite.

"No, thanks," she said. "You won't be that long; I'll just wait here." The words felt thick in her mouth.

"But you'll roast," Reilly persisted. "I closed all the windows this morning to lock in the cool air. It's the stucco that keeps the temperature down."

She knew he wouldn't give up so she got out of the car. Smiling he walked her to the door, took out his key and opened it, allowing her in first.

Her immediate impression was that while the home's exterior may have looked like illustrations from those French foreign legion adventures by P.C. Wren, the interior was pure cowboy with ranch-style furniture and an adobe fireplace in the corner of the living room.

The contrast just added to the overall *weirdness* of the place, Leslie thought. But he was right about the temperature inside. It was quite comfortably cool.

"Have a drink while I change," he offered, pointing to a small bar on wheels near the fireplace. "I won't be a minute." With that he bounded up a short flight of stairs into the master bedroom. Momentarily, Leslie could hear water running into a sink.

Not wanting a drink but knowing that if she had at least a small one Reilly would be satisfied and they'd be out of there that much sooner, Leslie strolled to the bar, spotting a decanted red wine. She poured herself a small glass and took a large swallow to calm her nerves.

Reilly reappeared at the top of the stairs, buttoning a fresh white shirt, which he proceeded to tuck into his pants as he strolled down the stairs.

"All set?" Leslie asked, hopefully, as she put her glass on the bar.

"What's the rush?" Reilly said. "Sit down for a minute. I want to speak with you."

Uh, oh, this can't be good, Leslie speculated uneasily as he went to the bar and mixed himself a drink.

"What…about?" she asked falteringly.

"Sebastian Vane," he said with his back to her. "I got a phone call from him the other day."

"Oh, yes?" she said awkwardly.

He turned to face her and gestured for her to sit. She did, hoping it would please him and make this short—whatever *this* was. A dressing down, perhaps?

"Want a refill?" he asked. She shook her head and he took one of the ranch-style chairs opposite her.

It was then that Leslie noticed a white spot on the tip of his nose and suppressed a laugh at how ridiculous it made him look. If Leslie had been less naïve about the sins of this new industry she'd gotten herself involved with and was a bit more wise in the ways of the world, she would have recognized the white spot as powder—or, more precisely, the residue of a couple of snorts of an illegal drug called cocaine. She also would have noticed his wide irises and strung-out behavior for what they were—sure signs of drug use.

"It wounded me deeply that you went behind my back and talked to Vane," he said.

Leslie started to protest, but he held up his hand to silence her.

"If you were concerned about our being seen together so often and what Adela Grant was making of it, you should have come to me and said so," he went on.

"I guess I was just too embarrassed," she said, fighting for words.

"Free publicity is the mother's milk of this business, Leslie," he explained to her. "You take all of it you can get—even if it does strike you as being negative."

"*Negative?*" she exclaimed. "She practically wrote that I'm a gold digger and a tramp!"

"So you went to *Sebastian Vane*?" He looked more concerned than angry at this point. "Leslie, you have no idea what kind of man he is."

160

"He's always been kind and generous towards me," she said, coming to Vane's defense.

"And just what have *I* been towards you?" he protested.

"Kind and generous too, but—"

"But nothing," he shouted suddenly. "I worked my tail off to get you a starring role in *Phantom*—with only two other pictures under your belt, neither of them big roles, and at a thousand dollars a week!" Almost immediately, he shut up, realizing he had said too much.

"What do you mean a thousand a week?" she asked, perplexed.

"I meant $300," he responded quickly—too quickly—to cover himself.

But Leslie was having none of it.

"No, what you meant to say was *a thousand out of which you pay me $300*," she persisted.

"No, really, I—"

"That means you pocket $700 a week for yourself," she said angrily. "That's quite a commission fee!"

"Let me explain," he pleaded, knowing she'd caught him red-handed and that it was own doing. "It wasn't to be forever—just for the duration of shooting on *Phantom*. Then everything would go back to the way it was supposed to be—because I'd have enough to pay him off and no longer be under his thumb."

"*Whose* thumb?"

"I...I can't say."

"Why not?"

"*Because I like breathing. Okay?*"

She stood, exasperated with him. "And all the while you're warning me off Mr. Vane—it's *you* who's the swindler!"

"But I know him, you don't," he persevered. "He offered to buy out your contract with me to let you go. To show you where

161

his head is, he said you could be the next Mary Pickford—but with sex appeal."

"That sounds like something *you* would say," she returned dismissively.

"But it's true. He wants you all to himself!"

"That's ridiculous," she said in a huff. He looked so in earnest that she could no longer keep herself from laughing at the contrast with the white spot on the end of his nose.

He became indignant. "What? You think I'm *funny* now?"

She tried to apologize, but her laughter kept coming. "No, I'm sorry, it's just that you've got this white stuff on your nose…"

He quickly wiped it off with his sleeve but only succeeded in smearing it on his hand and across his cheek. She laughed even harder.

His face turned red and he lunged at her: "Why, you ungrateful—"

Startled, Leslie stepped back, knocking her chair askew. Enraged that he'd missed her, he lunged again, this time catching the shoulder of her blouse, which tore away in a cascade of buttons, exposing her brassiere and the swell of her left breast.

She flung open the door, pulling the torn fabric to her, not noticing the traces of cocaine that had passed from Reilly's hand onto her clothing.

To the accompaniment of Reilly's shouting of "Get back here!" she ran outside and slammed into the chest of a policeman on the steps. He was just about to knock.

Leslie screamed, not taking in at first the blue uniform and badge, and she tried to pull away.

"Whoa there, miss," the policeman said, holding on to her. "What's the hurry? Party getting a little out of hand?" He turned the torn flap of her blouse, revealing the flecks of white powder. He could also smell the faint aroma of alcohol on her breath.

"What do you mean 'party'?" Leslie protested. "He tried to assault me!"

"Is that a fact?" the policeman said.

"What she's saying is bull," Reilly bellowed from the open door where he was standing.

"Please, be quiet, sir," came a second voice from behind Leslie. She craned her neck and saw another policeman on the steps, plus two more poised on the steps below him. There were also several cars parked at angles on the street. She could tell they were police cars not only from the red lights on top but the black star on the white doors over which was painted the words "Los Angeles Police Dept."

"We got a tip that illegal drug activity was going on at this address," the first policeman said.

"Looks like we arrived just in time," the second policemen added.

Leslie turned back to the policeman holding her. "What's he mean 'just in time'?" she asked, in shock.

"He means that judging by that streak of white powder on your boyfriend's face and the traces on your ripped blouse, we got here before things went too far," he explained.

"And also before you could get rid of the evidence," the second policeman chimed in.

"What *evidence*?" Leslie objected, squirming in the policeman's arms. "I had nothing to do with this. And he's not my boyfriend!"

And then the world exploded in a flash of light that cut into the early evening dusk.

As Leslie's vision cleared, she saw that the light had come from a flash bulb set off by a photographer leaning up toward her from the bottom step.

"Got 'em," the photographer shouted, running to a car across the street that was idling in wait for him. Behind the wheel was an older woman with gray-streaked dark hair and a cigarette dangling from her mouth.

"Who *was* that?" Leslie wondered aloud as the car roared off.

"Probably the tipster," Reilly muttered dolefully, watching it go.

The first policeman nodded then ordered his cohort to cuff Reilly. "I'll get her," he said, turning Leslie around, taking the handcuffs from his belt, and snapping them on her wrists.

Then he announced sternly: "Victor Reilly and Leslie Paige, you're under arrest for the possession and use of illegal drugs."

NINETEEN

Stage 28
Universal Studios

"Take ten, ladies," Rupert Julian called out to the exhausted company of ballerinas gathered on the replica of the Paris Opera's huge stage. He watched them disperse then turned away and muttered irritably to no one in particular, "It truly escapes me why we are beginning this picture with a ballet sequence when the picture is called *The Phantom of the Opera!*"

From his place beside the camera on the platform erected at eye-level with the stage, cameraman Charles Van Enger, who had overheard Julian, thought to himself: "Probably because there's a lot more visual excitement to a ballet than to a lone figure singing an aria that the audience can't hear."

Instead he popped his head over the edge of the platform and said to the keyed up, pacing director, "You'll have to take that up with Uncle Carl. He gave the script the okay."

"Uncle Carl," Julian grumbled dismissively. "He just wanted his niece for the part of the prima ballerina. The nepotism in this company is incredible!"

"Don't say that too loud; one of his relatives might hear," the cameraman returned, continuing to egg on the distraught director.

"Very funny," Julian replied caustically. "But funny remarks won't get this picture done on time." Behind the director's back, the cameraman stuck his tongue out at him.

It had been a tough morning, the cameraman mused. Especially on the poor dancers whom the director put rigorously through their movements time and time again in order to capture the action from every conceivable angle. The dancers were so exhausted by the time Julian gave them a skimpy ten-minute break that they could barely walk let alone pirouette.

Using multiple cameras would have consumed half the time, the cameraman knew. But there was little use in making such a bold suggestion to Mr. Julian. If you had a better idea, the best approach, if possible, was to just go ahead and use it without his knowing and pretend later not to have heard his instructions. By then it would be too late for him to demand a re-shoot as Uncle Carl would already have seen and enthusiastically approved the rushes.

Turning from the camera to the hubbub behind him, the cameraman looked out past the orchestra pit to the row upon row of plush seats now being filled with costumed extras. He would be shooting their reactions to the ballet soon.

The capacity audience was nicely lit in partial shadow by the large prop chandelier built to duplicate the original in the Paris Opera. It had been electrified to give off an added sparkle.

Otherwise it was built to exact specifications although spun sugar and small, reflective mirrors stood in for the original's shimmering glass; light-weight wood painted brown for the beams and in a variety of colors and hues, including metallic, for the brass work and other filigree. It was an impressive sight, held together by a steel support structure.

In several days, they were scheduled to shoot the sequence where the chandelier, cut from its moorings by the murderous Phantom, falls upon the hapless audience. But for now, the schedule earmarked less complicated material.

By contrast to the morning ballet sequences, the rest of the day should go smoothly, the cameraman believed. The audience would remain in their seats for their reaction shots. All they had to do was applaud.

The ballerinas were strolling back on stage from their break. The director climbed onto the stage and quickly approached the prima ballerina played by Carl Laemmle's niece to go over the close-ups he still wanted of her—likely as a present to her uncle. Rupert Julian may have been a mediocre director, but he was not a stupid man, the cameraman mused as he watched the two of them.

Just then he heard a loud *tinkling* coming from somewhere on the set. He looked around but couldn't spot where the sound was coming from.

By this time, the director and the ballerinas too heard the *tinkling* sound, which was growing louder, and moved upstage to discover its source.

Then someone shouted: "Look, the chandelier!"

Everyone looked up at once to see the giant prop swaying precariously. In fact, the major link in the chain holding the chandelier to the ceiling had been cut through and the weight of the object was causing the hook to slip.

"Get out of there!" the assistant directors shouted in unison at the extras who'd just been seated as audience members. They emphasized those in the center and rear sections directly under the swaying chandelier.

Rupert Julian jumped from the stage and began signaling to the extras to move quickly.

The chandelier lurched again, the *tinkling* of its *faux* glass turning into the sound of a roaring stream.

Pandemonium broke out as the extras bolted seemingly at once, scrambling over seats and each other like the running of beasts in a mad rush to get out of harm's way.

From his platform perch, the cameraman joined in the chorus of warning shouts to the extras to get clear of the danger. But he quickly realized that his was a voice only among many and likely not even heard. He must do something productive to help out, he told himself as he glanced up once again at the bobbing chandelier which was now hanging by the proverbial thread.

Instinctively, he grabbed the camera tripod and spun it around so that the camera's lens now faced the mayhem below. He stepped behind the camera and immediately started cranking—just as the chandelier let loose.

There was a shower of sparks as the cable feeding electricity to the prop's concealed lights broke away from the ceiling.

With an enormous *whoosh*, the chandelier smashed into the almost-cleared seats, throwing up a cloud of dirt, wood splinters and other debris, as well as shards of flying "glass."

The cameraman had captured it all—or most of it anyway; the prop's fall had been so swift that he'd likely recorded only the tail end of it.

Balancing the camera on his shoulder, he picked up the tripod and climbed down from the platform. He hurried over to the panicked director and the crew who were busily pulling the remaining extras from under the seats where they'd flung themselves to escape the brunt of the crash. Some of them had small cuts and abrasions but otherwise seemed unhurt. There were no fatalities.

Setting up the camera, he began shooting more footage from a different angle of the demolished chandelier and the few remaining extras still scrambling to safety.

The cameraman caught the attention of Rupert Julian, who was not pleased by his resourcefulness, which some might interpret as callousness, and barked at him, "What the *hell* do you think you're doing?"

"Saving the studio money," the cameraman replied cryptically although the director seemed to catch his meaning right away. His stern face broke into a broad smile and he began directing the extras to keep moving quickly but to express more pain. Many were so confused they didn't know whether they'd been in a terrible accident or an elaborate set piece.

The director shouted to the cameraman appreciatively, "That was quick thinking, Charlie!" He winked his approval.

Taken aback by the unusual gesture, the cameraman shouted back, "Thanks!" Then added with a mischievous grin, *"Rupe."*

Carl Laemmle's Office
Universal Studios

From behind his large desk, Carl Laemmle read the letter presented to him by the stranger who now sat before him. When he had finished, he placed the letter among the papers on his desk and said to the stranger, "And how is old Gaston?"

"Still enjoying his meals," the stranger replied lightheartedly.

Laemmle smiled. "Ja, he does that, for sure." The studio chief steepled his fingers. "So, tell me vat can I do for the French judicial police?"

Pierre Donnay leaned forward purposefully. The time had come to reveal his mission. But how much dare he reveal? He'd been thinking about that for much of his journey. Most of the

169

readers of Leroux's *The Phantom of the Opera* here in America, including the authorities, and, perhaps, even Carl Laemmle himself, were not aware that the novel was based on fact. So, he felt he would likely be taken for some crazy foreigner if he were to begin by saying that he was on the trail of the *real* Phantom.

But what should he say?

As the *Superchief* had rumbled across the vast western part of this huge country, he had contemplated this problem and figured that the drug angle was the right approach to take initially.

When his train had arrived at East-Downtown Los Angeles Central Station this morning, he'd taken a taxi straight to Universal Studios to present Gaston Leroux's letter of introduction to studio head Carl Laemmle, and to begin his quest.

He'd dressed in a gray, pin-striped, three-piece suit that looked very continental, very chic, to make a good impression. What he hadn't counted on was the unusual weather for this time of year. His shirt was already damp with sweat.

Seeing Carl Laemmle had not been easy. Donnay was stopped at the front gate by a rather authoritarian guard who had refused him entrance without an appointment or proper pass. Donnay admitted to having neither, but told the guard he did have a letter from an important mutual friend that Mr. Laemmle would want to read.

Donnay had urgently requested that a call be placed to the executive's office. It was, and that had solved the impasse. The guard told Laemmle's secretary that "Uncle Carl" had a visitor from overseas with a letter from "a Mr. Leroux" (he pronounced the "x") and was told to send the man over.

Donnay found the surprisingly diminutive man who greeted him to be both amiable and warm. He was dressed in a slightly rumpled but expensive-looking dark brown suit and green tie. He was smoking a stubby cigar with a slightly bulbous shape. Donnay was not a smoker but he found the aroma to be not unpleasant.

Laemmle spoke with a thick, German accent. Unfortunately, Donnay's German was non-existent. His English was passable though; he had studied the language at the lycée and at university. As Laemmle's French was impenetrable, they agreed to communicate in English.

"I am looking for a man who has escaped French justice for murder and other crimes," Donnay began. "Interpol suspects, as do I, that he is now here in Los Angeles under an assumed name and new persona."

"Do you haff that name?" Laemmle asked.

"His real name is Arik Cassell," Donnay replied. "He works with a man named Darrass. Just that name alone. From what I've been able to learn, they've been in Los Angeles eight or nine years now, establishing themselves and setting up their illegal operation. It's taken that long for me to pick up their scent."

Laemmle's attention perked up. "Vat kind uf drugs are ve talking about?" he asked.

"The whole rotten smorgasbord," Donnay answered soberly. "From cocaine to opium."

"Dis ist a bit out uff mein line," Laemmle said. "Vat exactly vould you like me to do?"

"At first, introduce me to your contacts in the local police," Donnay said. "Then I won't be just some foreigner showing up to ask for help. I'll have some credibility."

Laemmle nodded. "I can do that," he said. "Vat else?"

Donnay jumped in quickly. "I hope I'm not being impertinent, but I noticed your reaction when I mentioned drugs. Has your studio experienced any problems related to drugs among your employees?"

"Funny you should ask," Laemmle said not at all mirthfully. He slid a newspaper across the desk to Donnay. "It was in this week's *L.A. Crier*. I had to let them both go," he added sorrowfully.

Donnay scanned the front page, which was taken up by a large photo and story bylined Adela Grant with a headline that screamed, "Rising Starlet and Manager Boyfriend Caught in Private Drug Den."

The photo showed an attractive young woman, her clothing torn, her face contorted in anger, grappling with a burly policeman on the steps of a Spanish-style stucco house. Behind them looking like a cornered animal stood a man in an open white shirt with a short white streak across his cheek.

Donnay took quick notice of the drug aspect of the story and knew that these were two people he wanted to talk to. They had to be getting their supply from someone.

"They're employees, you said?"

"*Former* employees," Laemmle returned, puffing on his cigar. "The young lady vas the female lead in the picture ve are currently making from Mr. Leroux's book," he explained. "Now she vill haff to be replaced and all the scenes she has made so far must be re-done. At great expense, I might add." He shook his head dolefully.

"The man in the background ist Victor Reilly, mein longtime casting director und talent scout," he went on. "Take the paper vith you if you like. It depresses me looking at it."

"Thanks. I will," Donnay said, taking the paper from the desk and folding it up.

"A very sad story," Laemmle continued with another shake of the head. "I did not think she vas like that. Und Reilly vas mein trusted associate for many years. But I had told them both, as I do everyone who comes to vork for me, '*no funny business*.' Bringing scandal und shame to the studio are verboten—an immediate firing offense." He ground the remnants of the cigar into an ashtray and his cherubic face took on a very dark expression.

Just then, the door to his office swung open and his receptionist poked her head inside. "Sorry for interrupting, Uncle Carl. But there's a call for you from Stage 28. It's an emergency," she said breathlessly.

He nodded and picked up the phone as she went out again, closing the door.

"Ja?" he said into the phone. Almost immediately his dark expression turned to one of alarm. "Mein Gott," he exclaimed. "Vas anybody hurt?"

Donnay couldn't pick up what was being said on the other end of the call, but the older man suddenly looked relieved. "I vill be there right avay," he said, hanging up.

"Forgiff me," he said to Donnay. "But something has happened I must attend to," he explained.

"Nothing *too* serious, I hope," Donnay said.

"Serious enough. You're velcome to vait here until I get back. Though I don't know how long I vill be." He paused, suddenly changing his mind. "Better yet, *kommst du mit*," he said, gesturing for Donnay to follow. "I vill show you vy in the picture business ve all haff ulcers."

As they left the executive office building, Laemmle's car and driver were already waiting for them at the curb.

It was a new Mercedes Benz Touring Car—black and white with a tan convertible top and whitewall tires. Laemmle and Donnay got in the back and the driver took them through the canyons of the massive studio complex to stage 28, the largest of the stages both inside and out.

On the way, Laemmle briefed Donnay on the incident that had occurred within stage 28 just minutes earlier. And so Donnay was somewhat prepared for the sight that greeted them of the shattered chandelier sprawled across several rows of auditorium seating.

What Donnay was unprepared for was not only the spectacular replica of the Garnier's grand chandelier but of the opera house itself that Laemmle's designers had constructed for the super-production. It was as enormous as the real article and as opulent down to the last fastidious detail. It was wondrous. He felt like he was back in Paris.

A small crowd had gathered around Laemmle, the buzz of voices all merging together to describe what had happened. Finally, Laemmle put his hands up to silence them and waved Donnay over.

"This is monsieur Pierre Donnay. He ist a friend uff the novel's author, visiting the United States," Laemmle began by way of introduction." Each member of the crowd acknowledged the Frenchman with a cordial nod. "He ist alzo a member uff France's judicial police."

Laemmle held out a short length of chain one of the technicians had given him. It was part of the longer chain rooted to the ceiling for holding the chandelier. "As you can see, the last link has been cut through at its veakest point," he observed.

Donnay examined the link and nodded. "Then this wasn't an accident."

"No," Laemmle said with a forlorn shake of the head.

Donnay looked closer. "You see this bubbling effect on the bent part of the link?"

Laemmle leaned in closer, as did the crowd around him, and nodded. "Vas ist?"

"It's the result of acid being applied to the iron to soften it up into gradually giving way," Donnay explained. "Like a slow-burning fuse."

Laemmle looked aghast. "But how? Who?" he stammered.

Donnay pointed up at the sprawling catwalk above the set that held the studio's heavy lights, and he sketched out a theory. "The perpetrator must have dangled from the catwalk to cut the chain and pour the acid," he surmised. "That means his legs must be incredibly strong and his hands both steady and nimble in order to avoid getting any of the acid on himself."

A man in riding breeches and a long, flowing blue scarf spoke up. "It sounds like you're describing a circus acrobat or trapeze artist," Rupert Julian suggested.

Donnay nodded. "That is what I believe," he said. Then to Laemmle: "Perhaps the authorities will be able to tell you more once they've investigated.

"In the meantime," he cautioned, "I would increase security throughout the studio and especially this stage. Someone, Mr. Laemmle, seems determined to shut your picture down."

In spite of his current woes, Carl Laemmle was gracious enough to have his niece cum receptionist arrange accommodations for Donnay at the Hollywood Roosevelt as the Frenchman had not yet made arrangements of his own for a place to stay.

A taxi spirited Donnay back over the pass to the train station where he picked up his stored suitcase, then took him on a brief tour of budding Los Angeles as they made their way to Hollywood Boulevard and the hotel.

Once settled into his plush room, he mapped out a plan for the next day, ordered dinner from room service then fell asleep in his clothes on the elegant sofa. He was dead tired.

TWENTY

Valley Division Headquarters
Van Nuys, California

Donnay awoke early the next morning feeling a bit stiff from having spent all night on the sofa. He got out of his still-damp, sweat-stained clothes from yesterday, washed up and put on a much lighter weight cream-colored suit. He had breakfast downstairs in the sprawling dining room then returned to his suite.

He called a taxi around eleven and it took him over the Cahuenga Pass again into the San Fernando Valley's central police station in Van Nuys where Laemmle had told Donnay to look up a Sergeant Tom and to use Laemmle's name as a referral.

The police station was located in City Hall in the Civic Center building on Sylvan street. Donnay paid the taxi driver and went inside where he asked the first man in blue he encountered to direct him to Sergeant Tom's office.

That office consisted of a desk with two chairs among many others in a room crowded with people, not many of them in blue, either talking into phones or chatting among themselves. Sergeant Tom got up from his desk as Donnay was led over.

He was heavy set, most of it muscle, with a round, ruddy face and sandy-red hair. Donnay said that Carl Laemmle sent him.

"How is Mr. Laemmle?" Sergeant Tom asked, offering Donnay a chair.

"Tearing his hair out, what's left of it," Donnay quipped, sitting.

The sergeant laughed and sank back into his chair behind the desk. "So, you've come all the way from France to our dusty little cow town," he said. "Whatever for?"

"Before I get into that, should I be calling you sergeant, Sergeant Tom or what?" he asked politely.

"Call me Thomas," he said with a grin. "My folks had a sense of humor, but I got the last laugh. I go by 'Thomas' rather than 'Tom-Tom,'" he remarked, holding the grin.

"I go by 'Pierre,'" he returned. "Not as creative but thoroughly French."

The two shook hands firmly.

"So, Pierre, how can I help you?" Sergeant Tom asked, getting straight down to business.

Donnay laid out why he had come to America, filling the officer in on what he knew of Arik Cassell's background.

"And you said he's disfigured?" Sergeant Tom remarked once Donnay had finished.

Donnay nodded.

"Seems to me he'd be pretty easy to spot under those circumstances."

"He most likely uses makeup when needed to disguise himself," Donnay explained. "And he has an accomplice to do much of the leg work for him."

"Any thoughts on the identity your guy's been using here?" the officer inquired.

"I have my suspicions. Strong ones," Donnay responded. "But until I'm sure, I'm keeping them to myself. I want to hook him this time so there's no chance of his wriggling away."

"That's good because we don't have the manpower here to help you with any investigation, short *or* long-term," Sergeant Tom said.

Donnay looked crestfallen. He'd been counting on the department's help.

"You see, we have less than a dozen deputies here to cover the two hundred square miles in our jurisdiction," the sergeant explained. "And our first order of business is tracking down rum runners and bootleggers. Drugs must take a back seat—unless we get a solid tip that we can act on right away, as was the situation with Victor Reilly and his starlet girlfriend. You may have read about it. Caught 'em red-handed."

"Mr. Laemmle told me about it," Donnay said. "Any idea where the tip came from?"

"Like you, I have my suspicions, but I can't reveal them," the officer said.

Donnay nodded that he understood. "Any chance of my talking to this Reilly fellow and the woman?" he asked.

"You can try," Sergeant Tom replied. "But he's not saying very much and she maintains she doesn't take drugs and doesn't know anything."

"Do you believe her?"

The sergeant shrugged without answering. Then he suddenly leaned toward Donnay and lowered his voice. "This didn't come from me," he insisted, "but you might try Adela Grant at the *L.A. Crier*. Her paper has been digging into this dirty business and she might have some answers for you."

"Will *she* talk to me?" Donnay asked.

"Worth a shot," Sergeant Tom said. "She's always threatening to name names in some future column though she hasn't yet. She's full of innuendo. Some of it might just correspond with your own suspicions."

"Do you have her number? Or should I just go there?"

"I'd say just go there," Sergeant Tom offered. "Harder to ignore you that way."

Donnay smiled. "Thanks, Thomas."

"You're welcome, Pierre. And good luck."

They shook hands again and Donnay left.

TWENTY-ONE

Sebastian Vane Residence
Hollywood Hills, California

Darrass picked up the week's *L.A. Crier* and began reading:

"IS UNIVERSAL'S PHANTOM JINXED?
LAEMMLE SAYS NO!"
By Adela Grant

"A run of bad luck—or worse—has plagued Universal's Super Jewel spectacular The Phantom of the Opera almost from the first day of production, sources close to the picture tell us.

"First, some expensive costumes and props went permanently missing and had to be replaced at considerable cost.

"The cast and crew are said to be at odds with director Rupert Julian.

"Then, only last week, an enormous prop chandelier broke away from the ceiling of Stage 28 and crashed onto the opera house set below. Many of the extras playing audience members were

181

injured, none fatally. 'Thank God for that,' studio head Carl Laemmle was quoted as saying.

"The incident mimics a scene in the picture where the title character cuts the chandelier's restraints and it falls upon the unsuspecting audience. The scene was scheduled to be filmed in the coming days, but plans are now in limbo.

"'Thanks to the quick thinking of my director, Rupert Julian, and his cameraman, some of the accident was captured on film, so we didn't suffer a total loss,' Laemmle said.

"'The sequence now may not be as suspenseful as it might have been,'" added the director, "'but it will still be very spectacular.'

"On top of all this, the production has lost its leading lady, rising star Leslie Paige, whose services were terminated on grounds of 'moral turpitude,' sources have revealed.

"Along with the studio's casting director Victor Reilly—with whom Miss Paige was allegedly in a relationship—the pair was arrested on illegal alcohol and drug charges at Reilly's Woodland Hills home.

"The two have posted bail and await trial.

"As a result of being let go, Miss Paige's completed scenes in Phantom must all be retaken at considerable expense with her replacement, Universal contract star Mary Philbin.

"'It's almost as if someone was trying to shut the picture down,' Laemmle noted with exasperation. "'But whoever he is, he won't succeed. We are committed to getting this picture done and making it great.'"

Darrass tossed the paper aside, furious that his difficult acrobatic feat of bringing down the chandelier prematurely had not had the desired effect of closing the picture down.

Arik and he were sure that Laemmle would sink no more of Universal's money into the benighted production after the chandelier catastrophe. But that had not been the case. Laemmle was a stubborn old coot.

What neither Arik nor he had foreseen was that sufficient footage had been captured of the chandelier falling and then crashing upon the panicked extras to be inserted into the finished film. Thus the calamity wasn't a total loss for the studio.

Arik was initially chagrined that he would now have to come up with another way to interfere with the production. But he quickly seized upon an idea that he liked even better. He told Darrass, "If you can't beat them, join them."

He began concocting his scheme, which this time around focused not on sabotaging "things," but the star of the picture himself, Lon Chaney.

Arik expressed sorrow over what had happened to Leslie as a result of being caught up in the aftermath of the tip to police that he was sure had come from that nuisance Adela Grant. Clearly the meddling reporter was hoping to "turn" Victor Reilly following his arrest and public shaming. But that hadn't happened and the young actress was snared in the crossfire. She had lost her breakthrough lead role in *The Phantom of the Opera* and was now a pariah to all the religious blowhards, power-hungry state censor boards, and spineless studio heads who listened to them.

Arik had been powerless to do anything for her other than post her bail, which he did under a false identity. She was released to the supervision of her cousins, the Paganos.

Arik had posted Reilly's bail using the same pseudonym in the belief that Reilly was savvy enough to figure out who his benefactor was and would keep silent. Reilly had been released under his own recognizance and was now holed up in his house. The man was fast outliving his usefulness.

As far as the pernicious Adela Grant was concerned, Arik calculated that removing her from the scene would be a mistake. He and Darrass had already taken care of one nosey reporter, the late Ted Alexander, whom Grant had essentially replaced. Two would be pushing it. Besides, if Reilly kept his mouth shut, her best source would dry up, and so would she.

Darrass was unaware that Arik had entered the room and seen him looking at the latest *Crier*.

"You'll ruin your eyes if you keep reading that garbage," Arik quipped. "We've got more important things to do anyway," he continued as he crossed the floor. "Ready to go down and start getting the 'Room' ready for our guest?"

Darrass nodded enthusiastically and the two of them proceeded to the door that led down to the "Room" in the secret basement.

Pagano Chicken Ranch
Canoga Park, California

Leslie Paige took a pen and some sheets of writing paper from the hutch in the dining room and went into the kitchen. She sat down at the table, listening to the mournful howls of coyotes way off in the distance.

It had taken her a while to get used to their sound. It seemed to her so lonely and full of pain. She had taken to calling her cousins Uncle Arno and Aunt Elena. Uncle Arno told her the time to take notice of the coyotes was when they got quiet; that meant they were drawing close by and probably had their hungry eyes on the chickens. Then he'd go outside with his shotgun, shoo them off, and stand guard for a bit. But not tonight.

She started writing:

> *Dear Mama and Papa,*
>
> *This is the most difficult letter I've ever written to you. By now, stories of the scandal I've been caught up in have probably reached the newspaper there too, though perhaps not on the front page, as they are here.*
>
> *First of all I want to say how sorry I am for the shame the accusations against me have brought on the family—especially as those accusations have since proven to be false. Here's the truth: My manager (not boyfriend) Victor Reilly offered me a ride home on a particularly hot day a few weeks ago; on the way he stopped at his home to grab a fresh shirt. What I didn't know was that he also refreshed himself with a drug called cocaine. After that we had an argument about my salary at the studio and I started to walk out. He grabbed me and in the scuffle some of the white powder transferred to me and the police arresting us jumped to the wrong conclusion.*
>
> *A mystery benefactor paid my bail. I suspect it was Sebastian Vane, who has been very kind to me at the studio, but I don't know for sure. I cannot think who else it might have been. In any event, Victor Reilly has substantiated my claims of innocence on drug charges, which have since been dropped, and I am now a free woman.*
>
> *Uncle Arno and Aunt Elena have been wonderful to me throughout this ordeal. Right now they are helping*

me lay low from the reporters camped outside, who are not interested in questions of guilt or innocence but in fanning the flames of scandal to sell more newspapers. Out here, even a whiff of scandal is enough to derail a career. I have lost the female lead in The Phantom of the Opera to Mary Philbin, the director's first choice for the part whose shrinking violet histrionics he much prefers.

As to my future plans, I cannot say. Some colleagues have advised me to just sit tight until the storm blows over, though it shows no signs of blowing over yet. My career had just started, they say. I could change my name again and begin anew, no longer a pariah. But as I wrote earlier, one scandal seems to be enough in this business to retain that status.

I wanted to let you both know that in spite of it all, I am doing fine, especially with the love and support of the Paganos. So, please don't worry about me. Look at it this way, I'll have more time to write and keep you up to date.

Your loving daughter,
Leslie

She tossed the pen aside and suddenly burst into tears. It had taken everything in her to stay upbeat and not let her true feelings of total devastation show through.

All she'd ever wanted was to be an actress—a *good* one—on the silver screen. The premieres, the parties, the nightclubbing and all the other baubles that went with a career in moving pictures meant nothing to her. Maybe that meant she was too much of a small town girl to have a movie career. If so, it was better she find out now rather than later when she might have so much more to lose. But that didn't make it any less of a bitter pill to swallow.

186

She bolted upright and wiped away the tears, hoping she hadn't spilled any on the letter and smudged the ink. She hadn't. She stuck the letter in an addressed envelope and sealed it as she listened to the coyotes keep up their nightly serenade, still far away.

Then she felt the plump but strong arms of Aunt Elena circle her from behind and heard a soft whisper in her ear that said, "My poor girl. Go ahead and cry all you want. Let it out."

So, Leslie did.

TWENTY-TWO

Offices of the *L.A. Crier*
Los Angeles, California

Donnay rose early the morning after his meeting with Sergeant Tom. He had a full breakfast of sausage and eggs in the hotel restaurant then spent an hour in his suite going over the notes he had brought with him from the Phantom case file. He wanted to be fully prepared for his hoped-for meeting with the reporter Adela Grant.

Mid-morning, he called the newspaper to see when she'd be in and was told her hours that day were noon to eight p.m. He arranged for a taxi to pick him up at his hotel at quarter to one. He spent the remaining time trying to control his impatience.

The offices of the *L.A. Crier* were located on the second floor of a large, gray building sandwiched between other large, gray buildings in an older part of downtown Los Angeles—not that any part of the city was "old" in the conventional sense, certainly not when contrasted with a city like Paris.

The bottom floor was taken up by a pawn shop, its front window overflowing with pawned items for sale, everything from a banjo to home-made tap shoes, a cavalry bugle, top hat

and tails, and a worn pair of cowboy boots made of snakeskin—
all of these items the temporary leavings, Donnay surmised, of
all those newcomers to Hollywood in search of fame and fortune
in the movies who had run out of money for food or a place to
live in the meantime.

Donnay went upstairs and through a door marked *Editorial*
to find himself in a room full of desks, typewriters and
telephones. The cacophony of people banging away on their
machines, shouting to each other or into their phones was almost
deafening. Donnay wondered how anyone could think in a
noisy environment like this, let alone get any work done.

He asked a young brunette at one of the desks closest if she'd
be so kind as to point him in the direction of Adela Grant. She
paused from typing to push her thick-lensed glasses up her nose
and pointed to a corner where an older woman with dark hair
streaked with gray was pounding away at her typewriter with
the fastest two fingers Donnay had ever seen.

Donnay thanked the brunette and maneuvered his way
through the sea of noise until he arrived at Adela Grant's desk.
A cigarette dangled from her lips as she worked, dropping ashes
and leaving burn marks on an apron or smock of some kind
worn to protect her clothes. The ash tray beside her typewriter
was filled with stubbed-out butts.

She didn't look up as he approached her but continued
assaulting the typewriter keys with her miraculous two fingers.

He tapped on the wall. "Adela Grant?"

"Who wants to know?" she barked, again without looking
up.

"My name is Pierre Donnay," he said politely over the din.

"From your accent, I'd say you're not a disgruntled reader,"
she quipped.

189

"No, madame. I come from Paris. From the Ministry of Justice," he said.

That got her attention. She stopped typing, turned toward him and pulled the cigarette from her lips with two stained fingers. "Just to see me? Whatever for?"

"Well, not *just* you," he offered with a wry smile. "I've read two articles from your newspaper about the supply of illegal drugs in your community, one written by you and one by your predecessor—"

"Ted Alexander," she interjected.

Donnay nodded. "He met with an accident, I understand."

"That's what the police say."

"Do you think they're wrong?"

"Not for me to second-guess the police," she answered. "But it was an awfully convenient accident."

Donnay nodded again. "Yes, Mr. Alexander did seem on the verge of naming names, but then he held back. The same with you. Why did you hold back?"

"What's this got to do with you?" she asked irritably.

"I'm on leave to pursue a lead of my own on a case of drug smuggling, multiple murder and kidnapping in Paris some years ago where the culprit got away," he said. "We have reason to believe he came here eight or more years ago to begin setting up operations under a new identity."

She eyed him skeptically, but with interest. "Do tell." She lit another cigarette.

"His real name is Arik Cassell."

"Never heard of him." She exhaled the smoke his way. "Pull up a chair and take a load off," she said.

"Excuse me?" He looked baffled.

"Sit down," she explained.

"Oh." Donnay did as she suggested. "Cassell works with an accomplice who goes by the single name of Darrass but has probably established a new identity too. Darrass cannot speak. His tongue was removed under torture in prison. Cassell belongs to a crime organization known as the Unione Corse."

He knew he had struck a chord when her eyes suddenly widened. "I think our respective investigations are on a parallel track," he went on. "So, why not share what we've each uncovered to help catch these two?"

"And how do you suppose we go about this sharing?" she asked with returned skepticism.

Donnay tapped the papers on his lap. "I'll show you what information I have," he suggested. "And you show me yours."

"And what if I've got more evidence than you do? You could scoop me," she said warily.

"I'm a public prosecutor, not a reporter," he countered.

"And a scoop is a scoop," she added quickly.

"Then how about we establish some trust between us first?" he offered. "Any ideas?"

She pondered the question for a moment. Then: "As a matter of fact, I just might," she said.

She lit up a fresh cigarette off the one she'd lit moments ago to help gather her thoughts.

Then: "How's this?" she said "You believe our investigations seem to be running parallel. Okay. Then probably we've each come up with a suspect."

He nodded.

"As you'd figured out, Ted and I held back until we could be sure. But both of us felt we had a strong suspect. The same one, it turns out. So, here's what you and I do." She tore a piece of typing paper in two, kept one half and gave the other to him, along with a pencil.

"We'll both write down the initials of the person we have in mind and then compare them," she went on to explain. "If the initials don't match, then neither of us will have given anything away. But if they do match, we'll both know we're on to something and ready to join forces. How's that sound?"

He agreed and they both scribbled away in secret, then handed their folded paper to the other.

"Ready?" Donnay said.

Adela nodded and they each opened their sheets and silently read what the other had written.

"S.V.," they said simultaneously. "Sebastian Vane."

Now, all they had to do was prove it.

Woolworth Building
Los Angeles, California

Adela suggested that she and Donnay adjourn up Broadway to the Woolworth Building's lunch counter for some coffee and some quiet as the noisy lunch hour crowd had probably thinned out. Woolworth's boasted the largest lunch counter in the world, she told him. Donnay marveled at the long line of seats that stretched the length of the cafeteria.

Adela was right that at this hour they would be able to hear themselves think as only a dozen seats were currently occupied. She and Donnay took the two at the far end of the counter, away from the stragglers. Most of the lunch room's waitresses were now off shift. The cute blonde (read: show business hopeful) who remained took their coffee order.

Donnay re-opened Grant's file and resumed looking through her and Ted Alexander's notes as Adela pulled out yet another cigarette and thrust it between her lips. She began searching for her matches.

"Do you *always* have a cigarette in your mouth?" he asked in wonderment. "Even when you sleep?"

"Not then. But the rest of the time. Helps me think," she replied, lighting up. "Why? Does the smoke bother you?"

"No," he answered.

"Good to know," she said with a wink. "Though it wouldn't have made any difference."

He smiled, amused at her forthrightness—the hard-nosed reporter with printer's ink in her veins instead of blood. But he could tell from the wink that it was a façade. Mostly.

The waitress brought them their coffees and asked if they'd like anything else. They said no and she went away, leaving them alone. Donnay added sugar and took a sip, then began fanning his lips from the hot brew.

Adela added lots of cream and sugar to hers and then stopped abruptly, looking impatient. "Don't you think we have enough between us to get this bastard charged?" she inquired of Donnay.

"Circumstantially," he replied. "As a prosecutor I could certainly make a case, but it might not be sufficient to hold up in court."

"Why ever not?" she asked, bewildered.

"Too much reasonable doubt," he said. "At least any good defense counsel could make it seem that way. What we need is some direct, incontrovertible evidence that Sebastian Vane and Arik Cassell are the same person beyond any shadow of doubt."

"Like what, for example?" she asked. "Short of catching him in the act of doling out the white powder to one of his customers, that is."

Donnay thought for a moment then suddenly snatched up his papers from in front of her. He flipped through the pages of notes, letters and reports until he came to what he was looking for and held it up to her—a square white card with some black smudges on it.

"Like these," he said. "*Fingerprints!*"

She looked at him in awe. "Where did you get them?"

He almost confessed "From his lair within the opera house," but caught himself just in time. "They were lifted from his rooms in Paris after he'd flown. They were in his original file. I brought them with me."

"That's all well and good," she said, looking suddenly deflated. "But we have nothing to compare them to." She eyed him hopefully. "Or have we?"

"No," he answered. "We'll have to get near him to collect something he's touched. Without his seeing us, of course."

"Easier said than done," she responded sourly.

"How well do you know Vane?" he asked.

"Not at all," she answered. "I've seen him around the Universal lot when he's been making a picture, or at some studio events," she added. "And he certainly knows me from my columns. I couldn't get near him with a ten-foot pole. How about you?"

"Me?" He shook his head as he reflected upon his brush with death at the hands of the fiend in the opera house's underground lake. Nothing of which he could reveal at the moment. "Like you, he knows me from my investigation," he said, leaving it at that.

"And so what do we do? Follow him around, hoping he doesn't notice, until one of us gets lucky?" she proposed facetiously.

He almost laughed. Then: "Are you familiar with his movements?" he asked seriously.

She shook her head. "As I said, I've only seen him occasionally at the studio in makeup and costume when he's making a picture or at events where he's accompanied by his manservant and bodyguard. Name's Bahram. Arab, I think. About six three, six four with a black beard. A real giant. I figure he's this Darrass character in your notes."

Donnay looked puzzled. "Hmm. I haven't read anywhere of Darrass' being so imposing," he said.

"Maybe he wears lifts in those big boots of his," she suggested. "One thing I do know. Rumor has it he can't speak. At least I've never seen his lips move. And when he's with Vane, he waits on the man hand and foot. So, anything touched would have Darrass' fingerprints on it mostly."

"That's a problem," Donnay admitted. "We'd have to get near Vane himself—somewhere he feels comfortable and where he won't be inclined to be waited on. His home, perhaps."

"Good luck with that," she said, finishing her coffee and cigarette.

"Know anyone who visits there? Someone we can trust?" he asked. "What about Victor Reilly?"

She laughed. "You've got to be kidding? Under his present circumstances, he wouldn't risk going anywhere near Sebastian Vane. And he certainly wouldn't do it for me. He's too furious with me for tipping the police to finding him with coke on his nose. But you could ask him. Maybe even sweeten things by offering him less prison time or some other kind of deal?"

"Unfortunately, I don't have the authority in this country to offer him any deal," he said. "And Reilly's not wanted in mine."

Adela Grant snapped her fingers suddenly. "What about the girl? The young actress—Leslie Paige—who was arrested with Reilly and lost her co-starring role in *The Phantom of the Opera* because of it?"

He nodded. "Yes, I saw the headlines," he said. "Is she still charged?" he asked.

"No. Exonerated and released," Grant said. "Paige met Vane on her first picture and, according to studio gossip, he was so impressed with her that he insisted her role be expanded. And he helped get her a bigger part in a next picture—a lowly Western. But that led to her being cast in *Phantom*."

"Think you can talk her into visiting Vane for us?" Donnay asked, excited now.

"Not me," she said emphatically. "Leslie Paige wouldn't give me the time of day after that photo I published of her being arrested at Reilly's home."

"Yes, I saw it," Donnay replied glumly.

"You and everybody else," Grant said. "She probably holds me responsible for derailing her career."

"Do you burn *all* your bridges behind you, Miss Grant?" he said, trying to sound lighthearted.

But then she gave him another of her subtle winks. "Not *all* of them, no," she said. "Could be that a charming, dapper-looking Frenchman I know just might have better luck."

TWENTY-THREE

Victor Reilly Residence
Woodland Hills, California

Sergeant Tom pulled the police car into the driveway behind Reilly's convertible, blocking it from any attempt at a fast getaway. The top was down, indicating that Reilly had possibly been out and about already this morning enjoying the sunshine. It had rained heavily the previous evening.

As the sergeant's deputy got out the passenger side and started heading up the steps to Reilly's front door, Tom noticed that pools of water were gathered in the folds of the convertible top of Reilly's car. He reached into the open car and touched the seats, which he found to be wet. This indicated to Tom that Reilly probably hadn't used the car this morning—in fact, he had left it out in the rain unprotected all night.

The deputy rapped heavily on the front door. He called out: "Mr. Reilly, open up, please. Police!"

Sergeant Tom saw that Reilly's mail box was overflowing. This was not surprising as the disgraced studio executive had been incommunicado for weeks, refusing to answer his phone or, it appeared, pay his bills.

197

"Mr. Reilly, it's the police. Open up," the deputy called out again, knocking even harder this time.

Sergeant Tom pulled the volume of accumulated mail from the box and glanced through it. Most were even more bills but there were two letters from Reilly's attorney, who had told Tom that his client had gone completely dark even to him.

As a result of his hibernating and lack of response to his own attorney, Reilly had missed a preliminary hearing of his case the previous day. The judge had immediately revoked his bail and issued a bench warrant for his arrest, which is why Tom and his deputy were at Reilly's home now.

"Not answering," the deputy said as Tom trudged up the steep steps, huffing and puffing. Maybe some of the weight he'd put on recently wasn't just muscle, he chastised himself.

"Gathered that," he said, catching his breath. "Go round the side and look in the windows, see if there's any sign someone's there," he added. "I'll stay here in case that someone tries to make a break for it." *Assuming he hasn't already flown the coop*, Tom thought but did not say.

The deputy acknowledged his instructions with a nod and left the porch, disappearing around the side of the house.

Meanwhile, Tom pounded on the door again. "Mr. Reilly, this is Sergeant Tom of the Valley Police. Don't make this more difficult on yourself, sir. Open up!" But again there was no response.

He put his ear to the door to judge if there was any movement inside. Nothing.

The deputy returned, remarking, "Somebody *was* there. Place is a mess inside."

"Well, they're not answering now," Tom returned. "Guess we'll just have to break it in."

"Want me to try kicking in the door?" the deputy offered.

Sergeant Tom reached into his pocket with a shake of the head. "Too hard on the knees," he said, pulling out a key ring with a dozen lock picks dangling from it.

The deputy watched in fascination as the sergeant considered each pick before settling on one of them. He inserted the key into the lock and jiggled it back and forth until there was a faint *click*. He turned the knob and the door fell open, revealing a short foyer littered with unread newspapers and mail as well as a disaster of a living room just beyond.

Guns drawn, they moved into the foyer where the sergeant added the mail he'd brought in to the pile on the floor.

As the living room came into full view, they saw empty liquor and wine bottles scattered about the floor and end tables.

Wonder where he gets his hooch from? Sergeant Tom couldn't help from thinking.

Ash trays overflowed with cigarette butts. Open newspapers were strewn about the floor along with plates of dry, spoiling food. And their noses were assailed by the stench of rotting garbage, probably drifting in from the kitchen.

"Whatever he was up to, it sure wasn't housekeeping," the deputy remarked, covering his nose with a handkerchief.

They picked their way cautiously through the debris on the way toward the kitchen as the stench grew worse. And as they crossed the living room past the stairs, they saw the body of Victor Reilly hanging from a rope fastened to a banister on the second floor.

The body had been there for some time, Sergeant Tom quickly realized, as it was already decomposing. There wasn't much left of the man's face other than a slick, gray ooze covering the cranium. The eyeballs were sunken and shriveled. And the tendons in the neck were visible, and stretched to the breaking point due to the taut rope around the deceased's throat.

"See if you can find a phone and call the coroner," Tom ordered the deputy, who moved quickly to start looking.

Sergeant Tom studied the body as a wave of nausea struck him. Then he too covered his nose and mouth with a handkerchief.

The Phantom's Lair Set
Universal Studios

Moving pictures are typically filmed out of sequence. This is done to keep the budget manageable and for logistical reasons also. The two are frequently related.

Today, Friday afternoon, director Rupert Julian would be shooting the ending of the film whereas Monday, the Phantom's unmasking scene, which was to come earlier in the picture, would be filmed. Everybody was looking forward to that moment as it would be the first time that anyone on the lot, including studio executives, witnessed Lon Chaney's allegedly horrific "living skull" makeup.

In the meantime there was the ending to deal with. Scenario writer Elliott Clawson had developed the novel's brief conclusion into a full scene. Whereas the novel had ended with a dismissive passage about the Phantom's dying "somewhere" of a broken heart, Clawson had set this "somewhere" in the Phantom's lair within the opera house.

In the scene, the Phantom, again wearing a mask, was to release the two lovers he had been holding captive and order them to "Go! Go!" Then he was to sit down at his organ, but rather than play music, he would hold his head in his hands, his body slouched, as if he were sobbing.

Overcome suddenly with sympathy for her former tormentor, Christine, the kidnapped opera singer, was to move slowly toward him until she was at his side. Then she would place her hand affectionately upon his shoulder.

His own hand would cover hers and he would wish her a long and bountiful life, gently repeating his order to "Please, go."

With tears in her eyes, Christine was then to run to her lover, Raoul, and the two of them escape—as the Phantom slumped over dead of a broken heart onto the keys of his organ. Fade to Black.

"Places, everyone!" the director shouted, stroking his long, green scarf. Then he called quiet from all but the violinist who was to accompany the scene with mood music.

Having already rehearsed the scene to his satisfaction earlier in the day, Julian called "Action!" The cameraman began cranking and the actors went through the scene without mishap.

As the take ended, the cast and crew burst into applause for Chaney's moving performance of the Phantom's final moments, all of them expressed entirely with his body, his back to the camera. As if on a string, the actor popped back to life, spun around, and took a deep, grateful bow just as...

...*a tormented howl like that from a wounded animal echoed across the stage from the catwalk above, chilling everyone's blood.*

Blinded by the bright studio lights illuminating the stage, no one could make out the source of the unearthly sound, except for a brief clattering of footsteps on the catwalk. Then all was silence.

Rupert Julian was the first to speak, and only loud enough for the cameraman beside him to hear:

"First, things disappear. Then the chandelier is cut. And now *this*!" he muttered irritably. "There's too many weird things going on with this picture. I'll be glad when it's over."

The cameraman mumbled back he would be glad too—for that reason, and for some others he left unstated as Julian instructed him to corral one of the assistant directors and shoot the remaining inserts and close-ups for the scene. Then he walked from the stage and out the door.

Subsequently, the howl was judged to have been a strong gust of wind that somehow got into the rafters, or, just as possibly, a minor electrical malfunction that somehow righted itself. And the incident was dismissed.

TWENTY-FOUR

Lon Chaney's Dressing Room
Universal Studios

Lon Chaney stepped into the private dressing room Universal had provided him on the lot.

This was one of the great perks of being a major moving picture star—the privacy and solace of having one's own personal living space away from the noisy hubbub of the studio floor. The place included a small kitchen and full bath as well as a bed for energy-saving naps between scenes.

He was grateful the dressing room hadn't been snatched away from him given that *Phantom* would be his last picture for the studio before moving over to Metro. But that kind of pettiness wasn't Uncle Carl Laemmle's style. He was very much like an idealized favorite uncle in that he always seemed glad for your success regardless of whether or not his studio benefitted.

Uncle Carl's sixteen-year-old son Carl Jr., whom everyone called "Junior," was a different kettle of fish, however. Forever at his father's side and being groomed to take over the studio one day, the always-grinning "Junior" Laemmle would occasionally be overheard grumbling about his father's propensity for nurturing talent only to let it get away from him once it had ripened. "Junior" would have taken the dressing room away from Chaney for sure if he'd been head of the studio.

Rumor had it that in opposition to his father, "Junior" was opposed to going ahead with the production of *Phantom* because he thought the story was too old-fashioned—that it had gone out of fashion with the performed-to-death stage version of George du Maurier's novel *Trilby*.

First Chaney got out of his costume then removed the small amount of makeup he'd worn for that day's scenes, which required only that his character disguise himself behind one of his several full-face masks.

On Monday they would be shooting the scene where Christine unmasks him—for which he would have to be in full "living skull" makeup for the first time.

Concealing his craggy, working man's features and thinning hair behind the spectral visage of the Paris Opera's worst nightmare would be a challenge that would likely take the weekend of experimenting to address. Then, beginning Monday, there would follow several hours in the morning making himself up followed by several more hours at the end of the day taking it off, then repeat the next day and the next for as long as it required to film all the scenes in which he appeared in his Phantom make-up.

Chaney lit a cigarette then fell back into the plush sofa-chair he'd sat on to relax and luxuriate before he had to get moving again. He smiled as he thought of the vacation he had planned during the picture's upcoming temporary hiatus. His wife Hazel and boy, Creighton, would be joining him.

"Mr. Chaney...?"

It was almost a whisper and seemed to come from outside the door to the dressing room.

Lon Chaney's eyes snapped open. Only then did he realize he had dozed off in the chair. His fingers burned and he looked down to see the long ash of his cigarette ready to fall on the carpet. He quickly extinguished the cigarette in a potted plant then glanced toward the door.

"It's open!" he shouted. But no one came in and for a second he began to wonder if he'd imagined the voice in his half-asleep-half-awake state.

But then he heard it again.

"*Mr. Chaney…?*"

It was louder and this time came from the short dark hallway that led to the kitchen and bath.

"Is someone there?" the perplexed actor called out.

"*Lon Chaney…?*"

It was more of a hiss this time, coming from very close by, practically in his left ear.

Startled, Chaney swung around to the source of the sound and found himself staring into the scarred, bone-white countenance of…

…*a living skull.*

"They call me Erik, the phantom," the skull said. Then its hand shot up to Chaney's face. It was holding a rag moistened with chloroform.

As Chaney struggled, the phantom closed the rag over the man's nose, until Chaney's body went limp.

The "Room"
Sebastian Vane Residence

Lon Chaney awoke with the burning sensation of chloroform still in his throat. He was surrounded by pitch darkness, his body on a thick layer of white sand.

Was he outdoors somewhere? On a hillside, perhaps? The beach? Or the desert?

He looked up but there were no stars. Just more pitch blackness. There wasn't even an evening breeze.

Which meant...*what?*

That he was shut up somewhere *indoors?*

He grabbed a handful of sand and let it sift through his fingers. But where indoors? It made no sense that he'd be inside, not with all this sand beneath him.

But then nothing about this entire episode made sense.

Why had he been kidnapped? And by whom?

The last thing he remembered before being chloroformed was resting in his dressing room on the studio lot, and suddenly looking into the terrifying visage of an almost-exact duplicate of the "living skull" makeup he had created for his role of the phantom of the opera.

But how was that possible when he'd taken every precaution to keep even his working sketches under wraps?

Even *more* unsettling was the fact that while his makeup for the phantom was wholly an illusion manufactured of greasepaint, wax, spirit gum, false teeth and other odds and ends of his trade, the "living skull" that had confronted him with the words "They call me Erik" spilling from its lipless mouth seemed utterly *real*.

Chaney could clearly see the nicks and slash marks in the skull where the facial flesh had been cut away. He could see in the creature's blinking eyes the only remnants of that flesh — the eyelids. And he could see the holes where the man's ears had once been. If indeed he was a man and not some nightmare come to life.

Chaney was startled by a metallic grinding sound as his prison was semi-illuminated by a dim light from above. It took a few minutes for his eyes to adjust before he could take in his surroundings.

He was confined to a large, octagonal room that was, he presumed, enclosed within a much larger room. He could make out his reflection in the octagon's mirrored walls that surrounded him from floor to ceiling. As his eyes moved about the room he spotted a vent in the ceiling.

What manner of hell is this place? he wondered.

Chaney spotted a large bowl in the far corner of his mirrored prison. He crawled over to it and found that it contained water. He dipped his finger, and found the water cool to his touch; he tasted it, rolling it around in his mouth before he swallowed. It was fresh and clean so he scooped up a handful and drank thirstily. It felt good going down his parched throat and helped take away some of the still-lingering burn of the chloroform.

All the same, what he craved even more than water right now was a cigarette. But he had none. His pockets were empty.

"Mr. Chaney..." came the same ominously quiet voice he'd heard in his studio dressing room. Only this time there was a slight echo, as if it were coming through a long, hollow tube.

"Mr. Chaney, I know you've regained consciousness," the voice continued. "I can see you moving about."

Chaney's eyes quickly inspected the mirrored walls then the ceiling but discovered no portals or peep holes that he could make out. Could it be that the mirrors were of two-way construction, allowing his tormentors to watch him but not vice-versa?

"What do you want?" Chaney bellowed. "Why have you brought me here? And where *is* here anyway?"

"You are in a room originally of Persian design," the voice explained. "A torture room to be exact. But I've created some modifications of my own—to make it more *efficient*."

"Torture?" Chaney exclaimed. "What have I ever done to you? And who the hell are you anyway?"

"I've already told you who I am," the voice said impatiently. "Erik. The Phantom. The disfigured monstrosity you've been playing in your latest moving picture!"

"You talk as if he's a real person," Chaney shouted. "He's a *fictional character*. In a *fantasy!*"

"I grant you that Mr. Leroux's novel is indeed mostly a fantasy. But you can take it from me that his Phantom of the opera was very real—because *I am he*."

The man was insane, Chaney said to himself.

"By the way, your designs for my makeup are quite good," the disembodied voice went on, sounding almost complimentary. "Taken from the book, no doubt—another detail Leroux got right in his otherwise shamelessly romantic melodrama."

"Come Monday when I don't show up at the studio, they'll be looking for me, you know," Chaney warned.

"I doubt it," the voice returned with nonchalance.

"What do you mean?" Chaney shouted indignantly. "They'll even call in the police when I can't be found."

"But you won't be missing," the voice egged him on. "You'll be right there on time and ready go through with the unmasking scene."

How did this lunatic know what scene they'd be shooting? Chaney wondered. Had he been there among the crew and bystanders all this time?

"I've been watching the picture as it's been made," the voice divulged as if having read Chaney's mind. "And I haven't much liked what I've seen."

Chaney recalled the unearthly howl they'd heard at the conclusion of shooting the farewell scene and the phantom's death on Friday. Could that have been a reaction by this lunatic of a critic to their playing of the scene?

Again, as if reading Chaney's thoughts, the voice bemoaned, "I had two options: create enough production problems to get the picture cancelled, which hadn't worked so far—that Laemmle can be *so* stubborn—or take your place and play the part myself with more accuracy. I'll begin Monday with the scene of my unmasking, where my true face and not your makeup will be revealed for the first time."

"And what's in store for me?" Chaney demanded of his persecutor. Instantly on his feet, he smashed his fist against one of the mirrors. It flexed but did not break.

"Shatterproof glass," the voice remarked almost with sympathy. "As to what's to happen to you, I haven't made my mind up yet. You'll be okay here until I do—once you *warm* to the idea." At this he let out a chuckle which metamorphosed into a maniacal laugh that chilled Lon Chaney to the bone.

"You won't get away with this, you devil. Let me out of here. *Now!*" Chaney shouted but to no avail as he continued banging on the mirrors.

The voice was silent. The fiend either was gone now or just mutely observing him.

Chaney dropped to his knees in the sand and thought scornfully: Kidnapped and held prisoner by a maniac claiming to be the *real* phantom of the opera. It's insane!

Was there an actual Phantom of the opera like the maniac insisted?

Chaney remembered reading somewhere that Leroux's gothic fantasy was based on the actual case of a madman who had terrorized the Paris Opera a decade or more ago. But that was all he remembered. Were this maniac's claims true?

The actor put his head in his hands. Was there no way he could get out of here on his own? His mind sifted through the incidents in Leroux's book, which he had read so long ago, but came up with nothing.

His mind then turned to the Clawson scenario of more recent vintage. It had incorporated all the major plot points from the book. As Chaney went over them in his mind, he recalled a scene where Christine's lover, Raoul, and a mysterious Persian secret service agent on the phantom's trail were being held prisoner in a mirrored chamber not dissimilar to the room Chaney was in now. And they had almost perished because of…

Chaney heard a metallic *whir* and looked up to see a panel open around the vent in the ceiling, revealing several spotlights pointed at the mirrored walls of his cell. And he suddenly remembered with mounting dread the diabolical nature of the torture chamber in the book and the scenario.

As if on cue, the spotlights came to life simultaneously, filling the room with light that reflected blindingly off the mirrors. Now he knew the reason for the white sand. It too acted as a reflector of the heat that would soon be burning through his clothes and shoes.

Already Chaney was feeling the building temperature. He loosened his shirt collar and felt the perspiration on his skin soaking through the fabric.

Shrinking from the scorching "sun" all around him to which there was no shade, he cringed at the madman's infernal purpose in putting him here, which was now horrifyingly clear.

He was to be burned to a crisp.

TWENTY-FIVE

Pierre Donnay's Accommodations
Hollywood Roosevelt Hotel

[From the *L.A. Times*]

"Disgraced Former Studio Executive Dead, a Suicide"

Victor Reilly, 37, a former casting director for Universal Studios was found dead in his Woodlands Hills home, the victim of an apparent suicide.

"We saw no evidence of foul play," remarked Van Nuys police Sergeant Thomas Tom. "He hung himself by a rope tied to the second floor railing of his home," Tom said.

Sergeant Tom was investigating why Reilly, who was out on bail on an illegal drug possession charge, had failed to report for a preliminary hearing.

"Those who knew Reilly best say they had not seen or spoken to the disgraced movie executive for some time," Sergeant Tom explained. "They told me he was severely depressed over the scandal that had cost him his job and reputation," Tom added. "He seemed determined to just lay low."

Pierre Donnay closed that morning's edition of the *Times* and placed it next to his breakfast dishes on the room service cart. This initial notice of Victor Reilly's death was on page 2, a sad commentary on how far the former executive's fortunes had fallen.

Most likely there would be more items with more details in the days to come. On the other hand, the *L.A. Crier* would probably splash the full story with all the gory details across its cover and inside folds when it came out this week. But that was the trouble—it was a weekly. And he was impatient. He wanted the full story with all the details *now* because his prosecutor's nose was telling him there was more to Reilly's alleged suicide than met the eye. Regardless of what the *L.A. Times* claimed, he suspected murder.

No one in Sebastian Vane's orbit died naturally, no matter how ashamed or depressed that person may have been. Victor Reilly had too great a story to tell about Vane to have voluntarily taken it with him. Mum out of jail, he very likely would have wanted to talk his head off to the state for a favorable deal once he'd been incarcerated for a few weeks. And Arik Cassell a.k.a. Sebastian Vane would have taken this into account.

Donnay knew Adela Grant wouldn't be sitting back twiddling her thumbs but be all over the story of Reilly's death. Very probably she was already in possession of a great deal more about Reilly's demise than the *Times* was able to report. And she would tell him all she knew.

He snatched up the phone and quickly dialed her direct number at the scandal sheet.

"Grant, here. Talk to me," she answered on the second ring. The Frenchman smiled. Her tough façade always amused him.

"It's Donnay," he said.

"With an accent like that, you could have fooled me," she responded.

He smiled again. "You've heard the news about Victor Reilly, I assume?"

"Crack of dawn," she said. "I've been working the story ever since."

"You convinced it was a suicide?" he asked.

"No. You?"

"I have my doubts," he said.

"So does the coroner," she admitted. "I just spent the morning with him."

"What does *he* say?"

"On the record, probable suicide. He's plenty pissed off at the *L.A. Times*, I'll tell you that—for leaving off the 'probable' in its story. Off the record, he believes possible foul play," she revealed.

"What makes him think so?" he asked as he heard her light up a cigarette and take a long, deep drag.

"According to what he shared with me, in order for Reilly to have broken his neck from hanging he would have had to jump from the second floor railing with lots of momentum so that when the noose snapped tight it would do so with enough force to break his neck," she explained, expelling smoke. "Applying that theory to the facts, however, the condition of the railing becomes a problem."

"In what way?" Donnay pressed her.

"The same force of impact should have pulled the railing away or at least cracked it, neither of which happened," she said. "Ergo, his belief is that Reilly was killed first, then his neck was broken, and then he was hung to make his death appear a suicide. He told me they'd have to re-construct the incident with proper weights to see if he's right. But they don't want to take time or go to the expense. So they left it as a 'probable' suicide.

"And then there's the matter of Reilly's hyoid bone. It was crushed," she added.

"Indicating strangulation," Donnay responded.

"Very good," she said with a wink in her voice. "You must have done this before."

He smiled at her sarcasm. "Once or twice," he answered.

"Unfortunately, the body was apparently too badly decomposed to reveal any abrasions or fingerprints on what was left of the throat for the coroner to be definitive," she went on. "The rope could have crushed the hyoid bone, the doc said, though he didn't think so. A noose cinches tight as it moves upward at impact, he told me. Whereas the hyoid bone breaks as a result of inward pressure. But in the end, he couldn't confirm either way."

"Or wouldn't," Donnay said skeptically.

"If he could have proven homicide, he would have said so on the death certificate," she said defensively.

"Listen to you, supporting the authorities. I'm shocked." He laughed. "Is that how you're going to write it?"

"Not if I want to keep the doc as a source," she replied. "But don't worry. There's plenty of room for nuance. So, I'll give the alternative theories of Reilly's death as much play as possible before dismissing them. Enough to make Vane and company nervous that maybe they haven't been as clever as they thought.

"By the way, when are you seeing Leslie Paige about Vane's fingerprints?" she asked, changing the subject.

"I'm going there soon as I hang up," he said.

"I'd offer you a lift, but if she caught sight of me, you'd never get her to cooperate," Grant said. She wished him good luck and they each rang off.

Donnay collected his suit coat and his papers on the Phantom/Vane case and went out the door.

Once in the lobby, he handed in his room key at the service desk and was told he had a telegram. He took the telegram — addressed to M. Pierre Donnay Hollywood Roosevelt Hotel — and went outside onto Hollywood Boulevard where he asked the doorman to raise a cab. Meanwhile he tore open the telegram and read quickly:

"DONNAY—THE 'LARGE ONE' GREATLY ETHUSED BY YOUR PROGRESS. STOP. VERNEUIL SNIFFING AROUND AS TO YOUR WHEREABOUTS. STOP. HAVE BESMIRCHED YOUR WORK ETHIC TO HIM. STOP. INTENDS TO DISMISS YOU IF/WHEN YOU RETURN TO ARCHIVE. STOP.—BLIER"

Donnay folded the telegram and put it in his pocket as the taxi pulled up to the curb. Good old Blier was holding the line on his end, keeping Gaston Leroux (the "large one") informed and Verneuil ignorant of Donnay's activities just as they'd planned.

He got into the taxi, gave the driver the destination in Canoga Park and the automobile pulled away. Now to put into motion the key element of the plan: Capturing Vane's fingerprints on the sly and matching them to the elusive Phantom's. He could only hope that Leslie Paige was up to that risky task.

As important, he hoped his powers of persuasion would be sufficient to get her to accept that risk.

The "Room"
Sebastian Vane Residence

Lon Chaney awoke with a start to the sound of gears turning in the vented ceiling. The accumulated hot air was being pulled from his mirrored jail.

That prison was now dark again; he couldn't see his hands in front of his face. But he knew that would change as the room continued draining its oppressive heat to take on an uncomfortable chilliness. By then his eyes would again have acclimated to the darkness and he could resume his search for an escape route, which was otherwise impossible to even look for in the blazing artificial "sun."

Far from being a welcome respite from the eye-straining brightness thrown off by the mirrors—and certainly not a kindness to him—the changeover to cooler darkness, he'd learned from experience, was pure sadism on the part of his tormentors, an attempt to wear him down with alternating extremes of hot and cold. The cold only seemed extreme, however, when contrasted with the burning heat.

His captors—he didn't know why he assumed there to be more than one, just a gut feeling—had taken away his wristwatch, so he had no idea how long he'd been imprisoned.

Judging by the stubble on his face, he guessed no more than a day. He'd been through six changes from high heat to middling cold so far, but again, without his watch, he had no idea how long each session had lasted. But he estimated a couple of hours per.

He'd also guessed the changeover was on a timer and not operated manually. And he had concluded that switching over regularly to the cooling darkness was also to prevent the build-up of heat from sparking a fire.

Once his eyes had adapted that first time from glaring brightness to enveloping night, he took the opportunity to insulate himself as much as possible from the next scorching session. The suffocating heat played havoc with his lungs and he found breathing to be a labor.

First, he'd tried to move the water bowl closer, but it was bolted to the floor—perhaps to make re-filling it easier for his tormentors, or just as likely, to prevent him from using it as a weapon. So, he had moved himself closer to the bowl. He had to keep himself hydrated.

Chaney would also sometimes find a couple slices of bread next to each fresh bowl of water—although when or how his captors came and went he had no idea as he was either too groggy to notice or had passed out from heat exhaustion.

Next, he'd removed his suit coat and folded it into a pillow to keep his face off the burning sand. Then, he'd torn off the tails of his white shirt into strips and submerged them in the water bowl. As the heat began to build, he applied the strips to his face and the top of his head for some protection against the blistering light. And that was about all he could think of to do to help shield himself.

When the cell was dark he gave himself over to searching for a way to extricate himself. Logic said that if there was a way in through the mirrors there had to be a way out; all he had to do was find it. But so far not even a glimpse was forthcoming.

At his most dispirited, he began to think that, perhaps, his search was useless and there was no way out.

This *was* a torture chamber, after all.

Which meant that by its very nature, it was designed to thwart any and all attempts at escape.

TWENTY-SIX

Pagano Chicken Ranch,
Canoga Park, California

It always amazed Donnay how in a few short miles through the Cahuenga Pass into the San Fernando Valley, the bustling cityscape of Los Angeles proper almost magically transformed into the rural landscape of California's not-so-distant past.

It was no wonder that Carl Laemmle's Universal Studios made so many pictures set in the Old West. Authentic locations were everywhere just outside the studio's front gate. And the farther into the Valley you ventured, the more rural and Old West-looking it became.

Donnay's taxi pulled into the Pagano Chicken Ranch just a few minutes past noon in a cloud of dust. If it weren't for the Ford truck parked outside the ranch house next to a freshly-painted red and white barn, one might have thought the year to be 1894 not 1924.

Donnay got out of the idling cab and quickly brushed off his light blue suit. He paid the driver, instructing him to wait and see if the Paganos let Donnay in. "If I am, come back and get me in about an hour," he said, then smiled wanly. "If not, I'll be right back."

Tucking the Phantom papers under his arm, he set off for the ranch house. The cab driver watched and waited in a carefree manner. One way or the other, he already had his next fare.

On the far side of the barn was a fenced-in area where scores of chickens were milling about, pecking at the ground. The noise of their clucking, Donnay thought, would have been deafening—and a whole lot more annoying—if the barn didn't act as a buffer. A couple of leghorns, as he would soon learn to call them, wandered freely outside the fence.

He knocked on the front door of the ranch house. When there was no response, he knocked harder. Eventually, the door opened, but only a few inches. Donnay could see an older, plump woman with a face burned brown by the sun looking up at him.

"Yes?" she said suspiciously.

Donnay slapped a friendly smile on his face. "I was told that Leslie Paige is staying here. I'd like to speak with her, please," he said.

"You a reporter?" the woman asked.

"No," he answered firmly with a shake of the head.

"Friend?"

"Not that either," he said.

"Then who *are* you?" she persisted.

"My name is Pierre Donnay and I'm with the public prosecutor's office at the Palais de Justice in Paris. I need to ask Mademoiselle Paige some questions about an old case I'm working on," he said.

"She doesn't talk to strangers," the woman responded intractably.

But a voice from behind her suddenly intervened. "Let him in, Aunt Elena. This I've got to hear."

"You sure?" the aunt asked over her shoulder as she slowly widened the door.

A shadow moved behind her, stepping into the light of the opened door. "Has news of my 'scandal' reached all the way to France?" Leslie Paige inquired impishly.

Donnay recognized her at once, having seen her photograph in the *L.A. Crier*, and also somewhere else that nagged at his memory. And then he had it! She'd had a small but memorable role in the pirate picture he'd seen in Paris that had provided him with the first clue that the "Opera Ghost" might still be alive and the possibility of Cassell's new identity.

Leslie's smooth skin was much darker now like her aunt's. She had also cut her long, black hair into a bob.

"No, it is not your 'scandal' that brings me here, although I have read about it and regret that it has wrapped itself around you, especially as you have been declared innocent of all charges," he explained politely.

"Not so the studios have noticed," she said caustically. "I'm still damaged goods as far as they're concerned," she added.

"I *am* sorry," he said sincerely.

"Nothing for you to be sorry about," she said. "Not your fault." She gestured to a table in the corner of the kitchen. "Come on in where it's cool and have a seat."

Still eyeing him suspiciously, the aunt stepped aside to let Donnay enter.

"Would you like some lemonade?" Leslie asked as her aunt closed the door behind him.

"Very much," he said, sitting at the table. "Gets a little dry in this part of the country."

"That's why it's important to keep yourself hydrated," Leslie said taking a pitcher from the kitchen's centerpiece icebox. "I've learned that from working on the ranch."

She poured a glass of the cool liquid, returned the pitcher to the shelf and sat opposite him. "Been in Los Angeles long?" she asked.

He drained the glass thirstily and sighed with contentment. "That was refreshing. Thank you," he said. "No, just a few weeks. Not long."

Still skeptical of her vulnerable niece talking with this foreigner, the aunt moved to another room where she was out of sight but could easily overhear.

"Would you like another lemonade?" Leslie asked.

"No, thank you. That should do me for a while," he replied, dabbing his lips with a handkerchief.

Leslie studied the dapper Frenchman closely. He was handsome but very formal and ill at ease in her presence. She opted to get him to relax so that he would be more forthcoming and talk more openly. "Go ahead and loosen your tie," she suggested. "I won't report you."

He laughed and did as she proposed. "I'm not exactly dressed for this California weather, am I?" he said self-deprecatingly.

She liked that.

"And to think it's almost winter," she said. "We've been having a heat wave. Probably turn to rain soon. It's the season." She leaned toward him, her expression serious. "So, tell me, *Monsieur* Donnay, what's the nature of this old case you're working on that's brought you to my door?" she asked forthrightly.

She seemed older and more mature than her years would suggest, he thought. But from what he'd seen of the City of

Angels so far, he concluded the vagaries of the burgeoning picture business made many young hopefuls grow up fast. And here he was about to ask her to put herself out there again—this time to snare a man who could be very dangerous indeed when cornered.

"It is a case of kidnapping, theft and murder that started more than a decade ago with a campaign of terror visited upon Paris' luxurious landmark, the grand opera house Garnier, a setting with which you are now quite familiar due to your film role as Christine," he explained.

"Former film role," she corrected him.

He nodded. "Yes, I meant former," he apologized, then went quickly on. "These criminal acts were all committed by a man who, I believe, is well known to you."

"To *me*? I've never even been to Paris!"

"Nevertheless, it has come to you," Donnay assured her. "His actual name is Arik Cassell. But after his escape from France, he came here to Hollywood where he has made a more famous name for himself—*Sebastian Vane*."

She looked stunned.

The time for holding on to secrets was over, he told himself. And so, he revealed everything to her, beginning with what happened in that icy lake beneath the Paris opera house so many years ago.

The Phantom's Lair Set
Universal Studios

Arik Cassell strolled onto the set punctually at eight a.m. He was fully dressed in Chaney's Phantom costume—long, flowing dark cape, black cloth cap to cover his naked cranium, flesh-colored mask to conceal his disfigurement until the moment of the unmasking.

It amused him that the high cheek bones of the mask gave him a strangely oriental look. The peepholes in the eyes made it a bit difficult to see where he was walking and the mask fit a tad more snugly than it apparently had Chaney. Otherwise, the overall costume fit him quite well as he and Chaney were of roughly the same height and build.

What Cassell hadn't had time to master was a convincing impression of Chaney's voice so he decided he would compensate by speaking in a raspy whisper that he would attribute to a cold he'd caught over the weekend should anyone ask.

As he walked by several of the crew, they greeted him warmly and respectfully with a "Good morning, Mr. Chaney." Cassell offered a slight nod but otherwise ignored them.

Approaching the ornate organ where he would be seated for the unmasking scene, he observed the director and cameraman lining up the first shot as several crew arranged the lights above.

"Morning, Lon," Rupert Julian greeted him. "Ready for the grand unveiling?"

"Why have you put the camera here?" Cassell asked critically, pointing at the machine.

Judging from where the director and cameraman were setting up the camera, Cassell saw that the unmasking would occur with the camera taking Christine's point of view of the Phantom's back.

"As Christine approaches from behind and rips off your mask, you bolt to your feet with your back to the camera, and slowly turn to face her, gradually exposing both her and the audience to the shocking sight of your disfigured face for the first time," Julian explained. "We talked about it last week. Remember?"

"And I offered no objection?"

Julian shook his head. "As I recall, you didn't say anything."

"That's because I must have sensed then, as I'm sure of it now, that this approach is all wrong," he rasped imperiously.

Chaney was not above openly disagreeing in front of the crew with some of the director's choices and insisting that his own ideas be used, but Julian had never seen him this *vehement*.

"Well, we can work on it," Julian said agreeably although he was miffed by this latest challenge to his authority by his intractable star.

Cassell walked to the other side of the organ. "Place the camera here, *facing me*," he demanded. "So that when the mask is pulled away, the audience experiences my disfigurement first."

"But, Lon, the girl *is* the audience," Julian persisted. "It is through her reactions that they understand the meaning of what they see and how to feel about it."

Cassell remained steadfast. "On the contrary, this scene is about putting the fear of God—or the devil—into the audience, then into Christine for her betrayal.

"It is about shocking each of them to the core with this grisly example of man's inhumanity to man." His voice rose passionately. "And how each is complicit in that inhumanity whenever they turn away on the street at the sight of someone maimed, disfigured or crippled.

"But the audience *can't* turn away from the Phantom because what they're seeing is in close-up, thirty feet high!" he added. "And Christine is paralyzed with guilt and fear by what she has done!"

Sandwiched between them like a forlorn referee, the cameraman silently watched Chaney and Julian stare each other down. He had never seen Chaney confront the director so defiantly. Yes, the actor and director had often disagreed before, mainly about Chaney's approach to his character, and the actor would insist on going his own way. But Chaney had never challenged Julian about where to put the camera to film a scene, which was the director's prerogative.

Rupert Julian was no pushover though when it came to his position of authority and stood his ground. The cameraman wondered if they would soon come to blows. But after a few moments of growing tension, the director relented.

He pointed to the spot where Chaney had insisted the camera be set up and instructed the cameraman, "Ok, we'll try it from here and see how it plays."

Almost immediately, the satisfied actor threw back his cape in a flourish and sat at the organ. The camera was moved to his front. And the crew went about re-lighting the scene at the cameraman's command.

The director turned to one of his assistants and barked, "Where's Miss Philbin?"

"In makeup," the assistant responded.

"Tell her we're ready," Julian said, pulling anxiously on his aquamarine scarf. "By the time she gets here, we probably will be."

The assistant nodded, spun on his heel and took off running.

Checking possible angles to show the director, the cameraman observed silently: "Ah, the start of another stress-free day of production on *The Phantom of the Opera*. I wonder what's in store next."

TWENTY-SEVEN

Pagano Chicken Ranch,
Canoga Park, California

Leslie Paige closed the Phantom papers on the table before her as Donnay finished walking her through with his absorbing narration.

"And you're positive this person Cassell is the man responsible for all these terrible crimes," she said rhetorically.

Donnay nodded. "If we'd gotten him into custody, he'd be on Devil's Island right now."

"How you must hate him, for all that he put you through."

"I don't hate him, even for that," he said. "I just want to see him brought to justice."

"And you're certain, he and Sebastian Vane are the same man?"

He nodded again. "Yes. But that isn't proof. Which is why I've come to you."

She shook her head in disbelief. "I just find it difficult to accept that they could be the same man. I mean, on the pirate picture where I met him, I only ever saw him made up as his character. But how could he conceal his facial injuries so completely, even with makeup? And yet I never caught even a glimpse of his disfigurement showing through."

Donnay said nothing. He had no answer to this.

"Besides that, Mr. Vane has always been so supportive of me," she went on. "I'm positive he was the one who put up my bail money."

Donnay offered no reaction for he wasn't at all surprised. Such "generosity" was wholly consistent with the behavior of the Phantom, especially where talented and attractive female ingénues were concerned.

But then a strange look crossed her face, as if she were suddenly remembering something that troubled her.

"What is it?" he probed gently.

"Something Victor Reilly told me on that awful day," she muttered, looking away uncomfortably.

"What did he say?" Donnay pressed.

"That Mr. Vane offered to buy my contract from him," she replied after some contemplation. "That Vane wanted me all to himself and wasn't the man I thought him to be." She paused again. "But I wanted to get out of there and thought Mr. Reilly was just being vindictive."

"But now you're not so sure."

"How *can* we know for certain? Perhaps from the cocaine he was using, Mr. Reilly was clearly unbalanced enough to have taken his own life."

"You feel a bit sorry for him, don't you?" Donnay said sympathetically.

"I feel badly over his suicide," she admitted. "For all his duplicity in keeping most of my weekly salary for himself, I wouldn't have had a salary worth stealing but for him."

"Or lost it all either," Donnay added.

"Yes, and lost, too," she conceded. "Although that wasn't so much his doing as that of Adela Grant, the witch."

"There are some who don't believe Reilly did kill himself," Donnay offered. "Me, for one. And the coroner, for another."

She looked at him in astonishment. "What? You think he was…"

"Murdered," Donnay interjected, nodding.

"And you think who did it is Mr. Vane?" Leslie responded skeptically.

Donnay sat back in his chair, arms folded, and kept silent, allowing her time to ponder these questions for herself.

"But why? Over my contract?" she asked dubiously.

"That's one possibility," Donnay suggested.

"But it wasn't worth anything. No one will give me a job!"

"Not right now, perhaps," he said. "But generally scandals do blow over. Especially if there's no truth to them."

She contemplated this for a second. "And so Reilly wouldn't sell."

Donnay nodded.

"Another possibility is this," he said. "I have it on good authority that Reilly was heavily in debt to his drug supplier. We know that Arik Cassell is a veteran drug smuggler connected with the Corsicans. If Vane *is* Cassell, it's feasible he feared being exposed should the authorities get Reilly to talk. The man had to be silenced. The coroner told me the evidence suggested homicide, but he held back from making that final judgment because he couldn't be 100 percent positive," the Frenchman concluded.

The two of them fell silent, the only sound to fill the room that of the non-stop squawking of the chickens outside.

Donnay noticed that Leslie's dark-as-a-nut complexion had lost some of its tan as she'd listened. It was no wonder she'd grown paler, he considered; everything in her young life had been turned upside down—beginning with her career, which was snatched away from her almost as quickly as it had begun. And now she was going to be asked by him to come to terms with the idea that of the two men who'd done so much to help launch that career, one was dead, possibly murdered, and the other may have done it as part of a ruse to turn her into another Christine. He knew that it was almost too much for her to absorb, but he pressed on anyway.

"But if we can prove beyond any shadow of doubt that Vane is the drug smuggler and murderer Arik Cassell, we can perhaps achieve some measure of justice, even for Reilly," he said.

"Prove it how?" she asked. "Get him to confess? From what you've told me about him, he'd *never* do that."

Donnay agreed with her.

"Then how?" she asked again.

Donnay again turned the pages of the Phantom papers on the table, flipped through them, and pulled out an envelope. "With this," he said, withdrawing a 5" x 7" photograph from the envelope.

All she could make out in the picture he showed her was a series of black smudges. "What is it?" she inquired.

"A photographic copy of Arik Cassell's fingerprint card," Donnay explained. We were able to lift his prints from the keys on the organ in his chambers within the opera house. Christine told us he was the only one she saw play it, so we're confident they're his—all eight fingers plus the thumbs of his right and left hands. They were lifted with surgical adhesive and then transferred to a white card for comparison once we had him in custody—which, of course, we never did.

"Fingerprints are the surest way of establishing a culprit's identity. A clerk in the office of the prefecture of police in Paris refined the technique, which dates back to Babylonian times. Police departments all over the world now use it in criminal cases to catch their man—or woman." He paused for a moment as she studied the photograph, then went on:

"What we need to determine if Vane is indeed Cassell is a sample of his fingerprints—off a drinking glass, for example. Then I can compare them with this photograph, and we've got him!"

"Or not," she put in, playing the devil's advocate.

"Right. Or not," he admitted. "But I'll eat my hat as the saying goes if the prints don't match!"

"You don't wear a hat," she remarked. "Besides, you'd look pretty silly," she added with a smile.

"I'd *feel* pretty silly," he confessed. "Which is why I'm so sure my hat, if I ever do wear one, is safe."

They were quiet for a moment as she looked him searchingly in the eye. "And what you want from me is to get this sample of his prints for you." She spoke with deep seriousness.

He nodded. "Believe me, if I could leave you out of it, I would," he said. "But you're the only one I know who can get close enough to him to pull it off without arousing his suspicion or that of his bodyguard. Cassell would remember me."

"What if he catches me in the act and demands an explanation?" she asked, again playing the devil's advocate. "What then?"

"It's a dangerous gambit, I won't tell you it's not," he owned up. "But I'm sure you'll be so convincing that he'll never notice," he assured her. "You've got every reason to seek him out for advice on your career and the limbo your contract is in."

She nodded her head, albeit with uncertainty. After all, she had turned to Vane once before with regard to the Victor Reilly situation, though now, should the Frenchman's suspicions prove correct, she wished she hadn't. But if she does go through with this and the experiment fails to prove Vane is Cassell, she will have achieved nothing but the betrayal of a friend's trust.

On the other hand, if she refuses to help and Vane's identity as Cassell is later confirmed some other way, she will have let the criminal get away again—a criminal whose repugnant deeds numbered an attempt on Donnay's life, subjecting the Frenchman to years of unsure and painful convalescence. He deserved to be caught and punished—if he is that criminal.

She was torn, as well as scared, not knowing what to do.

Sensing her struggle to make up her mind whether to help him, especially on the heels of so much other upset in her life, Donnay was about to jump in to try and tip the scales when he heard the sound of an automobile pulling up to the house. He looked out to see his taxi.

Damn, he thought, *has an hour gone by already? I need more time with her; she's right on the edge!*

He turned to the young actress. "It's my ride," he explained. "I have to speak with him. Excuse me for a moment, will you, Miss Paige?"

"Given what you're asking me to do, don't you think you can call me Leslie?" she suggested, smiling lightly at him.

"Yes, of course," he said, smiling back at her. "Leslie—it's a pretty name. Be right back." And with that, he hurried out the door.

"Are you going to help him?" Mrs. Pagano asked her niece as she stepped from the shadows into the kitchen.

"Aunt Elena, have you been listening in?" Leslie returned, startled and somewhat annoyed.

"Someone has to look after you," her aunt insisted. "He seems quite smart. And sincere." She winked. "Handsome, too."

Leslie lost her annoyance. "Are you *ever* going to stop playing matchmaker?"

"Not until I succeed," the older woman replied with another wink. "It's an ill wind that blows *nobody* any good. With what you've been through, you deserve a nice fella. When he comes back, ask him—"

"I told the driver to give me ten more minutes," Donnay announced, coming through the door. He stopped abruptly when he saw Leslie's aunt standing beside her. Judging from the aunt's stern expression, he figured he'd be leaving a lot sooner.

But then, quite suddenly, the older woman unexpectedly looked upon him with favor.

"Young man, when was the last time you had a home-cooked meal?" she asked.

"Me? I...I don't remember. I think it was the last time I was home from university," he stammered. He never went there now as his folks had died in the Spanish flu epidemic of 1918 while he was in hospital.

"Would you like to join us for an early supper?" she offered.

Donnay was at a loss for words. He had no idea how it had been accomplished, but he appeared to have won the older woman over. Now all he needed was to convince her niece to come over to his side, as well.

"Yes, that would be very nice, if it's not too much trouble," he replied. He turned to Leslie. "And if it's OK with you."

Leslie took his arm with a teasing expression. "Come, I'll walk you to dismiss the taxi. We'll get you back to your hotel before dark," she said. "In the meantime, I'll show you around the farm," she added. "And you can tell me what I have to do to get you those fingerprints."

Donnay felt jubilant as they went out the door.

The Phantom's Lair Set
Universal Studios

"Places, everyone," Rupert Julian shouted from his chair beside the camera.

Arik Cassell's masked phantom was already seated at the organ so he didn't move except to flex his fingers.

Actress Mary Philbin emerged from the throng of crew and other technicians, one of whom was giving her makeup as Christine a last-second retouch. Then Philbin took her position behind the Phantom's back. The scene had been rehearsed several times already so everyone knew what their respective responsibility was.

From his chair, Julian glanced up at his cameraman and in a clear, stentorian voice said, "Roll camera." Immediately cameraman Van Enger began cranking away on his magic box. Julian then shouted, "Action."

Unlike Lon Chaney who had just mimed playing the organ, Cassell launched into a piece from Mozart's "Là ci darem la mano" ["There you will give me your hand"] from the opera *Don Giovanni* and the stage filled with gorgeous music from the Romantic Age. Cassell dived more and more into the notes as his fingers glided masterfully across the keys and his body swayed to the rhythm.

Philbin's Christine approached cautiously from behind, her arm outstretched as she reached tentatively for the corner of his mask. Suddenly his body shifted as his fingers pounded the keys. She snatched back her hand and withdrew slightly to await another chance.

The Phantom's playing settled into a more rapturous pace. The girl drew closer again, reaching out once more with her trembling hand. Her fingers rose tenuously toward the mask as she anticipated another sudden movement by the Phantom that never came.

Then she had hold of the mask and in one swift movement she tore it from his face, accompanied by a convulsive roar from the Phantom as his fingers pounded the keys, triggering an explosion of sound from the organ that ricocheted off the walls of the stage with a din that startled everyone—except for the cameraman whose professionalism wouldn't allow him to miss a steady turn of the crank.

There was a uniform gasp from much of the crew and the continuity girl let out a shriek as the Phantom's horrifically deformed skull-like face was revealed. Rupert Julian himself experienced shivers at the gruesome sight.

Lon Chaney had outdone himself with this ghoulish transformation, he thought. Perhaps, too much so. He envisioned the screaming and fainting reaction to the unmasking scene among a theatre audience and wondered if Chaney had come on *too* strong.

As the actress drew back from the Phantom with the mask in her hand, he rose from his seat and turned slowly towards her until she had a full-on view of the cadaverous visage she'd exposed, its tongue sliding like a serpent's across crooked teeth in a wide-open mouth with only a blackened crust where the lips had once been.

The actress screamed so loudly that the sound echoed off the walls of the stage. Eyes saucer-wide, she folded in on herself as he moved toward her with his arm outstretched, pointing at her in an accusing manner.

Then, quite suddenly, he snatched a clump of her curly hair in his iron grip and pulled her close until their faces were just inches apart.

"You wanted to see, to expose my secret, now *look!*" he bellowed, tightening his fingers until the actress' already-bulging eyes bulged even more and she appeared to wince.

"I said *'Look!'*" He commanded again, and she did, her eyes seeming to tear up as she gazed upon the revolting sight of the dark nub of cranial bone that was all that was left of his nose.

Transfixed by what he was seeing, Rupert Julian was on his feet and leaning in to his cameraman, who continued cranking away with an amazingly steady hand in spite of the shocking display.

"I hope you're getting all this," Julian whispered to him. "It's pure gold."

Before them Cassell's Phantom pulled back the actress' head and forced her to look into his eyes.

"See what your betrayal has unmasked," he exhorted her.

Her mouth opened as if to scream, but no sound came out as the actress' eyes rolled back in her head, and she seemed to faint dead away. The Phantom let her crumpled body slip to the floor.

"And *cut!*" Julian shouted, applauding the two actors. "Mary, Lon, your performances were sublime. They transcended acting."

Cassell spun around and fixed him in a furious stare as the make-up and costume crew moved in to attend to Mary Philbin.

With a flourish of his cape and a silent, over-the-shoulder dismissal of all around him, Cassell told the director in an imperious manner to call him when ready to shoot the other angles and then he departed the stage for Lon Chaney's dressing room.

He's getting a bit of a head, isn't he? The director said to himself as he watched the actor go. Then he turned his attention to Mary Philbin.

"You were absolutely brilliant, Mary," he enthused. "I was scared *for* you."

One of the costumers looked up at him from the floor where she was cradling Philbin's head. "I don't think she was acting, Mr. Julian," she said.

"She's out cold."

TWENTY-EIGHT

Executive Projection Room
Universal Studios

"*Mein Gott,*" Carl Laemmle exclaimed as the lights came on and the operator in the booth behind him finished showing the day's rushes.

His face was taut and serious from the chills he'd experienced watching the unmasking footage. His cigar smoke hung in the air like a yellow mist.

"How did Lon Chaney effer come up mit zuch a face?" He grimaced with distaste.

"Then you think the scene is too intense?" Rupert Julian asked from his seat to one side of the studio boss.

"I think it's inspired," Junior Laemmle beamed from his seat on the other side. "You were right about doing this picture, papa. It's going to make Universal a fortune!"

"Not if it gets around dat it ist too scary to see," the elder Laemmle put in. "So scary dat de lead actress fainted." Turning to Julian, he asked, "How ist Mizz Philbin anyvay?"

"Mostly she's just embarrassed," Julian responded. "She told me later that Chaney was just doing his job and got so deeply into his character, that's all. She apologized for ruining the take."

"Apologized?" Junior Laemmle exclaimed, dumbfounded. "She fainted right on cue—and for real. You can't buy that kind of publicity."

"NO! Dat kind uf publicity dis picture doesn't need," the elder Laemmle thundered. "Ve don't vant vord uf her fainting to get out."

"Then you've decided to do a toned-down re-shoot of the scene?" Julian inquired.

"I don't vant to, but ve may haff to," the older man replied. "But for now let's tink about adding zome comic relief to de picture. It's too macabre—too *morbid*—as it ist now."

Rupert Julian was nodding his head in agreement, but Junior Laemmle looked appalled.

"Some people said the same thing about Chaney's hunchback of Notre Dame," the younger Laemmle countered forcefully. "And look at the business that picture did!"

His father shook his head impatiently. "*Hunchback* vas a tragic story," he explained to his son. "Dis picture ist ein melodrama. People von't accept being hit so hard on de head."

Junior Laemmle fell silent. His father had a point.

"How much more do you haff left to shoot?" Carl Laemmle asked his director.

"Just the subterranean lake scenes and it's a wrap," Julian replied. "But we'll be stalled a couple of weeks as this weather blows through and be on hiatus due to the wind and rain. It's an outdoor set."

"Dat's OK," the studio boss said. "You can use de time cutting de picture und making it ready for a preview as zoon as de final scenes are included," he suggested. "Den ve vill see how it plays mit ein audience und if it needs some comic relief."

Rupert Julian once again nodded his head.

The elder Laemmle turned to his son. "Meanvile, find a good gag man to cook up some funny scenes to add to parts uf de picture," he instructed.

Junior jumped right in. "I know just the man," he said enthusiastically. "Eddie Sedgwick." He knew his father would agree as Sedgwick was the man behind some of the studio's most vibrant and popular comedies.

"Perfekt," his father averred as Rupert Julian nodded his agreement with the boss a third time.

"OK, if dere's nutting else, let's all get back to vork," Laemmle said.

Then, as they each got up and moved toward the door of the projection room, he added with a smile: "Lon Chaney can take his monsters to MGM from now on. Let dem deal mit de headaches."

Rupert Julian chuckled, but Junior looked chagrined by his father's remark, for he had several other unique monsters in mind for future Universal pictures, with or without Lon Chaney's participation. But that battle with his lovable but stubborn old man would have to be for another day.

Valley Division Headquarters
Van Nuys, California

Sergeant Thomas Tom glanced out the window closest to his desk. The sky was darkening. A strong wind was picking up that was getting much stronger. Rain was on the way.

So much for a weekend of outdoor activities, he thought irritably. What else was new? It was winter in normally sunny southern California; cold and rain had to be expected.

The phone rang and he snatched it up.

"Van Nuys, Sergeant Tom speaking," he said into it.

"Please hold for Mr. Carl Laemmle Junior," a woman's voice intoned.

Tom heard a click and a man's voice came on. "Hello, Sergeant?" the voice said.

"What can I do for you, Mr. Laemmle? How's your dad?" Tom returned.

"He's fine, Sergeant; in fact he's the one asked me to call you on this matter," Junior said.

"What matter is that?"

"My father got a phone call this afternoon from Mrs. Hazel Chaney—the wife of the actor Lon Chaney?" Junior explained hurriedly.

"I've heard of him," Tom said patiently.

Junior laughed. "I'm sure you have," he continued rapid-fire. "Anyway, she's worried about her husband. Seems she hasn't heard from him in several days and says that's not like him."

"Isn't he busy making a picture for you?" Tom asked.

"Right. *The Phantom of the Opera.* But we finished temporarily on Monday and aren't going to resume shooting until this weather lifts," Junior said. "There was no reason for him to stay around so we naturally thought he'd gone home. But his wife says no and she's very concerned."

"Where do they live?" Tom asked.

"Beverly Hills," Junior told him, adding, "I know it's probably not in your jurisdiction, but Father said to start with you because you've been a great help to us in the past."

"I'll get right on it, Mr. Laemmle, and see what I can find out," Sergeant Tom replied. "Can you give me the address and phone number?" The policeman wrote down the information in a small pad as Junior reeled it off. "I'll get back to you as soon as I know anything," he added.

"Thank you, Sergeant, I appreciate it, and so does my father. Goodbye," Junior said and hung up.

"Goodbye to you too," Tom mused into the dead phone and then hung up as well.

He pondered the situation. Don't most actors go incommunicado for a few days after a long stretch of work? He asked himself. Out here, picture actors tend to disappear briefly like that, much to the consternation of their wives or girlfriends. Most of them have just gone off on a bat somewhere. He wondered if Chaney was a drinker. He'd never heard any rumors in that direction.

Sergeant Tom decided he'd better look into the whereabouts of Mr. Chaney—if only to stay on the good side of Universal Studios and the two Mr. Laemmles.

The headquarters building was thinning out for the weekend so he opted to head home as well. But first he'd make a detour to Beverly Hills and find out what he could from the worried Mrs. Chaney. Then he'd turn the matter over to West L.A., which had proper jurisdiction.

He signed out his respective destinations at the front desk and left the building, pulling on his rain slicker.

The sidewalk was already dotted with fat raindrops. He hurried to his police car and climbed in, starting the car up and turning on the windshield wipers in one smooth, practiced motion.

The car pulled out and Sergeant Thomas Tom headed off in the direction of southern California's fastest-growing domain of the rich in the hills of Beverly.

TWENTY-NINE

Pierre Donnay's Accommodations
Hollywood Roosevelt Hotel

Pierre Donnay paced the floor of his hotel nervously. He would be like this until later that night when Leslie returned with a sample of Sebastian Vane's fingerprints.

That is, if all went according to plan.

Leslie had driven in from the San Fernando Valley earlier that afternoon. As her uncle was not scheduled to make any egg deliveries that day, she was able to borrow his truck, which she'd parked on the street outside his lavish hotel, making for a unique contrast.

The French prosecutor and the young actress had spent the entire afternoon together getting to know each other better as well as going over details of Donnay's plan for capturing Vane's fingerprints on the sly.

The first part of the plan had gone smoothly. She had placed a call from the hotel room to Vane's home several hours earlier, requesting to see him to offer her gratitude in person for all that he had done for her.

Vane had been both surprised and delighted to hear from her, adding that thanks were not necessary. She insisted, however, and he relented easily. "It would be my pleasure," he said. "How about tonight? Before the weather gets too bad and flash flooding makes it too dangerous to go out." They settled on seven p.m.

Vane couldn't have been any nicer, Leslie thought as she hung up the phone, and she told Donnay so. Hearing from her out of the blue hadn't seemed to put Vane at all on his guard, she said. In fact, if anyone was vexed about how agreeably he'd taken to her idea of meeting, it was Leslie herself, she admitted.

Vane was so welcoming and considerate over the phone that once again she had a difficult time imagining him as the monster Donnay believed him to be.

"It's so underhanded. I feel like such a rat," she said to Donnay. "If you weren't so positive that Vane is this Arik Cassell character, the phantom of the opera, I wouldn't go through with this. I *couldn't*, not in good conscience!"

Donnay had reassured her that he was not wrong and that the fingerprints would prove it. There was no doubt in his mind, he insisted again, that Sebastian Vane was the elusive murderer, kidnapper, and thief he had been hunting for so long. For the moment, this seemed to persuade her.

Leslie was a talented actress, Donnay mused. She hadn't betrayed an ounce of tension or misgiving on the phone with Sebastian Vane. He admired her skill at delivering what was required of her in the face of her own feelings of hesitation, even guilt. She was an honest person.

He suggested they go for a late lunch (or early dinner) in the hotel's extravagant restaurant. "Great! I'm starved," she said and okayed the idea.

244

All through the meal, he'd been on tenterhooks worrying that something would go wrong with the plan later that night, and he ate little. But Leslie consumed every bite of her food as if nerves were something completely foreign to her digestion.

"Unlike most people, anxiety doesn't kill my appetite, I get hungrier," she admitted to Donnay. "I don't know whether that's good or bad."

"I suppose neither," he'd returned, pushing his plate away. "It's just *you*."

She grinned at him. "That's what I mean. In my line of work, anxiety is constant. I could wind up getting very fat, very fast."

Donnay laughed. He enjoyed her self-deprecating sense of humor. In fact, he enjoyed everything about her and liked being with her. He got the impression that, mission aside, she liked being with him, as well. He wondered if, perhaps, he was falling a little in love with her. If so, he hoped the feeling was mutual.

But he hadn't the nerve to ask. He was too wound up worrying about her safety tonight if Vane or his manservant caught on to what she was doing. Broaching a question like that now would only add to her mind's disquiet.

Donnay paused from pacing back and forth to look out the window of his suite. The drapes were open, revealing the dying light and the gloomy weather conditions outside.

The rain had stepped up over the past hour to where he could now hear its steady drumbeat against the glass. This deteriorating weather only added to his concerns over Leslie's safety in the face of the dangers she would be up against.

Fortunately, she wouldn't be facing those dangers entirely on her own. Her Uncle Arno had insisted on driving her in his truck both to the Vane house and then later to Donnay's hotel. Although, the urbanite Donnay could not drive, accompanying Leslie on the clandestine mission was a job he'd wanted for

245

himself but could not risk taking for fear of scuttling the plan. He would have to remain in the truck, tucked somehow out of sight, while she was inside.

But Cassell and his manservant Darrass were also drug smugglers, after all, and therefore always on the alert. If Darrass broke away from his master's side long enough to check the truck and found the Frenchman inside, it was unlikely that Donnay would be able to overcome the other's strength and subdue him. So, Donnay would be captured and taken to Cassell who would very likely recognize the prosecutor as his nemesis from that long ago confrontation in the Grand Garnier's subterranean lake. Leslie's uncle wouldn't be able to overpower Darrass either should the two go up against each other. But Donnay doubted that would happen for if Darrass discovered the older man in the truck, Leslie had already concocted a logical explanation for his presence there that she was sure would be believed.

Although Donnay didn't know Leslie's uncle well, he felt sure the man was a sound alternative to look after her tonight. He'd met her uncle only several days ago when Donnay had been invited to stay for supper.

Looking a bit tired and bedraggled from dealing with chickens, Mr. Pagano had shambled into the kitchen that afternoon. After washing up, he and Donnay had been introduced, and he'd shaken the Frenchman's hand with a firm but not show-off vice-like grip. He was a tall, slim man in his early fifties with streaks of silver in his already thinning hair. He sported a trim salt and pepper goatee and had an infectious laugh.

Over a delicious Italian meal that Donnay couldn't name but had chicken in it, Donnay asked as the operators of a chicken ranch how often they ate chicken.

"Sometimes, but never our own. We're an egg farm not a hatchery. We raise chickens to lay eggs," Uncle Arno had answered proudly. Then with a twinkle in his eye, he took a dig at the chicken ranch run by Universal. "We don't raise 'em to be slaughtered for box lunches on studio tours." They each smiled.

Donnay glanced at the time on the wall clock. It was a bit past six. Leslie would be leaving for the rendezvous in less than an hour. All he could do now was wait—at which he was admittedly quite terrible due to his prosecutor-cum-investigator instincts.

He wanted a drink to relax himself but knew his head had to be clear for the fingerprint analysis later on. Nevertheless, he gave in and went to call room service for a bottle of red wine. He desired a Bordeaux but considered "When in Rome..." and chose to give the California vintners a try and opted for a bottle of the region's cabernet instead.

He resolved to have just one glass and save the rest of the wine for when Leslie and her uncle returned and they would hopefully have cause for celebration. If she failed to get a sample of Vane's fingerprints, then they could get drunk under the old adage that misery loves company.

And so does disappointment.

With that, he reached for the phone.

Lon Chaney Residence
Beverly Hills, California

Sergeant Thomas Tom bid goodbye to Hazel Chaney and closed the door to the two-story Italian Revival home. He had assured the woman that he and/or the West L.A. police would be in touch with her very soon.

He realized now that he was as much concerned about her husband's sudden disappearance as she was. From what she had told him about her husband's habits, it definitely wasn't in the actor's nature to go dark like this, even for a day. But where had he gone? And why?

Could his disappearance have been an adult kidnapping? Such crimes weren't uncommon these days. But if so, why had there yet been no ransom demand? The actor had now been missing for four days!

It was raining steadily but not yet teeming as was predicted for later on, Tom mused, walking down the stone steps to his car. The raindrops were thick though and splashed noisily on the pavement—an omen of worsening weather to come.

As he approached his car, Sergeant Tom glanced across the street where another car was parked illegally directly opposite him. A woman got out of the car almost as soon as he'd looked her way. She wore a dark raincoat and wide-brimmed hat. Opening an umbrella, she leaned against the car as if waiting for him.

He crossed the street to her. "Following me?" he asked.

Adela Grant shook her head. "Just dumb luck," she answered. "I came to see Mrs. Chaney about her missing husband and I find the law is already on the case. That *is* why you're here?" she finished rhetorically.

"How did you hear he was missing?" he asked disconcertedly.

"Ah, then you confirm it," she said with satisfaction. "One of my many little birds at the studio told me," she continued. "Everything's a bit chaotic over there as you can imagine. Lots of scuttlebutt going around."

"Such as…?" he asked pointedly.

Grant shook her head, teasing him: "Uh-uh, tit for tat. Like always, remember? You first. What did Mrs. Chaney say?"

He shrugged. "Not much," he answered vaguely. "She has no idea what might have happened to her husband and wants us to comb every ditch between here and Universal."

Adela Grant looked surprised. "That's *all* she told you?"

"I said it wasn't much," he replied, adding: "Chaney called her last Friday to say he would be staying at the studio over the weekend to work on his make-up for Monday's filming. That wasn't unusual, his wife said; he's a perfectionist and always worried how effective his creations would be on the screen. But that was the last she's heard from him, which *is* unusual, especially as they'd planned a camping trip to Inyo National Forest as soon as there was a long break in filming."

"How did he sound to her?" Grant asked.

"Tired, she thought. His voice was a little raspy—as if he was getting a cold," Sergeant Tom revealed.

Grant was about to hit the policeman with another question when he put up his hand to stop her. "Your turn," he said. "What's the scuttlebutt about?"

"I'm not sure what to make of it," she replied.

"Make of *what*?" he probed.

She shrugged. "My sources tell me Chaney came on pretty strong during Monday's filming," she said.

"Strong how?"

"Imperious," she replied. "Which was not at all typical Lon Chaney behavior, they said. In fact, they tell me he was so intense and frightening—even violent—that he made his co-star faint."

"Isn't that called acting?" he suggested.

"Up to a point, yes," she returned. "But he was so horrific, even mad, they said, that he also shook up the crew. And when he was done he just walked blithely off the set."

"Sounds like an attack of temperament," the sergeant offered.

"Except that next to Rin Tin Tin, Lon Chaney has a reputation for being one of the least temperamental stars in this business," Grant countered. "When he returned that afternoon to finish filming, my sources described him as being even more imperious and intense. And when work was done, he again just walked off—without saying goodnight to anyone, which was also unlike Chaney."

Sergeant Tom pondered her words. "So, what are you suggesting?"

Grant shrugged once more. "I don't know. Nothing, I guess. Except that by all accounts, Lon Chaney wasn't himself that day."

"And now he's vanished," Tom interjected. "So, it's clear that something odd was going on with him."

Adela Grant's eyes suddenly lit up. "Come on, I have an idea," she said excitedly, opening the door to her car. "I'll drive."

"Not on your life," Sergeant Tom said, pushing the door closed. "We'll take mine. Where to by the way?"

They crossed the street in the rain to his police car.

"The Hollywood Roosevelt hotel," Grant said. "Ever been there?"

"On my salary? You've got to be kidding," he said as they got into his car. "What's there anyway?"

"Someone who just might have a thought or two about the missing Mr. Chaney," she replied.

"Who?"

"You already know who. You sent him to me, remember?" she told the puzzled official.

"Monsieur Pierre Donnay of the Paris police."

THIRTY

Sebastian Vane Residence
Hollywood Hills, California

Leslie's uncle pulled into the circular drive fronting Sebastian Vane's elegant Spanish mission–style house. He killed the delivery truck's engine and turned to his niece beside him.

"Are you sure you want to do this?" he asked, pulling on his goatee with tense concern.

She nodded as she reached for the door handle. "I'll be all right," Leslie said even though her stomach was all-aflutter with nerves.

She forced a smile. "I won't be long," she assured him, wishing someone could reassure her as well.

"If anything goes wrong, just let out a blood-curdling scream and I'll be right there," he said.

She kissed him on the cheek. "Thanks, Uncle Arno."

Leslie got out into the now pouring rain. The Valley's dirt roads had gotten thick with mud. Even the paved roads were getting slick from flooding and mudslides. It was a wild night already and from her perspective was now about to get a whole lot wilder, she thought with trepidation as she hurried to the front door and pushed the chime button.

Moments later, the door opened and a giant in a long, flowing dark robe filled the doorway. His heavy, brown boots with thick soles and his turban-style headgear added even more height to his considerable frame.

"I'm Leslie Paige," she said, suppressing the tremor in her voice. "I have an appointment with Mr. Vane."

The giant said nothing and remained stoic behind his thick, black beard and piercing eyes. His only response was to widen the door a bit more, allowing her to slip inside.

"I'm in here, Leslie," came a muffled shout from elsewhere within the house.

The giant closed the door and held out his hands to help her off with her raincoat, which she shucked quickly trying not get the floor wet. He hung the coat in the foyer and gestured for her to follow him.

Vane was waiting for them in the sunken living room. He rose from his easy chair beside the fireplace where the flames from the logs in the grate cast a warming glow.

Vane extended his hand and Leslie took it. He didn't look at all like he had on the pirate picture they had made together, she observed. He wasn't in make-up for one thing. And he was comfortably but elegantly dressed in a wheat-colored cardigan over a light blue shirt and dark pants, not a pirate's costume.

Donnay had instructed her to look at him closely for any sign of his wearing a mask. But she could spot none. What she could see were some of the pores in his skin. If it was a mask, she thought as they shook hands, it was the most convincing one ever made.

"It's very nice of you to see me, Mr. Vane," she said humbly.

253

"Nonsense. The pleasure is all mine," he replied, turning to the giant. "This is Bahram by the way, my manservant."

Leslie had heard of the manservant from people around the studio, but she had not seen him herself until now. She wondered why he hadn't accompanied Vane during filming to take care of the actor's needs. The two seemed paired at the hip otherwise. Perhaps Vane just felt the crew was adequate to take care of those needs and had decided to give his manservant some time off.

Leslie smiled at the giant and held out her hand. "Nice to meet you, Bahram. I'm Leslie," she said, then added, somewhat sheepishly, "But I guess I already told you that at the door."

Bahram shook her hand but otherwise didn't move.

"He doesn't speak," Vane explained.

Leslie nodded uncomfortably. If these two were the criminals Donnay believed them to be, she already knew that Bahram had no tongue, and that his actual name was Darrass. It would be up to her to test Donnay's theory and to confirm or deny it with a sample of Vane's fingerprints. But how to get them without arousing Vane's suspicious nature. She couldn't just *ask* for them.

"You are not curious as to why Bahram can't speak?" Vane broke into her thoughts.

She now wondered with growing unease if he was already ahead of her and knew why she hadn't asked. But he couldn't know. There was no way. Despite the warmth of the fire, she felt a chill.

"I…I thought it would be impolite to ask," she replied. "And I didn't want to offend him."

"You wouldn't have," Vane returned. "Bahram's used to people being curious about his silent ways. Aren't you, Bahram?"

254

The giant remained impassive.

"Is it because of a birth defect of some kind?" Leslie asked, feigning ignorance.

"No, it was torture in a Persian prison," Vane said with nonchalance. "Please, have a seat."

Leslie sunk into a plush chair opposite Vane as he returned to his own comfortable seat. The chill that had suddenly gripped her slowly began to dissipate from the heat thrown off by the fire.

Bahram moved behind Vane's chair and stood there regally. His silence unnerved her. Out of the corner of her eye she caught him occasionally glancing her way as if watching her closely. Or was it all in her mind? She asked herself.

"You found us with little difficulty?" Vane interjected through tightly pursed lips.

"Just the weather," she replied. "It's getting worse out there. But your directions were perfect. My uncle drove me."

"Where is he now?"

"Waiting for me. Out in his truck."

Vane looked surprised. "We can't have that," he said adamantly. "Let's invite the poor fellow in. Bahram, please go and—"

Leslie held up her hand. "That's okay," she interrupted. "I told him I wouldn't be long due to the weather and he insisted on waiting in the truck. You see, he's been working the farm all day and says he smells like chickens. I think he's too embarrassed to come in."

Vane accepted this impassively. "Very well. But please tell him I extended the invitation."

Leslie assured him she would. Again she was plagued with doubt about what she was doing there. How could such a considerate man be concealing such a criminal monster inside?

"So, how have you been doing, my dear, since...?" Vane paused, searching for the right words so as not to embarrass her. "...all the *un-pleasantness*?"

"The studios don't want me, but I'm learning the egg trade pretty well," she said with pretend amusement.

"I am *so* sorry," Vane said with considerable feeling.

Again, Leslie felt conflicted about this man and her mission to expose him—if indeed he was guilty. But Donnay was so *sure*. She couldn't let him down by getting cold feet now.

"No need to be," she said quickly. "I'm healthy. I'm not in jail. And I want to thank you for what you did to help get me my freedom."

"But I did nothing," he scoffed.

"I know it was you who put up my bail," she answered back. "There was no one among my friends or family who could come up with that kind of money. And there was no one else who would. Except you.

"You'd helped me out once before with Victor Reilly, so I know it was you. I just wanted to come here and express my gratitude to you in person.

"Don't worry. I'll keep silent," she added with a smile. "Anyway, that's all I really came here to say."

Vane didn't respond, his face expressionless.

She then decided to go off script for a moment with a direct question of her own to see how Vane would react. Perhaps he might slip and give himself away to her, if just slightly, and that would assuage her guilt over deceiving him.

"Oh, yes, there was one other thing," she put in suddenly. "Victor Reilly told me you offered to buy my contract from him and he accused you of wanting me all to yourself," she said pointedly.

Vane offered no response, just pursed his lips tighter, his face stark.

She studied him for any sign that she had hit on the truth. But there was none. Vane just sat there undemonstratively, his hands folded on his lap.

"Of course, I didn't really believe him," Leslie went on. "What good is buying up a contract on an unemployable actress?"

She wanted this to be over and to get out of there. Maybe if she asked him for a glass of water? She reconsidered—he'd probably just ask Bahram to get it.

She eyed an open bottle of Chardonnay in a bucket of ice next to Vane's chair away from the fire. His empty glass was sitting next to the bucket. How could she get hold of it?

As if reading her thoughts, Vane suddenly offered her a glass of wine.

So as not to appear too eager, Leslie hesitated for a second, then said, "Yes, thank you. That would be nice."

Bahram drifted out to the kitchen and returned momentarily with another glass, giving it to Vane, who took it firmly in his right hand. With his other he poured her a glass of the chardonnay and held it out to her, his fingers curled around the glass. She took it by the stem and watched him refill his own glass.

"What will you do next?" Vane asked, raising the glass in a silent toast.

"Not sure," she said, toasting him in return. "Maybe change my name back again and start over since I've lost my big break."

"I wouldn't worry too much about losing the part in *Phantom*," Vane reassured her. "From what I hear, the picture is turning out to be a fiasco." He sipped his wine.

Still holding her own glass by the stem, she raised it to her lips, nervously thinking "Please don't let me smear the fingerprints!" and drank.

Aloud she said," Yes, rumor among some of the crew I'm still in contact with has it that Universal is thinking of turning the picture into a comedy."

"They're *WHAT?*" Vane thundered back, almost choking on his drink.

Shaken by his outburst, she forced a shrug. "Or at least they're thinking of adding some comedy sequences," she corrected herself. "I don't know how accurate these rumors are, but that's what I've heard."

Her correction did little to un-ruffle him.

"Those idiots!" he fumed through taut lips. "From the beginning, they haven't known what to do with this project."

Leslie continued to watch, fascinated, as Vane fought to control himself. She jumped in to change the atmosphere with another toast. "To better times," she said holding up her glass.

Vane's lips scrunched into a feeble smile and he held up his glass as well. "To better times," he replied, calmer now.

They each drank fully. Then Leslie went to put her glass aside and suddenly gasped as the stem slipped from her fingers and the glass fell to the floor.

Where it shattered against the tile into myriad pieces.

Pierre Donnay's Accommodations
Hollywood Roosevelt Hotel

Pierre Donnay resumed pacing the floor of his hotel room. But this time he had a relaxing glass of California cabernet in his hand.

Though by no means a wine connoisseur, Donnay had a fondness for the wines of his native country, which was not unusual as he had grown up in a household where a Bordeaux was served at every meal except for *le petit dejeuner*. But this California red was very nice indeed. He knew he would have a hard time keeping to just one glass until Leslie got here.

The door chime rang and Donnay's eyes went immediately to the wall clock, which showed slightly past seven thirty — much too soon for Leslie to be back.

Unless her objective was a failure.

The chime rang again. He hurried to the door and threw it open with foreboding only to find Adela Grant and Sergeant Thomas Tom standing there dripping onto the hotel carpet, their folded umbrellas in their hands.

As Donnay stared at them silently, Sergeant Tom spoke up. "May we come in?" he asked politely.

"Of course," Donnay answered. "I'm sorry, my mind was a million miles away." He widened the door. "You can put your wet things in the bathroom. Over there," he said, pointing.

He closed the door and strolled into the center of the room as the two returned from hanging up their soaked raincoats and umbrellas.

Donnay and Adela Grant had arranged for her to drop by much later in the evening so as not to cross paths with Leslie. So, why was she here now? He wondered. And why had she brought along Sergeant Tom?

Adela eyed the glass of wine in his hand. "Celebrating already?" she said with a wink.

"No," Donnay replied, taking a sip from his glass. "Just trying to subdue the anxiety of waiting. Would the two of you like some?"

"That would be most agreeable on a night like this," Adela responded eagerly. She glanced toward Sergeant Tom. "Even if he is on duty," she added with another wink.

"Then this isn't a social call," Donnay said to the policeman. He crossed to the folding stand with the room service tray and poured each of them a glass of the cabernet.

"The sergeant knows what's going on, Pierre. I told him on the way over," Adela hastily admitted as Donnay handed them their drinks. He frowned, not sure he liked the fact that she had jumped the gun like this.

Sergeant Tom admitted to being very surprised when Adela told him the man Donnay was after is Sebastian Vane.

"Posing as Vane," Donnay corrected him. "For which we'll have concrete proof, I hope, in a short while."

"Yes, I know all about Miss Paige's errand this evening," the policeman continued. "If he's the man you think he is, she could be in great danger."

"I know that. And so does she," Donnay returned defensively. "Her uncle is with her for protection."

"All the same, that's not quite how I would have gone about trying to expose him—"

"That's the point. You wouldn't have tried," Donnay interrupted curtly. "When we first met, you told me that catching drug dealers wasn't a top priority with the police unless you already had the evidence for an arrest. Remember?"

The policeman nodded.

"Well, that's what Leslie's doing—getting you that evidence," Donnay added.

"I look forward to receiving it," Tom said. "But that's not really why we're here."

Looking surprised, Donnay glanced at Adela, who had already drained half her glass.

"Lon Chaney is missing," she said bluntly.

"Missing how?" he asked, puzzled.

"Like up in a puff of smoke missing," she replied. "It hasn't hit the newspapers yet. Right now it's just a private inquiry. Mrs. Chaney says she hasn't heard from her husband since the weekend before Monday last."

"Universal called me," Tom explained. "Then I ran into Miss Grant here, who certainly does have her sources."

"Why come to me?" Donnay asked. "I don't have him."

"I thought you might have some idea what could have happened," Adela Grant interjected. "It's too suspicious not to be related to the case you're working on."

"I agree it's suspicious, but why do you think the two are connected?" Donnay asked her.

"Because last Monday they filmed the unmasking scene with Chaney in full make-up," she reported. "From what I was told, his performance was so extreme and disturbing, even sadistic, that he cruelly made Mary Philbin faint.

"Mrs. Chaney doesn't deny that her husband can be obsessive, but that behavior was *too* unlike him, personally and professionally, she says. Then the picture went on hiatus due to this streak of bad weather, and Chaney up and disappears—even when, according to Mrs. Chaney, the family had planned a camping trip for the hiatus," Grant finished breathlessly.

"At first I thought it might have been a kidnapping," the sergeant suggested. "But there's been no ransom demand and he's been gone for going on a week now. That's unusual for a kidnapping because no kidnapper would want to hang on to such a high-profile victim and risk having the full weight of the law come down on him."

"So, what's your theory now?" Donnay inquired.

261

"From the beginning, this picture has been plagued by bad luck to such an extent that time after time it's been close to being canceled. And that bad luck—or call it sabotage—is still happening," Adela Grant submitted. "Universal is considering whether to even release the picture because the unmasking scene alone may be too frightening for audience consumption. In addition to some final scenes that are on hold, the studio is contemplating putting in some comic scenes to help soften the overall tone. That means even more filming will be needed once the hiatus is over. And now their star has vanished!"

Sergeant Tom nodded, looking somber. "And my guess is that whoever took Mr. Chaney doesn't want him to be found. The question is who wants the picture stopped? And why?"

Adela turned to Donnay and jumped in. "From the start you've insisted to me that person is Arik Cassell a.k.a. Sebastian Vane. Tell the sergeant why."

Donnay looked toward the policeman and said: "No, it isn't due to paranoia if that's what you're thinking."

"Crossed my mind," Sergeant Tom replied with a subtle wink at Grant.

"Well, since Adela has chosen to spill most of it before I was sure, you might as well know the rest," Donnay added reluctantly. "Our quarry isn't just a murderous drug dealer, he's the elusive creature who actually terrorized the Paris Opera almost fifteen years ago.

"And whom French authorities have erroneously declared to be dead."

THIRTY-ONE

Sebastian Vane Residence
Hollywood Hills, California

Leslie Paige was quickly on her feet and apologizing profusely for the mess she had created.

She knelt and reached for the smashed wine glass when Vane abruptly stayed her with his hand. "Don't," he ordered. "You'll cut yourself. Bahram will clean it up."

"Bahram could cut himself too," she argued. "It's broken because of me."

Vane let go of her wrist and surrendered with a sigh, leaning back in his chair.

"Do you have a dust pan and a damp cloth I can use?" Leslie asked.

Bahram disappeared into the kitchen but was back in less than a minute with the items she'd requested, as well as a large brush. Leslie took them from him and as he resumed his position behind Vane she went to work, gingerly picking up the larger pieces of broken glass first and placing them in the dust pan.

"I'm so sorry, Mr. Vane," she said as she cleaned up.

"It was just a glass, my dear," Vane replied.

"But still, an expensive one, I'm sure," she answered with pronounced regret. He dismissed the apology with a wave of the hand.

Leslie swept the smaller fragments into the dust pan with the brush and then wiped the wet floor with the cloth, sweeping up any remaining bits that were too tiny for her to see.

"Where do you want me to toss this?" she asked.

"Bahram will take it," Vane began, but Leslie quickly interrupted him.

"Please, let me," she urged. "I...I don't want to embarrass myself further by leaving it to someone else," she added with self-recrimination in her voice, hoping she wasn't overplaying it.

Vane looked up at his manservant for support, but the giant simply shrugged ambivalently.

Vane gave in again. "Very well, if you insist on being a scullery maid," he said with amusement, smiling at her through still-tight lips.

"Call it my Midwest upbringing," she said, again studying the contours of his face and the tightness of his mouth for any sign of the mask Donnay was convinced Vane wore to disguise himself. But she perceived nothing.

"There's a waste bin in the kitchen cabinet beneath the sink," Vane said, interrupting her thoughts. "Bahram can help you find it."

"That's okay," she said, jumping up quickly. "I've got it. You two just relax and I'll be right back."

She hastened into the kitchen where she swiftly located two cabinet doors beneath the sink. She opened both of them. The waste bin was on the left. She pulled off the cover and found some old crumpled copies of the *L.A. Crier* and some other newspapers inside as well as scraps of lettuce and other refuse.

With a glance toward the living room to ensure no one was coming, she reached deep into the pocket of her pleated skirt and withdrew a handkerchief, which she quickly unfolded. In it she put the two largest pieces of shattered wineglass from the dust pan and dumped the rest into the waste bin. She folded the handkerchief again carefully and returned it to her pocket—just as she heard the loud *clomp* of Bahram's boots approaching the kitchen.

Trying not to panic as the sound grew nearer, she promptly swept all the minute splinters of glass from the dust pan into the waste bin and tossed the damp cloth on top of it.

"All done," she said to the giant as he stepped into the room. "I put the dirty cloth in the bin too. There's lots of little pieces of glass still stuck to it."

She felt herself shrinking back as the forbidding manservant came toward her with his arm outstretched, reaching for her. She didn't know whether to scream for her uncle or remain mute and just hope for the best.

Leslie was stunned when he took her hand in his own and gently pulled her to her feet. He took the empty dust pan and brush from her and hung them both on a barely visible hook at the rear of the cabinet. Then he returned the now-covered waste bin to its spot and closed the cabinet doors.

Breathing a long, silent sigh of relief, Leslie followed Bahram back into the living room where Vane was pouring himself another glass of wine.

Bahram took his place behind the actor's chair as Vane offered her another glass.

"No, thank you, I think I've made enough of a mess for one evening," she replied with a false chuckle. "Besides, my uncle's waiting for me and I've taken up too much of your time already."

"Nonsense, my dear. It was a joy seeing you again," Vane responded warmly in his old-world style.

"Then I think I'll take my leave before we put that to the test," she said, offering her hand. Vane took it in both of his and pumped amiably as Bahram looked on with his customary stoicism.

"Again, thank you for all you've done for me," Leslie said earnestly. "I just wish I could have repaid you in some way."

"You've repaid me enough already with your gratitude and friendship," Vane replied, letting go of her hand and rising to his feet.

Leslie bid him goodbye then turned and walked away. Vane watched her as she walked up the living room steps to the foyer, followed by Bahram, who helped her on with her coat.

She looked up at the giant and said goodbye to him as well. Then she was out the door.

She hurried to her uncle's truck and got in out of the driving rain.

"Well, I didn't hear you scream your head off, so things must've gone okay," her uncle said.

"I came close once, but it was a false alarm," she replied, drying her face with her hand.

"Were you successful?" he asked.

"I think so. I've got two big chunks of broken glass he touched. They're in my pocket. So, we'll see," she answered, feeling a mixture of exhilaration and shame for what she'd just done to a possibly innocent man, one who had shown her nothing but kindness and concern. Her shame could only be assuaged if he proved to be guilty, she told herself. She would know in a few short hours.

Her uncle started the truck and they drove off.

For a full half hour after Leslie Paige left, Darrass had listened to his friend and business partner, Arik Cassell, fulminate about Universal's intention, according to studio gossip Leslie had heard, to inject some comedy into their troubled production of *The Phantom of the Opera.*

"I give them the scariest scene in what is supposed to be the scariest picture of the year, and what is their reaction? *Where are the laughs?*" he thundered, pacing back and forth. "Why don't they go all out and get Chaplin to play the 'Opera Ghost'?"

From his sofa-chair in the living room, Darrass peeled an orange as he listened to his friend rip "those imbeciles" at Universal up, down, and sideways.

He peeled off another chunk of rind and dropped it into an ash tray. Then placed a piece of orange pulp in his mouth and crushed it, savoring the sweetness.

Darrass was deeply concerned—about Arik's mounting mania and obsessive vindictiveness over the picture Universal was making—and the impact his behavior was having on his moving picture career and their drug business supported by the Corsicans. Arik was paying less and less attention to both endeavors.

Paramount had sent him a copy of the best-seller *Beau Geste,* an exciting novel of the French Foreign Legion the studio was currently adapting into a big budget picture scheduled for production next year and release in 1926. The studio wanted Sebastian Vane for a major part—that of the brutal, bearded Sergeant LeJaune, a top legionnaire when the chips were down but a sadistic, greedy martinet the rest of the time. Arik had yet to acknowledge the studio's offer and had so far left the book unopened.

Even more alarming was Arik's increasingly careless lack of attention to their drug business. He had made a deal with the

Corsicans for more autonomy in his choice of clientele and a greater share of the profits. In return he had promised the Corsicans bigger overall profits because his plan was to use his moving picture connections to target the new high-rollers of Hollywood, who would be eager to pay his escalating drug prices once hooked.

Up to recently, the operation had functioned more or less smoothly and profits were heading steadily skyward as promised. But in the last few months, those profits had taken a dip of almost forty percent, a sign of trouble the Corsicans would not accept when they made delivery of the next drug shipment from Mexico in January. They would demand their full cut of the diminishing proceeds regardless.

Arik would have to explain the shortfall, but as clever as he could be, he would have a hard time doing so convincingly and would thus expose himself to some form of retribution. Darrass was properly worried, but Arik had just laughed off his concern. "What are they going to do? Cut off my face?" he'd countered joylessly.

What also disturbed Darrass was Arik's growing fondness for Leslie Paige, which was beginning to mirror his fixation with Christine Delfont at the Paris Opera more than a decade ago. He'd shared with Darrass his intention to acquire the actress' dormant contract from the estate of the late Victor Reilly and use his clout to get her career back on track and turn her into a big star. But to what end? Darrass wondered. Where would this infatuation lead? He and Arik had barely escaped with their lives when the entire Parisian venture began to collapse.

In his present state of mind, Arik Cassell was again listening to his ego rather than to his logic or reason. But the Corsicans were neither understanding nor forgiving—nor gullible like the French police. There would be no avoiding the clutches of the murderous Corsicans with an arranged escape and planted corpse. The Corsicans would never give up hunting for them to the ends of the earth.

Finishing his orange, Darrass picked up the ash tray full of rind and headed for the kitchen while his friend continued spewing epithets at Carl Laemmle and Company. Somehow he had to get Arik's head away from the mania overtaking him and back on track with their business affairs.

Darrass opened the door below the sink and pulled out the waste bin. Popping the cover open, he emptied the ash tray full of rinds. As he did this, the small bits and pieces of the broken wine glass the girl had deposited earlier gleamed up at him, capturing his attention. Something was wrong, but he couldn't put his finger on what.

Without knowing exactly why, he picked up a few pieces and placed them on the countertop. They were smallish in size and not large chunks. In fact, as he looked more closely, he didn't see any large chunks.

His curiosity aroused, he picked up the rest of the visible shards and added them to the small pile on the counter. Then he took out the still-damp cloth the girl had tossed away and plucked out all the remaining splinters, placing them next to the rest. When done, he studied the display he'd made with perplexed interest.

And, suddenly, he knew what it was that had caught his attention, then aroused his curiosity and finally made him suspicious. He snapped his fingers loudly.

It was the *volume* of broken glass—or rather the lack of it—that had caught his eye at first. But he had not been able to put meaning to what he'd seen until now when all the fragments were spread out before him.

Arik Cassell heard the loud finger-snap and strolled from the living room to the kitchen. He stopped in the doorway to look at his friend, who appeared to be scrutinizing a small pile of broken glass on the counter.

"What are you up to there?" he asked with some amusement. "We've got more wine glasses, you know. There's no need to fix that one." He almost chuckled.

Clearly not amused, Darrass turned his head slowly to look back at him. With a stern face, Darrass reached above his head and withdrew an intact wine glass from its shelf. He set it on the counter near the pile of fragments.

Cassell stepped closer. "What are you trying to tell me?" he asked, baffled.

Darrass turned the unbroken wine glass on its side and placed it next to the pile. He silently mouthed the words: "Not the same."

Cassell was not an accomplished lip reader, but over the years he'd become somewhat adept at understanding what his friend was trying to communicate, as long as the sentences were brief. "What's not the same?" he asked, still perplexed.

Darrass stretched his fingers and widened his hand into a measurement tool that he employed on the two countertop objects, first vertically, then horizontally. "Not enough pieces," he mouthed.

Cassell drew closer to examine the two objects himself. "Yes, I see what you're driving at. Are you sure you got all the pieces out of the bin?"

Darrass nodded fiercely.

"Then where's...the *rest*...?" Cassell began slowly, although the visibly increasing disappointment and wrath shown in his eyes indicated he already knew the answer.

Darrass gripped his friend tightly by the arm, hoping to control the eruption he knew would quickly follow.

"*Why?*" Cassell boomed, referring both to the girl he'd believed to be a friend *and* to the missing pieces she had clearly taken with her. But he already knew the answer to that too.

Darrass confirmed it mutely:

"*Fingerprints.*"

THIRTY-TWO

Pierre Donnay's Accommodations
Hollywood Roosevelt Hotel

Apart from the sound of rain and the distant *whoosh* of automobile tires along Hollywood Boulevard that filtered in through the open window of Donnay's hotel suite, the room was quiet as a tomb. All three occupants anxiously awaited Leslie Paige's arrival in their own private way.

Donnay broke the silence. "What time is it?" he asked Adela Grant.

She squinted at her wristwatch through the haze of cigarette smoke that circled her head. "Exactly ten minutes later than the last time you asked," she responded. "And approximately ten minutes earlier than next time—if there is a next time."

"Very funny," Donnay said.

He got up from his chair and walked impatiently to the window. He looked down on the busy sidewalks below where pedestrians scurried along undaunted by the downpour. It was almost eight thirty. *What was keeping her?*

Sergeant Tom shifted in his seat where he was folding a piece of blank white paper into ever-smaller pieces. "When you've

272

confirmed the fingerprints match, what happens then?" he asked of Donnay.

"Then you can arrest him," Donnay responded bluntly.

"On what basis? My good looks?" the policeman replied. "I'll need an arrest warrant and you forget that I'm just a lowly cop in an out-of-the-way district of the Los Angeles County Police Department."

"You're still a cop. And he's a criminal," Donnay countered irritably. "Besides, Interpol has a long-standing arrest warrant out on Arik Cassell for international drug smuggling. That and your badge should be all the authority you'll need."

They each snapped to attention when the doorbell rang.

Adela Grant was instantly on her feet and heading for the bathroom with her ashtray full of cigarette butts. She dumped them in the toilet then pulled the chain to flush them away. She grabbed her raincoat and umbrella and moved quickly to the bedroom where she and Donnay had pre-arranged for her to hide so that she and Leslie would not encounter each another.

Once Adela had closed herself inside the bedroom, Donnay rushed to the door of his suite and hurled it open.

And there stood Leslie Paige, looking cute as a button in her sopping rain hat and dripping raincoat. "I thought maybe you'd fallen asleep," she teased him.

Impulsively, he overcame his inherent reserve and shyness with women and pulled her close. "You can't imagine how worried I've been," he said, encircling her in a hug. He'd never been so happy to see anyone in his life.

Leslie was surprised by the sudden intimacy but eagerly reciprocated. "Oh, I think I can imagine. I was plenty worried myself," she said with a twinkle in her eye.

He closed the door and led her into the suite where she grimaced at the smell in the air. "God, this place stinks like an ash tray," she muttered, looking at Donnay. "I thought you told me you didn't smoke."

Donnay looked startled. Did Leslie know that Adela Grant smoked like a chimney? Had Grant given herself away? "Well, I...I...," he stammered.

"It's my fault," Sergeant Tom said rising from his seat and stepping out before them. "When I get overanxious, I tend to smoke one cigarette after another. Hope the smell isn't too unpleasant." He thrust out his hand. "The name's Sergeant Tom. Thomas Tom, Valley police," he introduced himself.

"The sergeant is helping out with some of the legal details," Donnay explained.

The sergeant and Leslie shook hands.

"I guess I can't go wrong if I call you Tom then can I?" she remarked jovially.

"Just as long as it's not Tom-Tom," he quipped back and the two of them laughed.

Sergeant Tom took Leslie's wet raincoat and rain hat and brought them to the bathroom to dry.

"Where's your uncle? Didn't he go with you?" Donnay asked her.

"Yes. And he brought me here as well," she replied. "He's out in his truck, waiting. You know Uncle Arno."

"Did you have any problems at Vane's?" Donnay solicited.

Leslie shook her head. "I was watched like a hawk the whole time by Vane's manservant—"

"Darrass," Donnay interrupted.

"Yes. Although Vane introduced him as Bahram," she explained. "But he never spoke a word the entire time I was there," she added, "as he has no tongue."

"How do you know that?" Sergeant Tom asked as he returned.

"Monsieur Donnay told me. And that's how Vane too explained his muteness to me," she said.

"Quite open about the disabilities of others, isn't he?" Donnay said with disgust.

"I almost came close to being spotted by Bahram—I mean Darrass—while getting these," she said as she withdrew the wrapped pieces of glass from her skirt pocket. "But I don't think he saw me take them."

"Are you certain?" Donnay asked with deep concern.

"I'm here, aren't I?" she said lightheartedly.

"That you are." Donnay beamed. "Let's see what you've brought."

He steered Leslie to a writing desk and offered her a chair. As she sat, he pulled the desk lamp's on-off chain. She began unfolding her handkerchief on the desk's surface as Sergeant Tom looked over their shoulders.

Leslie exposed the two pieces of broken wine glass. Each was spherical in shape and about the same size as a large piece of broken egg shell.

Donnay pulled on a pair of white cloth gloves, gently picked up one of the shards and began moving it back and forth in front of the light.

"Anything?" Leslie asked anxiously.

"I think so," Donnay said, sounding modestly enthusiastic. "We'll know for sure in a minute."

He put down the shard and took a small black box from one of the desk drawers. It was the size of a thick hardcover book. He opened the box, revealing his fingerprint kit.

"If it helps to know this, I took the glass from Vane by the stem," she said. "So as not to mix his prints with mine."

Donnay nodded appreciatively. "Did he offer you the glass with his right hand or his left?" he asked, sprinkling a layer of grayish graphite powder from a small vial over the surface of the shard.

"His right," she answered.

"Good to know," Donnay responded approvingly. He took a brush with long, thin and extremely soft bristles from the box and began lightly wiping away at the powder in a circular motion. Gradually the fingerprint impression emerged as a series of dark arches, loops, and whorls.

Donnay placed the piece of glass on the desk and tore off a strip of clear "lifting adhesive" from a roll in the box. He applied the strip to the glass, sticky-side down, to affix the impression to the adhesive. Then, very carefully, he pulled the adhesive from the glass and transferred the impression to a white card, thus making a permanent record of the impression for future comparison. Turning the white card to the light, he let out a long sigh of satisfaction.

Never having seen anything like this done before, Leslie was suitably impressed and said as much with a long, softly spoken, "*Amazing!*"

Sergeant Tom had taken fingerprints on the job but had never seen them lifted from an object before. He was impressed too, but remained quiet about it.

Donnay withdrew a magnifying glass from his kit and closely examined the print on the card. "It looks like a thumbprint," he remarked. "A complete one, too." He turned to Leslie. "Just perfect. Great job!" he added admiringly. She gave him an embarrassed smile.

"Now let's see what else you've got," he went on, putting away the magnifying glass and picking up the second shard. He applied the graphite powder and dusted it with the soft brush as before, revealing what looked to him like the partial print of an index finger—enough for a less than 50 percent identification, but not much more than that. The full thumbprint would have to do. Fortunately, he felt it would be more than up to the task.

Donnay asked Leslie if he could take her seat at the desk and she moved out of the way.

"Now comes the time-consuming part," he remarked, taking the photographic record of Cassell's fingerprint card from his coat pocket and placing it under the light next to Vane's card.

With the magnifying glass, he began comparing Vane's right hand thumbprint with the Phantom's, side by side.

"Would you like a glass of red wine while we wait," Sergeant Tom asked Leslie.

Her eyes went to the serving table where she saw a two-thirds empty bottle of California cabernet and three glasses. "Thanks, I think I will," she said.

The policeman opened the bottle and then reached for one of the glasses only to discover that it too had been used—by Adela Grant. Smeared traces of her bright red lipstick were still on the glass.

"This one looks a bit dirty," he said with some embarrassment. "I'll wash it for you."

"That's okay, I'll do it," she jumped in.

He quickly declined the offer. "I must have used it without knowing," he explained, still embarrassed. "Won't be a minute," he added and was off to the bathroom to wash the glass off in the sink.

Leslie glanced at Donnay, who was bent over the desk, painstakingly moving his eyes back and forth across the two thumbprints in absorbed silence. She couldn't even hear him breathing.

"Here you go," Sergeant Tom said, returning. He handed her the glass and filled it half way.

"Thanks," Leslie said. She took a long slow sip from the glass, the wine a bit tart but still satisfying, when she noticed a tiny speck of red caked under the lip of the otherwise spotless glass. Lipstick?

She and the sergeant jumped suddenly as Donnay slammed his palm on the desk. They turned to see him sit back and mumble something neither of them could distinguish.

"What did you say?" Leslie asked with concern.

Donnay looked up at her and spoke curtly. "I said *they don't match.*"

"But you were so sure," the sergeant put in, mystified.

Donnay rubbed his tired eyes. "I *was* sure," he said. "But apparently I was also wrong. Look for yourself."

The policeman leaned in and scrutinized the two prints. Even at a quick glance it was clear they were not the same. He stepped aside so Leslie could have a look.

"Not even close," Donnay whispered solemnly.

"Could he have altered his prints somehow?" the sergeant asked.

"No," Donnay answered. "Fingerprints can't be altered, only obliterated." He looked at Leslie beseechingly. "Are you absolutely sure it was Vane who handed you the glass?" he asked.

Her face reddened. "I'm unemployable, *Monsieur Donnay,*" she responded brusquely. "Not blind or stupid."

"I didn't mean—"

"Of course I'm sure," she spoke over him. "Vane was sitting across from me—about as close as I am to you now. He was talking as he poured the wine and offered me the glass, while this Darrass or Bahram character stood behind him like a statue."

"Maybe the prints lifted in the opera house belonged to someone else," Sergeant Tom suggested, hoping to defuse the growing tension between Leslie and Donnay. "Could there have been a mistake?"

Donnay shook his head. "We pulled samples from all his known roosts inside the Grand Garnier," he explained. "And they all matched."

Suddenly the bedroom door flew open, slamming against the wall, and Adela Grant stormed out, arms in the air, a cigarette between two fingertips. "Is that the story you expect me to write?" she fumed, her voice rising shrilly.

Leslie looked aghast, her eyes darting from Grant to the speck of lipstick on her glass back to Grant again. "What's...*this woman* doing here?" she shouted at Donnay.

"Same as you, dearie," Grant responded caustically. She glanced Donnay's way. "Helping out this junior grade Dupin here with his 'fool-proof' investigation."

"How? With another smear campaign?" Leslie demanded spitefully. "You've got a disgusting job, know that?"

"You're right," Grant shot back. "Some jobs *are* disgusting. You found that out yourself tonight."

Sensing the two women might be about to come to blows, Sergeant Tom stepped in front of Adela Grant while Donnay clasped Leslie's sleeve and tried to draw her to him. But she pulled away in anger and made for the bathroom where she quickly grabbed her rain gear then rushed to the door to the suite and yanked it open.

"Hold on, Leslie, please don't go...," Donnay pleaded with her. "I'm so, so sorry about the prints not matching. I'm as shocked as you are. There's got to be an explanation. Just give me a chance to..."

But she was having none of it and started through the door. He made another grab for her sleeve but she snatched it away.

"Promise me one thing then," he urged, still fearing for her safety in spite of what the comparison had shown. "Whatever you do, *don't go to Vane!*"

Leslie stopped abruptly. "Go to him?" she said, astonished. "I'll never be able to look him in the face again."

With that, she slammed the door and was gone.

THIRTY-THREE

Pagano Chicken Ranch
Canoga Park, California

Leslie's uncle parked the delivery truck in the muddy courtyard fronting the ranch house and killed the engine. He and his niece sat in relative silence. Except for the fierce drumming of the rain.

"Feel better now?" he asked, breaking the quiet.

Leslie shrugged. "Not sure," she said. "I guess I really flew off the handle a bit back there," she added with some embarrassment.

"Judging from the steam coming out of your ears when you got in the truck, I'd guess more than a bit," her uncle replied with amusement.

"It just made me so damn angry to find *her* there—Adela Grant," she admitted. "And learn that she's been helping all along, too!"

"Sure there's not a little jealousy mixed in there?" her uncle mused, scratching his goatee.

"Not hardly!" Leslie answered, turning red. "Why, she's middle-aged. Maybe older!"

Her uncle laughed. "You mean like your Aunt Elena and me?"

"No, not like you two," she said, giving him a hug and peck on the cheek.

"I think Mr. Donnay is an honest man who somehow made an honest mistake and feels terrible about it for a lot of reasons, not the least of them being what he put you through," her uncle suggested.

"You think I should apologize?" she asked contritely.

"If it'll help set things right," he answered with a nod.

Leslie thought this over for a moment, then said: "Okay, I'll call him first thing in the morning."

"Good," he said with a smile, squeezing her hand. He changed the subject to getting a move on with his final rounds ensuring the chickens were safely tucked in for the night.

"You must be exhausted from driving me around. Cold, too," Leslie jumped in. "Let me handle those chores."

"You don't have to ask *me* twice," he said with a grin.

"I thought so. But you wouldn't ask for help, would you?" she said, admonishing him with a finger-shake. "I'll make the rounds and you go to bed. Deal?"

"Deal," he said.

The two of them got out of the truck. Leslie's uncle headed for the front door to the ranch house while she buttoned her raincoat, pulled on her rain hat and sloshed to the barn.

Leslie worked the combination lock then tugged the large door open. She went inside, took a flashlight from the workbench near the door and switched it on.

Row upon row of (mostly) sleeping chickens in their straw beds greeted her as she worked the light over them. As it was pouring outside, and night besides, none complained about being cooped in. This meant her rounds would be short. All she had to do was make sure they had enough water and feed to sustain them until morning.

She also had to run the flashlight over the hatches that opened to the fenced-in areas outside where the chickens spent their days. This was to ensure that each hatch was closed and tightly secured against any determined coyotes, foxes, or worse looking for an illicit meal.

All of this now done, Leslie returned the flashlight to the workbench. She stepped outside, rolled the barn door closed, and secured it again with the combination lock. She hugged the outside of the barn to keep herself as dry as possible as she made for the ranch house where the porch light had been left on for her.

Leslie had gone only few yards to the edge of the barn when she felt a hand cover her mouth and an arm tighten around her middle, pulling her around the corner of the barn.

"Scream for help and you'll be dead before it gets here," a voice hissed into her ear. "And then the help will die too."

She couldn't see who it belonged to but she recognized the mellifluous voice well—though now it was tinged with anger.

Sebastian Vane.

"Nod if you understand," Vane ordered her.

Eyes bulging with fear, Leslie nodded quickly and Vane relaxed his grip over her mouth. She stayed silent.

"Who did you get them for?" he snarled.

"I...I...don't under—" she started to say, but his hand violently clamped down on her mouth again, silencing her.

"Don't play games with me, Christine, I haven't got the patience," he interrupted with fury. "Now, *who did you get them for?*"

In his mania, he'd called her Christine, she realized; the name of the ingénue the Phantom had terrorized in Paris to become an opera star and then, in his disordered mind, because she had betrayed him. Leslie fought to clear her head. Donnay had been right all along, she now believed. Sebastian Vane *must* be Arik Cassell!

But how could the fingerprints not have matched?

"Answer me," Vane roared brutally into her ear, almost deafening her.

She cried out in pain but the sound died as hot breath in his pressing palm. Slowly he eased the pressure as she tried forming words.

"Donnay," she gasped after he took his hand away. "Pierre Donnay of the Paris police."

"*Donnay?*" Vane muttered in a confused but calmer tone. "But I saw him drown under the rocks and beams that fell in the explosion," he remarked incredulously.

"He almost did," Leslie explained hoarsely. "He was in a coma for a long time and it took him years to come back from his injuries. Then he discovered you weren't dead either. And he's been on your trail ever since."

"Where is he now?" Vane/Cassell demanded. "And don't tell me you don't know."

When she didn't reply, he pressed her against the wall of the barn with his body and punched her hard in the kidneys.

Leslie gasped in pain. She thought she was going to pass out. But he held her upright against the barn.

"I asked you a question," he growled. "Unless you want some more, give me an answer."

"No…Please…," she pleaded. "He…he's at the Hollywood Roosevelt." Tears fell from her eyes in agony and shame.

He reached into his pocket and took out a rag and a small vial of chloroform. He moistened the rag and the next thing Leslie experienced was the harsh small of something she couldn't identify as he covered her nose and mouth with the rag.

In seconds, she went limp in his arms and he hoisted her body over his shoulder. Staying well out of range of the light from the ranch house, he carried her up the muddy drive to his car, hidden behind a thick clump of rain-soaked pepper trees.

He placed the unconscious girl in the passenger seat then got in himself. He fired up the engine, turned on the wipers, and as the rain beat like stones against the roof, he drove off to show Christine what comes from betraying him.

THIRTY-FOUR

Sebastian Vane Residence
Hollywood Hills, California

Darrass pushed open the door to the torture room cautiously so that the top-to-bottom mirror affixed to the opposite side wouldn't be in danger of cracking or coming loose.

The chamber's interior was in its reflecting light-oppressive heat stage; he felt like he was opening a furnace. He could see a dark lump in the far corner of the room. It was Lon Chaney, huddled in a fetal position under the rags of his clothes. Darrass guessed the man was pretty much out of it.

He widened the door to let in Cassell, who eased through the opening with the still-unconscious Leslie Paige in his arms and placed her on the sand. She groaned in discomfort from the searing granules and sleepily rubbed her arm from the burn she had received. She would soon be emerging completely from the heavy dose of chloroform she'd been given.

Cassell backed out of the torture room and Darrass closed and locked the door. The two of them went upstairs. As the latter reached the top step, he uttered a sharp grunt, and Cassell turned quickly to inquire what the mute was trying to say. He found Darrass standing there stiffly with a grim expression on his face. He pointed down to the torture room and mimed the question, "What now?"

"We get rid of them, that's what," Cassell responded, entering the sunken living room where he poured himself a drink—a scotch this time. He took a sip of the 86 proof liquid and then fell into his plush chair with a look of contentment.

As he sipped more scotch, feeling himself relax, he pondered how he hadn't originally planned on doing away with Chaney, but on letting him go once the production of *Phantom* was shut down for good. Chaney would have no idea who had imprisoned him, where or why. All he would be able to tell the police was his delusional belief that his captor was the "real" Phantom of the Opera.

But the picture had not yet been shut down and so it was too late to free the kidnapped actor. Leslie and Chaney were now imprisoned together; they would very likely talk, and she would reveal to him everything that she knew. So, now, they both had to die.

From the top of the stairs, Darrass pointed again at the torture room door. With a stern look on his face and a gesture of finality, he mimed washing his hands of the mess.

Cassell smirked. "What's this?" He laughed. "A rebellion? You don't want to stain your hands with their blood? Why so finicky all of a sudden?" He rose to his feet imperiously, putting his drink aside.

Poor old Darrass, Cassell thought. The heretofore loyal servant. True, the man had never killed anyone that Cassell knew of nor had Cassell ever ordered him to. Darrass had always believed he had a say in Cassell's affairs when actually he had no say at all—unless Cassell wanted him to think that way. Now was not one of those occasions.

Darrass was a puppet—a devoted one to be sure, but still a puppet—whose job was to do what he was told. It had been that way ever since their time together in the Persian jail where they had first met. Cassell needed a henchman to watch his back while imprisoned and to help carry out his plans once he had escaped—preferably a henchman who would never be able to talk to the authorities no matter how rigorously they leaned on him.

Cassell had already suffered horribly under his tormentors; he knew what they were capable of and so it was not terribly difficult to manipulate them into believing that Darrass was a spy and inveterate snitch and putting the suggestion in their Neolithic minds to remove his tongue during one of their torture sessions.

Afterward, by helping Darrass recover and enlisting him in his escape plans, the master illusionist and manipulator had maneuvered the mute into feeling forever beholden to him.

Cassell stepped up to the almost-as-tall but not as imposing Darrass and teasingly pinched his cheek. "My dear Darrass, I don't mean for you to do anything as nasty as chopping them up into little bloody pieces," he said. "Lord no. Just give them an overdose of something lethal from our drug supply and be done with it. Then we just dump them in some seedy lodge for illicit lovers, tip off the police and reporters and presto, we're in the clear. How's that sound?"

Darrass still looked unpersuaded but was slowly giving into his benefactor's intimidation and subtly nodded in agreement.

"Besides, we've got a more serious problem that must be dealt with," Cassell went on. "And I don't mean the Corsicans," he explained. "Someone is onto us and it was for him Christine got the fingerprint samples."

Cassell's reference to Leslie Paige as Christine registered unsettlingly on Darrass though he dared not show it. His mentor was breaking down.

"Who is it?" Darrass mimed.

"It seems *procureur* Pierre Donnay did not perish in our charade with the dynamite," Cassell said. "He's here now. In Hollywood. Working to expose us." Darrass looked startled but Cassell waved off the man's concern.

"Not to worry," Cassell said. "Donnay's kept whatever evidence he has pretty close to his chest, I'm told. So, once he's out of the way—for good this time—no one will be the wiser. Except you and me."

Darrass struggled to suppress his worried look.

"But first," Cassell said, lifting his forefinger theatrically, "there's one more task I must undertake. And I must do it while we are still being deluged by this wonderfully useful monsoon."

Darrass knew what that task was—a final act of destruction that would fatally shut down Universal's "bowdlerized and soon-to-be joke-ridden" *Phantom of the Opera*, as Cassell now scornfully described it.

"Very soon, all this will be over and we can get down to satisfying the Corsicans," Cassell continued. "And ourselves too, of course." He laughed. "*Capiche?*"

Darrass looked at him from the top of the stairs but said nothing as Cassell waited for a response. Instead his mind was scrambling for ideas how to get himself out of this mess before any more blood was spilled.

And then he had it!

He quickly thought through the idea and felt it was sound. And could free him of guilt when the bodies were found if he later got caught. Who knew, it might even give the pair downstairs a slim but fighting chance. Not that he cared. His only concern now was his own fate.

"Well?" Cassell said impatiently.

Darrass nodded slowly and mouthed, *"Capiche."*

The "Room"
Sebastian Vane Residence

Leslie Paige felt her nose, throat and lungs were all on fire from the lingering taste of whatever Vane had used to knock her out, and now from the suffocating temperature.

She cracked open her eyes to find herself on a bed of stinging hot sand in a room ablaze with blinding white light. She quickly snapped her eyes shut again.

Where am I? she wondered. And *why* was she here? The last thing she remembered was Sebastian Vane forcing a smelly cloth over her face and then everything went black.

Prepared now for the brightness, she squinted her eyes open to look around, using her hands for shade. She quickly noticed that she was not alone in this hellish prison. There was an inert dark form in the corner of the room.

She inched closer, using the folds of her thick skirt as a buffer to keep her knees protected from the scorching sand.

Slowly, she reached the figure whose dark clothes were torn and layered with dust and stained with sweat. She could tell from the clothes that they belonged to a man, but as she could hear no breathing, she didn't know whether he was alive or dead.

Leslie nudged him with her finger and the body shifted with a strained and raspy groan. She drew closer and carefully peeled the moist fabric covering his red face and blistered lips.

To her surprise, she recognized him immediately, even in this sorry state. It was Lon Chaney. His barely open and blinking eyes indicated he was alive, but only just.

"Mr. Chaney?" she said, nudging him harder but still gently.

His lips parted and he croaked, "*Who…are…you?*"

"Leslie Paige, Mr. Chaney. Do you remember me? We worked together briefly on *Phantom*," she said, straining for breath in the oppressive heat. "We're both here I'm pretty sure because of the same person. Sebastian Vane."

He reacted with astonishment. "Vane?" he said. "What's he got to do with this?"

"Long story," she replied. "But first we have to figure a way out of here."

"Where *is* here?"

"A room in Vane's house, I believe."

Chaney's face scrunched into a confused look.

"It's a wonder you're still alive in this unbearable heat," she observed, fanning her face with her hand.

"It's not always like this," he remarked in a throaty whisper. "The heat comes and goes every few hours so things can cool off. I think it's on a timer."

He pointed weakly and she followed his finger to the ceiling where she saw a round faceplate consisting of several movable shutter rings that were currently open to expose and direct the lights.

"When those lights go off," he explained, "the plate turns and the rings close over them, revealing a hole in the ceiling that vents the hot air." He started to cough.

"Let me get you some water," Leslie said. She rose and went quickly to the bowl she'd spotted by the wall at the far end of the room. She found it bolted to the floor, so she pulled her handkerchief from her skirt pocket and submerged it until it was soaked.

She returned swiftly to Chaney and daubed his lips with the wet cloth. He absorbed the droplets greedily and after a few moments the coughing stopped. He seemed to become more alive.

"You say the changeover's on a timer?" Leslie sought to confirm.

"I think so, yes," Chaney said. Then he looked downcast. "I don't know when the last one was. After a while the heat gets too much to bear and I just go to sleep. But there'll be another changeover pretty soon I expect."

Leslie looked up once more, thinking. "If that faceplate is on a timer, there must be a mechanism of some sort that moves it and the rings," she suggested.

Chaney nodded.

"If we could get to that mechanism, maybe we could stop the process," she theorized.

"We're always being watched," Chaney said, sounding defeated.

"How do you know?" she asked, refusing to give up.

"A voice comes through a speaker. Always the same one," Chaney replied.

"Soft and reassuring with a calming but firm tone?" Leslie described it.

Chaney looked surprised. "How did you—"

"That's Sebastian Vane's voice. I'd know it anywhere," she jumped in, then added caustically. "He's the only one of them with a tongue."

Chaney didn't get her meaning, but was too sapped by the heat to inquire further. He took the wet handkerchief from her fingers and pressed it to his lips, savoring the lukewarm droplets that rolled down his throat.

"Watched or not, we've got to chance it," Leslie spoke adamantly. "When the next changeover occurs, we've got to jam that mechanism so it can't work. It's the only way to keep it cool in here long enough for us to build up strength to fight back."

"My legs are a bit rickety but my upper body strength is still there," Chaney said. "I had to build it up for my picture *The Penalty* and kept at it ever since."

Leslie nodded. "From helping my aunt and uncle out on their chicken ranch, I'm in a lot better shape than I ever was back in Wyoming," she explained. "Can you stand?"

"Think so," Chaney said. "Can't swear how sturdy I'll be until it cools off a bit. Why?"

"Because it's time to join the circus," she said enigmatically with a wink. "I have an idea."

THIRTY-FIVE

Pierre Donnay's Accommodations
Hollywood Roosevelt Hotel

After his guests had gone, Pierre Donnay was left uncomfortably alone in his silent room with only his thoughts for company.

Sergeant Tom had left for home, as any official and unofficial duties for which he might have been required were at a standstill. Adela Grant had departed in a huff, most likely for her office at the *L.A. Crier*, Donnay guessed, as he'd never heard the woman mention having an apartment, let alone a home. And Leslie Paige had walked out of his life—perhaps for good— feeling betrayed and angry. .

Donnay couldn't blame her. He considered how he'd botched his own investigation, chastising himself over and over as he sprawled on his bed in the dark, asking himself again and again how everything could have gone so suddenly and irrevocably wrong.

So far, he'd come up with no answers.

The fingerprints of the "Opera Ghost" had been lifted not only from his lair within the Grand Garnier but everywhere else in the opera house he was known to have been—from the managers' offices to the numerous secret rooms and storage spaces to the private *galerie* he "haunted" to frighten paying customers away.

In addition, the prints of every performer and employee had been taken for comparison purposes in order to rule them out as being the culprit. In the end, only the known fingerprints of the "Opera Ghost" had matched each other, so there was no question in Donnay's mind that the prints on the card he'd brought from Paris were those of Arik Cassell—unless, of course, the card itself was misidentified, which he did not believe was feasible in such a high-profile case.

This left a second possibility—that the fingerprint sample Leslie had gotten belonged not to Sebastian Vane but to someone else. Perhaps Darrass had been playing Vane in front of her while the actor himself played his mute manservant as a parlor trick for their own private entertainment.

What eliminated that possibility, Donnay reasoned, was that Leslie said she and Vane had been conversing, even after she'd dropped the glass, and *Darrass could not speak.*

What other possibilities remained? Donnay asked himself repeatedly. As far as he could figure only two:

The first was that Leslie might have grabbed pieces of a different glass object from the waste bin. But Donnay figured this was very unlikely because, according to Leslie, she had dumped the pieces of her wine glass into the bin herself. Clearly, she would have been careful not to pick up any other broken glass that might have been in there.

The second was that the prints belonged to an unknown third party who was not mute and could mimic the voice of Sebastian Vane. But *who*? And *why the pretense*? Surely it was too much of a coincidence to suggest that Vane, Darrass and this unknown third person would have chosen this particular night to perpetrate their hoax when Vane was so looking forward to Leslie's visit. And surely it seems senseless that they would have gone to such lengths if there were no one to fool but themselves.

For every possible explanation there was a solid reason to contradict it, and Donnay's head hurt from going over each of them only to come up with the same result: Zero.

He thought he was going crazy. Perhaps if he were able to clear his mind and focus on something else for a bit, the solution would come more quickly to him, he thought.

He rolled roughly onto his side to get more comfortable just as the wall phone rang in the hall. He got up to answer it, musing: Perhaps after all Arik Cassell *is* the consummate magician—an illusionist who actually can walk through walls, not just talk through them.

As he picked up the ear piece and spoke "Hello" into the receiver, an exhilarating new theory popped unexpectedly into his head, but it was pushed away by the voice of alarm on the other end of the line.

"Mr. Donnay, this is Arno Pagano, Leslie's uncle, I'm sorry to bother you so late, but my niece has disappeared," the man said in a breathless rush.

"How do you mean 'disappeared'?" Donnay asked with mounting anxiety.

"I think she was kidnapped," Pagano explained. "I found her rain hat by the barn along with some footprints in the muddy grass that looked like there'd been a struggle."

"When did this happen?"

"Sometime after we got home. She offered to make my last rounds of the ranch for the day, and I stupidly let her," Pagano said with self-recrimination. "I got up after midnight to get a glass of water and saw she hadn't returned. So, I went looking and found what I told you."

"Was she still angry and upset with me when you separated?"

"No, she felt bad about how she had left things and was going to call you this morning to apologize," Pagano said. "That's how I know she was kidnapped and didn't just run away voluntarily."

"I agree," Donnay said, thinking hard.

"Who could have taken her?" the man beseeched Donnay.

"I can make a good guess," the Frenchman answered as his new theory elbowed its way back into his thoughts.

"Mr. Pagano, listen to me carefully," he instructed. "Meet me at Sebastian Vane's house in a half hour to forty-five minutes."

"You think he's the one?" the man inquired hastily.

"I'm positive," Donnay said firmly. "You want to avoid being seen so don't park too near the house. And for God's sake don't try going in until I get there. I'll have help with me. Okay?"

"Okay," Pagano agreed and they each rang off.

Donnay quickly dialed Sergeant Tom's work number in Van Nuys. He didn't have the man's home number and hoped the policeman might have stopped off at his headquarters building before heading home. But no such luck. The grumpy and officious voice that answered told Donnay that Sergeant Tom was off duty and, according to protocol, his contact information wasn't to be given out. The voice wouldn't budge and so Donnay offered a caustic "thanks" and hung up.

Next, he dialed Adela Grant, praying he was right about her going to the offices of the *L.A. Crier*.

"Grant here," came the answer. "Who's this?"

"Now don't hang up, Miss Grant," he urged. "It's me, Donnay."

"With another bad scoop for me?" she replied sarcastically. "Keep it. I'm trying to come up with a story that won't get me sued."

"Look, I'm sorry about what happened," he said contritely. "But I wasn't wrong. I'm convinced I've put together how the mix-up occurred. Vane *is* Arik Cassell. I'll explain when you get here. I need you and your car."

"What for?" she inquired dubiously.

"To drive to Vane's house," he explained hurriedly. "Leslie's been kidnapped and I'm sure Cassell's got her. And if I'm right, I think we may find the answer to where the missing Lon Chaney is too."

THIRTY-SIX

The "Room"
Sebastian Vane Residence

L eslie Paige's eyes popped open at a sliding sound coming
from above. She found it too much of a strain on her neck to
lift her head so she rolled onto her back and looked up at the
white ceiling. Someone was inching along the floor above—in a
crawlspace, perhaps?

Or was what she believed she was hearing entirely a product
of her own fevered mind?

No, she decided; she could definitely hear the sound of
someone crawling.

She nudged the sleeping Lon Chaney with her foot.

"Do you hear that?" she asked groggily. But he offered
nothing in return other than a low grumble.

Leslie cupped her hands over her eyes to shield them from
the painful brightness and listened intently. She was able to track
the crawling movement and its accompanying grunts of exertion
across the ceiling to the area around the vent—where the sounds
abruptly stopped.

Next she heard the soft *clinking* of metal on metal, as if someone were tinkering with a piece of machinery. Chaney had been sure the changeover was imminent. How much time had passed since he'd told her? An hour? More? There was no way of knowing. They'd taken her watch. Chaney's too. Was there something wrong with the timer mechanism or the vent itself? *What form of deviltry were Cassell and/or his evil manservant up to now?* she asked herself.

As abruptly as it had begun, the *clinking* stopped. It was quickly followed by more crawling, but this time all movement was in the opposite direction. Leslie again tracked it across the ceiling until a door closed and all was quiet once more, except for a low *buzzing* from the light fixture circling the vent.

Leslie's eyes began to lose focus from the glare and she could feel herself growing drowsy again. Her eyelids closed in spite of her determination to keep awake. But the unyielding heat was too strong an opponent and she lost the struggle once more as her mind slipped again into blissful unconsciousness.

When Leslie awoke again, she could barely breathe. Her throat felt lined with sand, making it increasingly difficult for her to swallow even the small handfuls of fast-evaporating water that remained in their un-replenished bowl.

Chaney was in even worse shape, she calculated. His breathing had become so shallow that she feared he was near death.

It seemed to her that the room had gotten even warmer than it was earlier when she'd heard the noises above. How long ago had that been? Mere minutes? Or hours? Was it possible that after falling asleep she had remained that way while the changeover came and went? Or was even a short respite from the heat now being denied them? If so, why?

Then she put two and two together and had it figured. It doesn't just *seem* warmer than before. *It is!* She realized instantly the reason why: Their captor's strategy had also changed. Torture was no longer the objective. She and Chaney were to be burned to a crisp now that there would be no more changeovers to cooler temperatures.

It was too late now to put in motion her earlier plan of escape. She'd talked the idea over with Chaney and he was eager to go for it, but there was no longer any chance of implementing it. The two of them would die unless someone found them in time—which was fast running out, and for Lon Chaney, she thought grimly, might already be up.

The plan was relatively straightforward though not simple, and most certainly not a sure thing. It involved her being able to stand on Chaney's shoulders so she could reach the ceiling unit when the changeover occurred.

Using strips of their clothing, she would try to jam the shutter rings from re-opening when the next heat cycle was to begin—perhaps permanently damaging the unit itself. Before long, Vane [or Bahram] would come to investigate, she reasoned; by then she and Chaney should have recovered sufficient strength to overcome him and flee.

It was a flawed plan but worth taking a chance on when considering the alternative. But now, even taking that risk was no longer viable. In his condition, Chaney would no longer be able to stand let alone support her weight, even if she were able to summon the energy to climb onto his shoulders, which presently was very unlikely. Also, she would undoubtedly burn her hands uselessly on the now-scorching metal rings trying to jam them.

Leslie sat up in the sand and wiped the salty tears of frustration from her eyes, contemplating the fact that she was destined to die here of heat stroke, along with Lon Chaney, and never again see her folks, her aunt and uncle or her hometown friends again. All because of a crazy dream to become a big-time moving picture star like her fan magazine idols.

Or like Sebastian Vane.

She would have spit his name except that her parched throat couldn't summon the moisture.

A loud *pop* from above startled her. She looked up to see a shower of yellowish sparks and pieces of bulb rain down from the light fixture. One of the four light bulbs had exploded.

Instead of wondering what had happened or why, Leslie's thoughts coalesced around other questions:

Was Lon Chaney too far gone to be roused?

If there was still any fight at all in him, could he manage supporting her on his shoulders as she'd once planned?

If neither of them had the capacity for such acrobatics, was there something long and flexible enough for her to swing at the remaining bulbs from below to shatter them?

Was Chaney wearing a belt or had their captors taken it?

Leslie crawled over to the prostrate actor. She struggled to turn him over and look for a belt when another loud *pop* resounded as a second bulb exploded. More sparks and pieces of bulb cascaded downward as a hopeful thought came to her. Might whatever was causing the damage to the unit do the job for her?

But then she saw something else and her heart skipped.

Wisps of black smoke crept into the room along the edges of the light fixture.

Almost immediately a third bulb exploded, this time taking with it a small chunk of the fixture—so that Leslie could now see the roaring circle of flames behind.

Leslie pulled at Chaney in a panic, shouting at him to wake up, shaking him, then shaking him harder until she began to cough. Somehow they had to get out of there fast or—

She shook Chaney so violently that he let out a loud grumble and eased himself into a sitting position.

"What's happening?" he groaned just as the last bulb blew. Part of the fixture gave way and hung there like a dire birthday decoration, swamped with flames that were now licking at the ceiling.

"Good God!" he muttered in consternation—and fear.

Leslie grabbed hold of Chaney's arm and pulled him from the immediate danger of having the destroyed light fixture and part of the flaming ceiling collapse on them.

Flames advanced across the entire ceiling now. With eyes transfixed, Leslie watched the plaster and paint darken and blister, crumbling to the sand. She pulled on Chaney again and moved them closer to one of the mirrored wall panels. Soon there would be nowhere else for them to go and the entire burning ceiling would fall upon them.

Over the noise of the fire, she heard the door to the crawlspace above bang. This was followed by a loud *whoosh* of the kind made by a strong gust of wind, and the door was quickly slammed shut again.

Chaney was more alert now. The two of them realized that it was not just their torture chamber that was being threatened by the inferno but the entire house itself. Leslie couldn't help wondering with a vengeful smile how Vane would explain the presence of two burned bodies in a secret room of his home to the firemen when they arrived with their water trucks to put out the blaze.

As Leslie and Chaney started to cough and choke from smoke inhalation, she became aware that the mirrored panel behind her was bumping against her back, as if someone were trying to push it open.

She slid away from the moving panel just as the floor-to-ceiling mirror covering it shattered from the force of a ferocious kick to the other side. Pieces flew everywhere into the sand around them. She and Chaney were lucky not to have been cut.

Vane rushed into the room. Leslie recognized him from the same dark pants and wheat-colored cardigan he was wearing when they'd met a day or so ago prior to her captivity.

In Vane's hand was a cylindrical object about two feet in length made of chrome. He looked quickly around the smoky room, spying Chaney lying inertly not far away. Leslie, also inert and apparently unconscious, lay near the broken panel-door.

With them safely out of commission, he looked freely up at the flames spewing from the ruined light fixture and racing across the ceiling. He'd been unable to get to the fire's source through the crawlspace as it was engulfed by flames. His only hope of containing the flames now was this new-fangled extinguisher he held in his hand.

The apparatus was operated by an integrated handle that when squeezed was capable of shooting up to two gallons of carbon tetrachloride onto a fire and quelling the flames. Or so he hoped.

Vane pointed the canister at the flames bursting from behind the angled light fixture and fired a thick stream of the liquid at the blaze. Miraculously the concoction, as advertised, worked almost immediately, suppressing the flames then extinguishing them outright.

The downside to this miracle was that the room, now engulfed in even more smoke, was making it difficult for Vane to see or breathe. Nevertheless, he continued shooting more carbon tetrachloride at the burning ceiling.

Leslie spotted one of the larger chunks of mirror that stuck in the sand. Her immediate thought was to grab it to use as a weapon. But it was just far enough away from her that any sudden movement she made toward it was bound to be seen in Vane's periphery.

But the open doorway, she realized, was much closer, and raised the possibility of her getting away unseen. She realized she would have to leave Chaney behind—temporarily at least until she could get to a phone and call for help. Her only hope was that she wouldn't be too late.

As the gray-black smoke from Vane's efforts to put out the fire grew thicker, Leslie managed to suppress a cough by holding her breath. She inched her way through the sand to the door's threshold, letting her breath out again with a gasp only when she had crawled through the doorway.

The stairs loomed before her. There was another open door at the top. With renewed strength and excitement, she started climbing the steps when suddenly *she felt a hand grip her ankle.*

Leslie twisted her body to see Vane toss away the now-empty canister and grab her other ankle, pulling her toward him. She tried kicking but his grip on her legs was too strong.

Leslie's terrified eyes met Vane's as he pulled her closer and closer. His face now contorted in fury, she could still not make out even the seams of a mask against his otherwise smooth skin.

She lashed out with her nails, shouting, "Let's see the monster you really are!" and raked his face hard.

With a strangled *yelp*, he let go of her legs and his hands went to his face.

Leslie looked down at her fingers in disbelief at his genuine pain and saw they were covered with blood and bits of torn flesh.

She looked up again to see Vane clutching at his clawed face, his mouth widening to let out a scream of distress. And in the light coming through the open door above, she saw in that mouth a deformed and twitching nub of what had once been a tongue.

This man she'd tricked for his fingerprints wasn't Vane at all but his vicious cohort Darrass.

And yet, she asked herself in bewilderment, how was that possible? They had spoken to each other!

THIRTY-SEVEN

**Enroute to the Residence
of Sebastian Vane**

"So that's how two people can masquerade as one," Adela Grant shouted above the noise of the rain and her rattling four-seater Model T. She struggled to keep the vehicle from sliding along the mud-slicked road. Beside her, Pierre Donnay bounced up and down as the automobile hit seemingly every bump in the Hollywood Hills.

"I'd always believed the stories about Cassell's talent for throwing his voice to be an exaggeration," Donnay shouted back. "But apparently he *is* the master illusionist that many people claimed. He can even put words in the mouth of a mute."

The Model T once more slid in the mud, but Grant reacted quickly and steered it back onto the straightaway, luckily escaping getting stuck.

"I'll have to get a new car after this trip," she fumed.

"Cut down on the cigarettes and you'll easily be able to afford one," Donnay teased.

She frowned at him and responded sarcastically: "Do you see a cigarette in my mouth?"

"No. But that's only because you don't have enough hands," he teased her some more. This time she gave him an outright dirty look.

"Anyway," he went on, still shouting over all the noise, "The way I see it now, Cassell learned from the facially wounded vets returning after the Great War that no mask ever created could convincingly simulate real flesh. Later, when he became Sebastian Vane, he could safely hide his deformity behind greasepaint, crepe hair and wigs when making a picture or publicizing one. He could be himself. But in other situations calling for him to be without make-up, he needed a surrogate normal-looking self.

"Darrass, a quite handsome fellow with unblemished, olive skin was about the same height and build as Cassell and a perfect substitute, except for one thing: He couldn't speak. He became Vane sans makeup, and the bewhiskered mute manservant Bahram was born so Cassell would always have a logical reason for being in Darrass' presence to feed him lines.

"It was a routine they had practiced and perfected, fooling everyone," he concluded. "Even Leslie, who mistakenly got hold of the wrong fingerprints."

Quickly, he changed the subject and inquired impatiently: "Can't you make this thing go any faster?"

Adela Grant scowled at him. "This 'thing'?" she mimicked petulantly. "Watch your mouth; Lizzie has feelings. She's taken you this far, hasn't she?"

Donnay patted the metal frame of his seat. "My apologies, Lizzie."

"That's better," Grant said.

Spotting something obscure up ahead, she leaned forward intently and squinted to see through the pelting rain as the car's wipers struggled to keep up. But in the dim glow from the car's headlamps she could not make out what it was.

Donnay followed her gaze. "Looks to me like a build-up of fog."

But Grant was already shaking her head negatively.

"It's not fog," she said forcefully, having just seen flames jump into the sky. "It's *smoke*."

Donnay looked again and saw flames himself. "How much farther is Vane's house?" he asked anxiously.

"My guess is we're already there," she said curtly.

She pushed the fuel to the floor and the automobile shimmied and bucked beneath them with a loud clatter as it lurched forward.

"Come on, Lizzie," Grant shouted at the straining vehicle: "*Move your ass!*"

Sebastian Vane Residence
Hollywood Hills, California

Minutes earlier, Leslie's uncle had pulled his truck to the side of the road leading to the circular drive fronting Vane's lavish Spanish-style home. He had killed the engine and, as instructed, prepared to wait for Donnay and company to arrive.

As he sat there impatiently twiddling his thumbs, he noticed that many of the lights were on, but there was no movement inside, not that he could make out anyway. What he did observe were tendrils of fine mist oozing from the window and door frames.

He stepped out of the truck into the rain for a less obstructed view and saw that the weird mist was now oozing faster and in greater volume, thickening into a white cloud. His eyes moved to the front windows and he saw smoke billowing inside.

The house was ablaze.

The man's thoughts went instantly to his niece: *My God, don't let her be in there!*

Ignoring Donnay's instructions, he raced for the house and in seconds was pulling on the front door, but it was locked. As were the two front windows on the ground floor.

He returned quickly to his truck and grabbed a shovel from among the tools he kept in the back.

At the house again, he swung the shovel with all his strength at the larger of the two front windows, then instantly stepped back as the window exploded in a shower of glass. The noise of the shattering glass was followed by a loud gust of smoke and flame drawn out by the fresh air.

When both had cleared, he knocked the remaining shards from the window frame and climbed inside, glancing every which way for a sign of his niece. Nothing.

Before actively launching a search for her, however, he unlocked the front door for Donnay and the others.

He moved into the sunken living room area where he heard what sounded to him like a fight coming from off to his right. He saw an open door. It led to another room downstairs. Smoke was moving up the steps.

Still struggling to get away, Leslie felt Darrass' returned hold on her ankle suddenly loosen then give way. Though severely weakened by coughing and trying to breathe, she managed to hasten up a few more steps.

Pausing to look back, she saw the reason why Darrass had let go of her. Chaney had the manservant in an arm-lock around the legs and was holding on with the strength of a rabid dog no matter how hard Darrass beat him about the head and shoulders to let go.

Leslie started to inch back down the stairs to help Chaney but was suddenly held back by yet another pair of muscular arms. She looked up into the beaming face of her uncle, who pulled her up the remaining steps and out to the living room. Her heart leaped. She was saved.

Just then the open front door burst wider and she saw a drenched Pierre Donnay shamble in followed by a second party she couldn't identify in all the swirling smoke.

Donnay dropped to his knees and took her hands, kissing them. "I'm so sorry," he said almost out of breath. "Please tell me you're not hurt."

"I'm...fine," she whispered hoarsely, feeling giddy at his touch. "But if you don't get downstairs to Lon Chaney, Darrass will kill him."

Donnay turned to Adela Grant and asked her to take Leslie away from the house fast. As the reporter helped to support the girl, it still hadn't dawned on Leslie in her weakened state just who this person was. But she was grateful for the help all the same.

As Grant led Leslie from the burning house, Donnay and her uncle hastened to the top of the stairs and looked below, seeing part of some weird room, the floor covered with sand and numerous pieces of reflective glass embedded in it. The room was engulfed in flame.

At the bottom, Darrass was clubbing Chaney with a large canister while the actor stubbornly held onto the manservant's legs.

Before Donnay could even react, Leslie's uncle hurtled down the stairs, snatched the canister from Darrass' hands and tossed it aside. He clutched the man's collar and pulled him from Chaney's grasp to his feet. Instantly Darrass struggled to turn around and fight back, but his stance was too awkward and

Leslie's uncle easily pitched him aside. Darrass fell face down on the sand in the burning room and let out a barely audible "*oompf*."

Leslie's uncle grabbed Chaney by the legs while Donnay took him under the arms and together they maneuvered the listless man up the stairs and out of the house.

Donnay charged back inside and stopped at the head of the stairs. Darrass had managed to roll over on his back and Donnay could see a chunk of glass protruding from his chest. His shirt was thick with blood.

"Where's Cassell?" Donnay bellowed, instantly feeling like a fool as he remembered Darrass couldn't speak.

The stoic manservant raised his right hand and pointed his finger at Donnay in an accusing manner, or maybe it was just a plea for help.

Either way it was too late for him. Darrass let out a guttural roar of fear, of pain, or of both as the torture room ceiling collapsed in flames upon him.

Adela Grant yanked open the door of her Model T and pushed Leslie inside. The girl was shivering and so Grant removed her raincoat, draped it over Leslie's shoulders and pulled it tight.

It was in this fleeting moment that Leslie recognized her benefactor at last. Instead of being furious at the sight of Grant, however, she was just confused.

"Why…are *you*…helping me?" the girl stammered.

Without missing a beat and in her best hard-nosed style, but with a wry grin, Grant answered, "You said it yourself. Because I'll do *anything* for a story."

They each laughed.

Grant shut the door and hurried around to the driver's side, where she climbed in out of the stinging rain. She'd no sooner closed her door than Leslie's uncle showed up with Lon Chaney and she got out again to let them in.

Chaney was standing on his own now and was able to clamber into the back seat without much help. Leslie's uncle quickly followed and Grant got back inside.

Through the rain-soaked windscreen, Leslie could see Donnay in the distance. He was hurrying towards them, backlit by the burning house, that was now entirely in flames.

Once assured that Donnay was not trapped inside, Leslie looked in the back at Chaney. "How are you feeling?" she asked with concern. He was shivering too. As was her uncle.

"Wonderfully cold," he responded with irony. "But what I wouldn't give for a thick, juicy steak and a cigarette, not in that order."

Grant reached into her purse and got out an open pack of Camels. "Can't help with the first, but I've got you covered on the second," she said, handing him a cigarette. She struck a match and lit his then one of her own.

Chaney drew in the smoke and let it out slowly with a look that seemed almost rapturous. "You're a life saver," he said to Grant. Then he turned to Leslie and offered with deep feeling, "You are too, Miss Paige."

The passenger door flew open and Donnay stuck his soaking head inside. "We're getting your car all wet, Adela," he said. She shrugged a "so what" and puffed away.

Donnay took Leslie's hand again and searched her eyes. "Are you sure you're okay?" he asked, his voice cracking slightly.

"Yes," she said weakly, her throat still raw from the smoke-filled torture room. "I'm feeling a lot better," she added with contentment, although she looked exhausted.

"Where's Cassell? Was he in there too?" Donnay asked hurriedly.

"I don't think so. Just Darrass. And us," Leslie replied. She started to cough and quickly cleared her throat. "I...think he went out somewhere."

"Any idea where?" Donnay probed.

She shook her head. "I only know that when I told him the rumors about the studio's plans to add some comedy to the picture, he got really upset. I could hear the rage in his voice — though it wasn't his."

"You've guessed the truth then," Donnay said with admiration.

"That Cassell spoke for him? Yes. Down in that room when I scratched Darrass' face bloody, still thinking he was Vane, I figured out the whole thing with him and Bahram must have been a charade."

"But where would Cassell have gone?" Donnay threw out to everyone in frustration.

"Back to the studio for more sabotage," Adela Grant quickly speculated.

"Like what?" Donnay countered. "He's already tried kidnapping and sabotaging every standing set."

Lon Chaney sat up straight as he was struck by a possibility. He looked Donnay squarely in the eye and said dramatically: *"Every set but one."*

THIRTY-EIGHT

Subterranean Lake Set
Universal Studios

There's a common joke among old time Angelinos about the 51-mile long L. A. River: "It ain't much to look at as rivers go. But it's all ours." The joke is the word *all*.

For most of the year, the L.A. River is practically a dry bed, a trickle. But during the rainy season, that trickle turns into a raging torrent that can overflow the river's banks and cause severe flood damage to structures and property nearby. Just as it did some years ago to Universal's back lot, which the river runs alongside on its way to the ocean.

This situation is made even more hazardous because the almost 365 days of dryness makes the river a good dumping ground throughout the year for outdated or unwanted junk— old appliances and furniture, damaged goods, old construction materials, and so on. As the river swells and surges forth during rainy season, this debris becomes a lethal part of the raging tide. As a result, should any hapless animals or other creatures accidentally fall in, drowning is not always the cause of death.

Universal's Carl Laemmle learned a valuable lesson from a destructive flood back in the teens and he reinforced the lot's banks along the river. It was upon a section of these banks that the studio constructed the elaborate outdoor subterranean lake set for its production of *The Phantom of the Opera*.

Unlike other large sets replicated for the picture, such as the opera house's spectacular auditorium, the subterranean lake set was neither designed nor built to scale. Only a square, proscenium-arch view of a portion of the original was constructed. It showed a representative section of the opera house's open underground rooms, a portion of the foundation itself, and the platform running along that foundation.

A small-scale Venetian gondola roped to the platform for the Phantom to move about in embellished the otherwise prosaic wooden boat the "Opera Ghost" had actually used for traveling. Finally, the set was given a vaulted ceiling for hanging lights as well as to keep out the elements in the event of a storm while shooting.

The drawings of veteran art director, sketch artist and painter Ben Carré were used as the basis for the design and construction of all the picture's sets because Carré had visited the actual locale, including the subterranean lake, and could attest to the authenticity of his work.

A low wall in the foreground of the set held back the water, which had been hauled in by truck. Built into the wall was an artificial dam that acted as a sluice gate. After production was finished, the crew would open the gate, releasing all the water safely through the sluice and down into the river. Movie magic.

As he looked over the set, which also included a small platform built over the sluice gate for the camera, Arik Cassell could see that a residual effect of all this rain was that the lake's man-made water level had risen considerably and was starting to spill over the top of the wall, weakening the set's support structure even without his intervention, much to his delight.

Perhaps because the design of the set replicated only a fraction of the actual locale, it impressed Cassell as more realistic and transported him for a moment back into the nether world of the Grand Garnier.

Only the presence of the gondola robbed him of his feelings of nostalgia. Gaston Leroux and Hollywood were made for each other, he thought derisively. Each traded in fantasy.

Cassell could see that one of the set's support columns in the front also seemed a bit shaky from the buffeting wind and rain. But this alone would not bring the structure down. *He* must do that. And he knew precisely how.

He had concealed his automobile, a cobalt-blue Isotta Fraschini luxury car imported from Italy, behind the large, makeshift work shed where the tools for constructing the set were likely kept. He guessed it would be locked as there was no guard around, probably due to the inclement weather. But he figured he could easily break in if needing something. The primary ingredient, he had in abundance—more than enough to bring Universal to its financial knees by bringing down their expensive set.

It amazed him how easily it was to obtain this lethal ingredient in America. Back in France, he would have had to jump through all kinds of regulatory hoops to get his hands on some dynamite legally. So, he had Darrass steal some sticks off a construction site. But in the land of the free, one could go into any farmer's supply store here in the Valley and buy out the place with no questions asked.

As raindrops trickled uncomfortably down his neck, Cassell pulled up the collar of his raincoat. It was time for the bastards to pay for trifling with his story. Morning was coming and so he got quickly to work.

Leslie's uncle pressed on the gas to make the truck go as fast as he dared through the thick mud of the Hollywood Hills. Dawn was coming on quickly and some welcome light was brightening the sky, an indication, perhaps, that the seemingly endless rain was at last slowing down. He knew of a back way onto the expansive Universal lot that would lead to the river.

Crowded into the front seat next to him were Leslie and Donnay. They had left Adela Grant and Lon Chaney behind in her car to await the arrival of the authorities, assuming some astute homesteader called to report the fire. Without access to a phone, the five survivors of the inferno were helpless to do so. The Vane house was now a smoldering ruin.

As the truck turned out of the Hollywood Hills, the sound of firefighters in their noisy water trucks and several police car sirens could be heard heading toward them. All that could be hoped for now, Donnay considered, was that the fire might be contained from spreading and scorching more earth and expensive homes.

The truck bounced hard as it left the mud and hit several ruts in the wet scrub grass. Leslie and Donnay covered their heads with their hands to prevent being concussed by the truck's low metal roof. Leslie's uncle though seemed used to such rough terrain and took the gyrations in his stride.

Within moments, the L.A. River came into view, the turbulent, debris-filled water churning swiftly along.

"There!" the uncle shouted, pointing his finger.

"I thought you said the riverbed was mostly dry," Donnay commented above the roaring water.

"What I said was it's *usually* dryer than a bone," Leslie's uncle shot back. "Except for the time o' year when it rains hard. Why? You're not plannin' on swimmin' across, are you?"

"I think I see the set—the back of it anyway," Leslie shouted.

"Must be," her uncle said upon sighting the looming structure. "It looks out of place in all this *emptiness*." He turned to Donnay and joked, "You're in luck. You won't have to swim over, the set is on this side."

"We'd better stop," Donnay said. "If Cassell's there we don't want him to see or hear us coming."

The uncle pulled the truck behind a large Valley Oak and killed the engine. The tree's branches were well shorn of their yellow leaves for the winter, but the tree was big enough to still provide plenty of cover.

Donnay started to get out of the truck when Leslie clutched his arm. "I'm going with you," she said.

"No, you're not," he replied firmly. "You know how dangerous Cassell is. With what you've been through, you're no match for him. Your uncle neither. And I can't be worried about you two while I'm in there." He looked pleadingly to her uncle. *"Please make sure she stays put."*

The uncle nodded, adding, "Look under your seat."

"Why? What?" Donnay mumbled as he did what he was told and his eyes fell on a pistol.

"Take it with you," the uncle urged. "I use it to scare off foxes and coyotes after my chickens," he explained. "It's only got blanks. But Cassell won't know that." He smiled.

Donnay stuffed the none-too-shiny Colt automatic pistol into the pocket of his raincoat, stepped out of the truck and set off into the downpour.

He approached the large set at the river's edge as furtively as possible It consisted of a huge false front supporting a vaulted ceiling, all held up by a network of two-by-fours, heavy cross-beams, steel bars and other construction apparatus.

Donnay glanced back at the truck. No one was following. So far, so good, he thought as he stepped between a pair of cross-beams and moved toward an enormous backdrop.

There was a slit in the backdrop through which he squeezed onto the set's recreation of the actual locale's platform and foundation. The painted backdrop behind showed a portion of the honeycomb of open rooms beneath the edifice.

The sealed tank that contained the set's artificial lake was full to the brim and was already sloshing over the top of the low foreground wall from the excess rain blown in by the wind.

Donnay couldn't gauge the depth of the artificial lake, but figured it couldn't be more than four feet, enough to slow him down significantly if he tried wading through it to look for Cassell. He opted for the gondola roped to the foundation instead. He climbed in, untied the rope, and pushed off with a long pole.

As he glided across the lake, he couldn't help but observe how realistically the set designer and his construction workers had fashioned their facsimile. It was almost *too real*—especially to him as his thoughts revisited his brush with death in the actual lake more than a dozen years ago.

He could almost feel the ice-cold water lapping against his face, then covering it, filling his nostrils and his mouth with the foul taste of subterranean waste water. He remembered choking, his eyes no longer able to discern anything but the bubbles carrying his dwindling supply of air to the surface.

"Monsieur le *procureur*," came a shout from off to Donnay's right, returning him to the present. "Again we meet," the mellifluous voice went on. "Although I would have thought once would have been enough for you."

Donnay dropped the pole, thrusting his hand into his coat pocket for the gun. He followed the source of the voice to the far rear corner of the set, and once more glimpsed the deadly, commanding figure of the "Opera Ghost."

Cassell had doffed his overcoat, but was still wearing the make-up and the long robe and costume of the manservant Bahram. He was tying an object to a wooden strut. Although Donnay couldn't make out what the object was, he could guess. And he realized Cassell was planning to destroy the set with a replay of his trusty dynamite trick.

"And yet here you are once more, having tracked me down this far," Cassell continued blithely as he finished tying off the bound-together sticks of dynamite.

"Once would have been enough, I agree," Donnay shouted back. "Except that you had escaped French justice, Cassell." His fingers tightened around the gun in his pocket.

"You even know my real name. I'm impressed," Cassell returned, sounding as if he really were impressed. "But this time you have no army of gendarmes of even *flics* to help you," the fiend scoffed.

"Nevertheless, you're *finished*, Cassell," Donnay thundered back. "Your accomplice Darrass is dead. Your estate is in ashes. Your career in pictures is over. Even your drug empire is coming to an end."

Cassell started to move closer to the dynamite, but froze as Donnay instantly had the pistol out and pointing at him.

Donnay gestured with the pistol for Cassell to move away from the dynamite. He did.

"You're a liar!" Cassell roared back.

"He's right, *Bahram!*" caustically shouted a female voice from the opposite end of the platform where Cassell was standing.

Donnay's eyes snapped to the source and he saw Leslie defiantly confronting her tormentor, the former Sebastian Vane. Her uncle stood beside her, a coil of rope slung over his shoulder.

"I told you to stay away," Donnay hollered at them, fearful they might get hurt. "He planted dynamite near where he's standing."

"You...you're...," Cassell stammered, his eyes still on Leslie, unable to comprehend how she could still be —

"Alive?" She sneered at him. "Yes, and so is Mr. Chaney, no thanks to you or that lapdog of yours, *who isn't*. That room got a little too warm after you left and finally lit up like a torch."

"*You betrayed me, Christine,*" Cassell accused her bitterly.

"How could I betray a fraud?" Leslie accused him back. "And I'm *not* Christine. *There is no Christine* —except in your own sick mind," she taunted. "There's only what *you* want, what *you* need. Nothing and no one else matters—including Darrass, who remained your faithful puppet right to the end."

"For God's sake, Leslie, don't goad him," Donnay started to warn her when the gondola suddenly shifted beneath his feet from the roiling water that was pulling the craft steadily toward the sluice gate.

The gondola thudded against the wall, knocking Donnay off his feet. The gun slipped from his hand and slid toward the bow as he tried to catch himself, but sprawled on his back.

Panicking, he saw Cassell pull two more bound sticks of dynamite seemingly out of the air, but more likely from beneath his robe in a display of his skillful sleight of hand. Then, with equal swiftness, Cassell held out his right arm, his finger pointed directly at Donnay.

The tip of the finger burst into flame in yet another display of the magician's prowess and touched the tip of the short fuse attached to the dynamite. As Donnay looked on in mounting fear, Cassell tossed the explosives with precision into the gondola, where they landed between Donnay's feet.

Leslie screamed and her uncle pulled her back.

With no time to douse the fast-burning fuse, Donnay reacted instinctively and threw himself over the side of the gondola into the frigid water, hoping to be shielded himself, at least somewhat, from the impact of the blast.

Even through closed eyes as he tried swimming away, Donnay could see the bright, orange light of the explosion as it consumed the gondola and much of the construction nearby.

More powerfully, he could *feel* the shock wave as it tossed him about in the rank water. His ears were ringing but otherwise he couldn't hear a thing. He struggled to keep holding his breath.

Within seconds the artificial lake's surface was showered with splinters and other small bits and pieces of the destroyed gondola and set. Donnay felt a much larger chunk—from the gondola's hull, perhaps—strike his back as it splashed down. His breath exploded and he fought to get to the surface before his lungs filled with water. In his mind, the nightmare beneath the Grand Garnier was happening all over again.

Leslie and her uncle were knocked off their feet by the shock wave from the explosion, which had prompted the entire set to shake for a brief moment. She could see Donnay struggling in the water as it swept through the now-jagged opening where the sluice gate had once been, plunging into the river.

"Uncle Arno, we've got to help him. He could be hurt," she cried out as she got back on her feet.

"We will. But first wait here and don't move," he shouted back. He took off in a run through the billowing smoke from the blast to the far end of the platform where Cassell had been, but found him no longer there. Cassell had vanished.

Quickly, Uncle Arno located the dynamite planted earlier by Cassell but left unlit in the clever fiend's haste to disappear.

He tore them from the strut to which they'd been tied. Then he took off, running back to his niece, the explosives cradled under his arm. He planned to dispose of them in the river the first chance he got.

Leslie was climbing down off the platform into the water. The level had now sunk by half as thousands of gallons had already spilled into the river.

"I told you not to move!" her uncle reproached her. "Is this how you mind your parents?"

He began uncoiling the rope from his shoulder. "I was planning to tie Cassell up with this when we caught him, but he's gone. We'll use it to wade across instead so we don't get carried off," he explained above the din. "Here, take this end." She did as he asked while he tied the other end to the foundation. He carried the bulk of the rope, un-spooling it carefully as they made their way across the roiling wet stage.

His back throbbing where the chunk of gondola had struck him, Donnay thrashed away until he broke the water's surface and gasped for air. He was able to get his bearings sufficiently to see that he was being swiftly pulled by the fast-draining artificial lake toward the huge opening in the ruined wall.

As the void left by the demolished wall neared, Donnay grabbed hold of a still-intact section and clung to it as more rain blown in by wind stung his eyes and the swirling current covered his face again.

A pair of arms seized hold of him. Leslie? Her uncle?

Donnay had once more submerged, but this time only briefly as two strong hands pulled him back up. Unable to do more than sputter, Donnay would like to have expressed his eternal gratitude—except that the two hands were now around his throat. Ferociously they squeezed as the contorted face of Arik Cassell—or rather his alter ego Bahram—stared back in false dark beard dripping with water.

Donnay grabbed at the man's hands and tried pulling them away, but as he did so, the force of Cassell's bearing down on his throat pushed him below the water again.

Letting go with one hand, Donnay managed to take a swing at his assailant's face. He only caught the man's chin, ripping away the beard, which came off with a strip of malleable "flesh" deeply tanned with greasepaint.

Donnay fought harder still, lashing out and raking the man's face with his fingertips, tearing off more strips of the false visage to reveal the hideous true face of the phantom of the opera beneath—that of a yellowish-white, ghastly scarred skull that lived.

The robe Cassell wore as the manservant was soaked and getting cumbersome. He unhooked the collar and shrugged the robe from his shoulders, where it bunched at his waist, sodden and heavy.

Gripping Donnay's throat with both hands again, Cassell dragged the still submerged Frenchman toward the void and the fast-moving river beyond.

Donnay's hands flailed at Cassell's face for another punch, but the effort proved useless. He was weakening from lack of oxygen intake, his lungs about to burst.

Donnay could sense himself being pulled along, topsy-turvy, through the filthy water when something large and solid banged painfully against his already aching back. He tried opening his eyes to see what it was, but the grit of the muddy water forced him to snap them shut again, and whatever the object was got swept away. River junk, he guessed.

No longer able to hold his breath as Cassell pulled him along, Donnay's mouth involuntarily snapped open to suck in air but what he got instead was a mouthful of muddy froth. His lungs screamed for oxygen, but got only silt from the river. He was drowning. *Again.*

The water now just above their ankles Leslie and her uncle hurried as fast as they could to get to Donnay in time — if they weren't too late already. As they increased their pace, they saw Cassell's upper body snap straight, then he fell back into the swollen river. His robe had caught on a large piece of driftwood. Still twisted about his waist, the fabric snatched him from his quarry. Cassell barely kept from going under himself by grabbing onto some thick roots in the riverbank and holding on for dear life.

Leslie's uncle climbed onto the river bank and made a grab for Donnay's legs. He'd taken the end of the rope from his niece and now coiled it around the Frenchman's ankles, tying it securely.

"Pull!" he shouted to his niece who was now holding most of the rope. She prayed for strength as she tugged.

With both of them drawing hard on the rope, Donnay's limp form emerged feet first from the river and was pulled to rest on a slab of some wreckage.

Uncle Arno pumped Donnay's arms frantically as Leslie blew air into the Frenchman's mouth, pleading silently for him to "Please, please, my love, come back to me."

But Donnay didn't respond. His eyes had rolled back and his chest was barely rising and falling.

"Look!" her uncle yelled.

Still covering Donnay's mouth with hers and blowing air, Leslie's eyes followed her uncle's stare.

The floundering Arik Cassell had since gained a foothold on the slippery riverbank and was trying to leverage himself out of the river to safety. But to paraphrase the old saying, he was a bit late and a lot short. He never saw the group of old, disused and rusted steel construction rods hurtling toward him in the flood.

One of the rods struck him squarely in the left eye, passed through his brain, and burst out the back of his skull. There hadn't been enough time for him even to scream as he never knew what hit him. His lifeless body sunk beneath the water to be carried eventually out to sea. The phantom of the opera was no more.

Donnay coughed suddenly as water spilled from his mouth and splashed Leslie in the face.

She eased Donnay upright and hugged him close, overjoyed. More muddy froth dribbled from his lips and he started drawing in deep breaths.

Leslie kissed his hand, his forehead, his cheek but saved his mouth for last. She had prayed for him to come back to her and he had.

Smiling on the two of them, Leslie's uncle withdrew the sticks of dynamite from his pocket and threw them into the river where they quickly sunk from the weight of their no-longer-lethal payload.

Pierre Donnay massaged his aching throat as he looked up into the lovely eyes of Leslie Paige, which were now wet with happiness. He took in another glimpse of her uncle's sober but relaxed face, as well.

He savored the sweet air and even the icy rain that continued pelting them but with much less force. He was grateful to be alive and kissed Leslie deeply to express his feelings.

She responded eagerly and pulled him closer still, noticing that he appeared much rested and even quite at ease.

Donnay stretched like a cat as he looked once more up at her. "And so," he inquired softly, "what have I missed?"

EPILOGUE

1925 and Later

THIRTY-NINE

Hollywood

Leslie Paige/Pagano, her uncle, and Pierre Donnay all survived without major injury.

Arik Cassell a.k.a. Erik, the Phantom of the Opera, perished in the debris-choked L.A. River. His body was never recovered. But this time two credible eye witnesses could affirm that he truly had perished.

Bowing to pressure from Universal, authorities ruled the deaths of the studio's popular star Sebastian Vane and his manservant to have been an accident caused by faulty wiring in Vane's home in the Hollywood Hills. The misinformation was widely reported and accepted around the world.

Studio head Carl Laemmle leaned heavily on his contacts within the Los Angeles County Police Department to hush up the identity and crimes of Sebastian Vane a.k.a. Arik Cassell a.k.a. the phantom of the opera. He did so in an effort to protect Universal's $1 million-plus investment from suffering commercially due to notoriety and scandal.

Laemmle next rolled the dice once more by authorizing repair of the sabotaged subterranean lake set and production of the much-debated comic relief scenes so that *Phantom* could be completed, sneak previewed with the public and prepared for release.

The preview was held in late January, 1925, and the audience reacted with a cascade of hisses and boos, catcalls and raspberries along with a stream of reaction cards chiding the studio for "diluting the horror." Uncle Carl ordered the comic relief removed.

Additionally, the low-key, death-from-a-broken-heart finale was replaced with a more harrowing *denouement* in which Lon Chaney's Phantom in skull make-up is pursued by the first of what would become a long line of revenge-seeking extras in Universal thrillers to come. They beat the ogre to death then toss his body into the Seine.

When released at the end of 1925, Universal's troubled production of *The Phantom of the Opera* was an audience smash. Most critics also gave it raves, lauding particularly Chaney's make-up as Gaston Leroux's skull-faced "Opera Ghost," especially in the unmasking scene, which, they warned, was not for the faint of heart.

The unmasking scene continues to shock audiences to this day with its power, and for good reason. It was eventually decided by Carl Laemmle that the original footage of the deformed Arik Cassell playing himself in this horrific scene was too powerful and shocking not to use. Lon Chaney urged this himself ("How could I ever top the genuine article?" he is alleged to have said.) The actor and Universal then made an agreement that word of the Cassell footage should never get out. It is the only instance in any picture where, with or without make-up, Chaney is, in movie parlance, "doubled."

Lon Chaney would continue to thrill audiences as the undisputed "man of a thousand faces" until his death on August

26, 1930, at age forty-seven of complications from bronchial lung cancer. He had made only one talking picture, *The Unholy Three*. In it, he plays a carnival performer and clever criminal who also is a master of disguise and an accomplished ventriloquist.

Reporter Adela Grant never got to publish her scoop. Under threat of an expensive lawsuit she was convinced by her attorney that she would lose, she accepted an offer from Carl Laemmle to write scenarios for the studio at $1,200 a week. Fed up when none of her scenarios got made, however, Grant turned her back on Hollywood in 1928 and headed for Chicago where crime and scandal were still the life-blood of newspapers, and reporters were seldom if ever hushed up. She scored a big following with her bylined exposés of mobster Al Capone's gangland activities (even he was said to have enjoyed her work) and her coverage of the infamous St. Valentine's Day massacre in 1929.

Adela Grant continued writing about Midwestern "crimes of the century" until her death from lung cancer on Sunday morning December 7, 1941, just as the Japanese were writing the first lines of the biggest scoop she ever could have imagined with their surprise attack on the U.S. Naval Base at Pearl Harbor. She was sixty-three.

Where Cassell and his accomplice had stashed their shrinking supply of illegal drugs was never discovered. And with his death, the Corsican mob's monopoly on the Southern California drug trade in opium and other illicit substances evaporated. It was taken over in the coming years by a succession of ethnic gangs.

The death by suicide or murder of tarnished studio executive Victor Reilly remains one of Hollywood's lesser known but still discussed unsolved mysteries.

Pierre Donnay was shocked when Adela Grant called with the news that his doppelganger, internationally loved screen comic Max Linder, had died in Paris on December 16, 1924, of an apparent suicide. Donnay recalled the many times he'd been mistaken for the film star, often feeling irritated at the mix-up. Now he felt as though he'd lost a twin brother. Later, after his return to France, he grew back his thin, dark mustache and resumed using a cane for a walking stick as a personal homage to his deceased look-alike.

For flamboyant director Rupert Julian (real name Percy Hayes), the back-to-back triumphs of *Merry-Go-Round* (1924) and *The Phantom of the Opera* (1925) were huge feathers in his swelling cap. He viewed himself as a master of the moving picture art—the "new Stroheim"—but was, in fact, just a journeyman craftsman who never enjoyed similar success again. He retired from filmmaking after directing *The Cat Creeps* (1930) and one other talkie that same year. He died in 1943 at age sixty-four.

"Junior" Laemmle was appointed Universal's production chief by his dad in 1928. He was just twenty years old. He lavished money on each picture, turning out a steady stream of hits (*All Quiet on the Western Front, Dracula, Frankenstein, The Bride of Frankenstein, Showboat, et al*) as well as a series of expensive flops. By 1935 the studio was so much in the red that his dad [who died in 1939] was forced to sell and "Junior" was fast out of a job. He spent the next forty-plus years cashing stock dividends and being a playboy, presumably never working another day in his life, which ended in 1979. He was seventy-one.

Frustrated by the closed-mouth outcome of his stateside investigation, Pierre Donnay made immediate plans to return to France where he hoped for a more receptive and open hearing. As soon as he completed his report for Gaston Leroux, he planned to submit a copy to the Minister of Justice as well, bypassing the police hierarchy and the office of the chief public prosecutor, M. Severin.

Leslie Paige and Pierre Donnay spent the Christmas and New Year's holidays together, much of the time at the Pagano chicken ranch, where Leslie's aunt and uncle treated him like a son. As the teary-eyed lovers parted at the Central train station the second week in January for Donnay's return journey to Paris, they promised to write each other every day. And they agreed that as soon as Donnay had re-established himself professionally and she had saved up enough money for a ticket, she would visit.

Through the efforts of Lon Chaney, Leslie was offered a seven-year contract by Metro at $400 a week. After she signed, her screen name underwent another change. She was permitted to keep her actual last name of Pagano but her first became Victoria, which she hated because it implied an unwanted image of royalty. Her lustrous dark hair and olive complexion made her ideal for roles as "that other woman," which she played in a series of marital triangle comedies and dramas over the next several years. But she eventually grew bored with the stagnancy of these parts and wrote to her lover with dismay, "This isn't acting, it's sleepwalking!"

Disillusioned with the picture business, Leslie decided to quit acting altogether, her bank account fat enough by then to afford a first-class passage. But before she could quit she was abruptly given the sack. Talkies had arrived and Leslie's flat, Midwestern accent didn't go with her somewhat imperious and mildly exotic screen persona. Studio head Louis B. Mayer told her in a blunt but fatherly way that neither casting nor any other department on the lot knew what to do with her now. Happily free as a bird, she eagerly wrote to the overjoyed Donnay that she would be seeing him soon. And set off for France via New York in the next few days.

Paris

Pierre Donnay spent most of his cross-country journey home by writing to Leslie as promised while also developing his report on the new world misdeeds of the infamous "Opera Ghost," Arik Cassell.

He finished the report aboard ship during the last lap of his journey. Soon he reunited with his friend Michel Blier in Paris. The following evening after Blier's shift at the "Three-Six," they holed up in Donnay's apartment—well-maintained by the always protective Madame Delon, who furnished them food and snacks—to polish the report.

Donnay had prepared himself as best he could for every conceivable reaction to his finished report by the minister of justice—except for the one he received. The minister's deepest concern was the image of laziness, incompetence, and outright deceit the report presented of certain individuals within the "Three-Six," the Ministère de la Justice, and thus the institutions themselves. And so the cover-up was preserved. But there were some reforms:

In keeping with the procedures of many governmental bureaucracies, Etienne Verneuil of the "Three-Six" and Chief Public Prosecutor M. Severin were severely chastised for their conduct, dismissed, and summarily *promoted*—albeit to positions of little consequence where they could do no damage as they had no responsibilities (except to keep their mouths shut).

Under current circumstances, which would require the former *procureur* to keep his silence as well, the minister suggested that the public prosecutor's office was probably no longer a good fit for Donnay, and the latter agreed. Pierre Donnay was thus free to pursue any employment opportunity he desired, including in law enforcement, but elsewhere in France. The minister offered to provide him with sterling references in exchange for never saying anything publicly about the phantom of the opera case. Donnay had reluctantly gone along, but added that he had no control over the pen of author Gaston Leroux. He had financed the overseas investigation and had a copy of the report, as well. But the minister appeared unconcerned.

Donnay was considerably heartened by the reaction to his report from the wealthy novelist himself. Leroux said he'd found the narrative of the investigation to be "chilling," "mesmerizing," "a riveting tale of crime and punishment" that "would make one hell of a book."

Donnay was overjoyed, but then shocked by what happened next. Leroux then explained that as a sequel to his most famous novel, Donnay's revelations would also make hash of the original's widely accepted embellishments and fanciful alterations of fact. "I couldn't do that to my friend Carl Laemmle who is about to release his expensive picture version to the world," he told the dejected Donnay. "If successful, the picture will likely boost sales of my book and that will ensure it stays in print," he concluded enthusiastically. "What's the government's response to the report?" he asked Donnay with trepidation.

"Same as yours," Donnay assured him, "but for different reasons." The novelist had appeared visibly relieved by this news.

Nevertheless, Leroux did entertain writing a new adventure featuring his infamous villain. But, alas, died suddenly at his home in Nice, France, on April 15, 1927, at age fifty-eight, having written just four words of a possible title: *Return of the Phantom*.

Pierre Donnay's professional fortunes took a dramatic turn for the better in the autumn of 1927 when he was appointed magistrate of the regional court for le département of Versailles by a special panel of the High Court of the Judiciary. There he presided over the investigative hearings of all regional criminal cases recommended to him by the local public prosecutor. The appointment was for life; he could not be removed from the position except by constitutional order or his passing.

In private, Donnay seldom talked about the "Opera Ghost" case even with intimates, and not at all in public—except once when he wrote a brief letter to Christine Delfont and her husband. He assured them they could now live their lives openly and without fear of any vengeful reprisal from their former tormentor. Donnay wrote that he had definitive firsthand proof that their nemesis was indeed dead. He felt this guarantee of safety was the very least the actual Christine was owed by French authorities.

Leslie Pagano and Pierre Donnay were reunited at last in the summer of 1928 with her promised visit. She never went back. Their mountain of correspondence had brought them even closer together, and they were married in a small ceremony the following June. It was attended by Leslie's beloved parents, her treasured aunt and uncle, as well as by Michel Blier ("Best Man") and Madame Delon ("Bridesmaid").

The newlyweds purchased a small farmhouse in the lush countryside midway between the town of Versailles and the Sanatorium Boldieu where Donnay's second adventure with Arik Cassell had its start.

Thereafter, Madame Donnay devoted herself to raising goats, some chickens, and a family. The couple had two children: Josette and Michel Pierre.

Josette grew up to become a successful actress in French films under the *nom de screen* of Josette Paige.

Michel Pierre followed in his father's footsteps and went into the law. He steadily rose in prominence as a trial lawyer and in 1958 achieved that which was denied his father when he was appointed the country's Chief Public Prosecutor.

Acknowledgments

Warm regards and heartfelt thanks to retired Universal Studios make-up artist, film historian and Lon Chaney biographer Michael F. Blake. Mike appeared in my video docu-series *The Fearmakers* (1996), most notably in the episode on director Tod Browning and his favorite star, Lon Chaney. With five books on Chaney to his credit so far, Mike probably knows more about the actor and his films than anyone alive, including Chaney's family. So, who better to turn to for the rarest information of all—background on the whereabouts and recreation of the subterranean lake set in *Phantom*? And boy did he deliver with full descriptions from his own research of all I needed to know—information he'd obtained himself from his firsthand interview with *Phantom*'s chief cinematographer, Charles Van Enger. You're the best, Mike!

Kevin Brownlow, dean of silent era film historians and preservationists. Kevin graciously loaned me a photocopy of the chapter on the set design of the 1925 *Phantom of the Opera* from the unpublished memoir in his archives of Ben Carré, the film's sketch artist. The chapter focuses mostly on the recreation of the Paris Opera's huge auditorium and giant chandelier plus the lobby's equally elaborate grand staircase. But Carré's descriptions of these actual locales he'd seen personally and sketched for Universal's construction department put the reader right there, a feeling I hope *Masquerade* communicates too. Many thanks, Kevin, for your professional and personal generosity.

My good friend Audrey E. Kupferberg, film historian, archivist, and co-author of a number of film books with her late husband, Rob Edelman. Audrey read the entire manuscript in installments as they were completed. Her enthusiasm for the project and excitement to get her hands on each new installment surely kept my nose to the grindstone, if only not to disappoint her. In addition, Audrey proofread the manuscript and checked it for any factual errors. I am in her debt. Any remaining mistakes are mine alone.

Film historian and archivist Scott MacQueen whom I also called on for his expertise in *The Fearmakers*, my video docu-series of the 1990s. After that, we lost touch. But we reconnected for *Masquerade* when I solicited information on the Lon Chaney version of *The Phantom of the Opera*, a film on which Scott is an expert. I refer you to his engrossing commentary to the 2003 Milestone Video DVD release of the best quality and most complete print of the original film available, which was restored by Kevin Brownlow's Photoplay Productions. Scott directed me to a treasure trove of ballyhoo, box office figures and other production information in *Universal Weekly*, a publication promoting the studio's current and future releases to theatre owners. I found copies on the Internet Archive. Those for the years 1924–1925 contained a wealth of nuggets on *Phantom*, including such tidbits as this: the film's director, Rupert Julian, had denied auditioning any hopeful starlet who showed up on set with "bobbed" hair. Go figure.

My sincere thanks also to film historian, film critic and author Leonard Maltin for interceding on my behalf and reconnecting me with Scott. Gratitude to you both.

John McCarty, 2025

About the Author

John McCarty is a full-time author and filmmaker. His book *Bullets over Hollywood: The American Gangster Picture from the Silents to "The Sopranos"* (Da Capo Press, 2004), was produced as a major documentary by the late Hugh M. Hefner's Alta Loma Entertainment, for the Starz/Encore cable network; it aired in 2005 and 2006. Additionally, he is the co-producer, co-writer, and co-director of *The Fearmakers: Masters of Screen Suspense and Terror*, a documentary series (and video companion piece to his book of the same name) profiling some of the world's most influential makers of classic suspense and terror films that was re-released as a two-volume set on DVD by Alpha Video in 2014 and is still selling. He also is the author of more than twenty non-fiction books on film and entertainment subjects. John has appeared in conjunction with his work on such cable network programs as Fox News Saturday, CNN.fn's midday news, A&E's *Biography*, the Bravo network series *Backspin*, the ICONS Radio Hour hosted by Stephen Bogart (son of screen icon Humphrey Bogart), Neal Conan's "Talk of the Town" on National Public Radio, and many other major market stations across the country. *Masquerade* is his third novel.

Curious about other Crossroad Press books? Stop by our website:
http://crossroadpress.com
We offer quality writing
in digital, audio, and print formats.

Subscribe to our newsletter on the website homepage and receive a
free eBook.

www.ingramcontent.com/pod-product-compliance
Lightning Source LLC
Chambersburg PA
CBHW031306280626
47169CB00017B/323